Y0-AFR-442

STUDENT NURSE

BY PATRICIA RAE

ZEBRA BOOKS
KENSINGTON PUBLISHING CORP.

ZEBRA BOOKS

are published by

KENSINGTON PUBLISHING CORP.
475 Park Avenue South
New York, N.Y. 10016

AUTHOR'S NOTE

The dialogue and behavior studies presented in Part IV of this book were taken from actual Psychiatric nursing clinical records which I prepared as a student nurse in partial fulfillment of a course in psychiatric nursing.

For the sake of preventing tediousness, I have omitted the sections of the clinical records which included the needs of the patients, nursing interventions, and the results of nursing interventions.

Names, initials, and certain personal details of the patients have been changed to protect their privacy.

Patricia Rae, R.N.

Education has for its object the formation of character.

—*Herbert Spencer*

PART ONE

Ninety percent of what you learn in nursing school, you learn on your own. That's what Carol had decided two years ago. Lecturers in nursing theory jumped from subject to subject like grasshoppers, indiscriminately leading the students to chew on a bit of theory here and a sliver of scientific principle there, never delving into any subject deep enough to allow the students to consume anything, much less to digest it. Clinical instructors were figments of the imagination; when you needed them to help you learn a technique, they had vanished. When you didn't need them—well, they were still absent.

And nobody taught you in nursing school how to manage a lesbian patient either. Carol wasn't sure about the patient she had been assigned to care for that morning, but . . . there was certainly something odd about Lanelle Godsby's behavior. However, Carol wasn't so interested in that as she was her particular illness. So she was studying Lanelle's chart at the nurses' station hoping to learn something—*anything*.

A patient's chart is a storybook, a medical storybook as dramatic as any movie or TV serial, only maybe more so. It contains many chapters, beginning with the admittance sheet and, hopefully, ending with the discharge sheet. Or it could end with the death certificate. Or with the epilogue—the autopsy report.

So Carol became engrossed in Lanelle's history and physical sheet, searching for some clue as to why she had developed ileitis which had resulted in surgery. She was hoping Lanelle's medical history would yield enough material for her final thesis, a thing that loomed like a menacing phantom in the minds of all the nursing students because it would count as one-third of their Medical Surgical II grade. The thesis, as outlined by the nursing instructors, had to present a medical nursing problem the students had encountered, the scientific principles involved in this problem, and its final resolution—or a description of the failure to resolve it. They were all sweating great drops of blood over the damned thing.

Suddenly the paging operator's voice sounded precisely and loudly, but Carol did not comprehend the page until two nurses at the nurses' station jumped up from their seats, overturning a desk chair. Her head snapped up to listen as the operator repeated the page.

"Dr. Heart, Jenson 308. Dr. Heart, Jenson 308."

The CPR code.

Wide-eyed, Carol watched the two nurses vanish down the corridor. The charge nurse yanked the CPR cart from its niche near the linen room and ran with it, pushing it before her down the corridor. A young man in a white lab coat dashed past the desk. Activity at the nurses' station had ceased.

The excitement was too much. Carol rose slowly, hesitantly, and glanced at the nurses who remained. Seeing that they were oblivious to her as always, she

8

started down the corridor. At first she simply walked rapidly, but soon, her heart thudding in her chest, she found herself running, running like the other hospital personnel who thundered past her and on down the corridor, converging and disappearing into what must be room 308.

She was a senior student nurse and had never witnessed cardiopulmonary resuscitation before. She couldn't wait to ask her instructor if she could watch. No telling where Ms. Child was anyway. As she and her student friends had discovered long ago, ninety percent of what you learn in nursing school, you learn on your own. And that was a hell of a lot.

Room 308 was full of standing people in white. Only six of them seemed to be doing anything when Carol entered; most were merely spectators. She had to get up on tiptoe and stare between the heads of two nurses; even than she was barely able to see the huge, nude, ashen body of the patient on the bed. A male nurse was doing cardiac massage, and with every compression of the patient's sternum, his abdomen jiggled like a bowl of jelly. At the head of the bed stood the only doctor in the room — a first-year resident, she had heard somebody whisper. He stood tall, thickset, puffy-eyed, morose.

"Fifty of Xylocaine," Carol heard him say. "And stop massage a minute so I can see the pattern on the oscilloscope."

All eyes went to the CPR cart with its portable cardiac monitor.

Carol could not see the electronic blip on the monitor and couldn't have understood it if she had. The resident scowled, obviously unhappy with what he saw on the oscilloscope, and the male nurse resumed cardiac massage.

A nurse was injecting something into the intravenous tubing in the patient's left arm. The resident elbowed the respiratory therapist and the therapist removed the black bag with its face mask from the patient's face and stepped aside. The resident then began to intubate the patient, inserting a breathing tube guided by the cold-looking metal instrument called a . . . a laryngoscope, through his mouth and into the trachea. It took the resident two tries before he got it in. Carol had watched intubation before, on surgery patients and on Felix Seifert in ER when they'd practiced it on poor old Felix . . . . Intubation wasn't easy and more often than not the doctors got the tube in the esophagus instead of the trachea. But now the resident nodded after having listened for air in the patient's lungs, indicating that he had gotten the endotracheal tube in the right place.

Tension in the room was almost unbearable. A life hesitated on the brink of eternity in those critical moments and Carol was acutely aware of it.

"Get ready to shock!" the resident said loudly.

She tried to elbow her way through the crowd to watch the nurse defibrillate. She'd read about the defibrillating procedure, but had never witnessed it. She was sure none of the other students had either. CPRs didn't happen often, especially on the wards.

"Stand back!" the nurse shouted.

The spectators stepped backward on each other's toes and Carol heard a thud like a rubber hammer on wood. She could see the patient's limbs jerk up and fall back into the bed. The male nurse continued cardiac massage.

Carol's gaze moved around the crowd in the room. They were all hospital personnel, lab techs, respiratory therapists, nurses, aides, physical therapists, assorted supervisors. But only six of the people in the room were necessary; the rest were just getting in the way—like herself.

To one side of the crowd, near the patient's sink, a petite, dark-haired nurse was scribbling in a chart. Impressed by the intensity of the nurse's scribbling, Carol edged over to see what she was writing. When she saw that the nurse was writing in a patient chart, she asked timidly, "What happened?"

The nurse's gaze brushed her face briefly. "A cardiac arrest, obviously," she snapped.

Carol saw the room number on the chart—308. The addressograph printing in the upper right-hand corner of the nurses' notes sheet informed her that the patient was James R. Proctor. Age 52.

"What was he in the hospital for?" she persisted.

"A T.U.R.," replied the nurse not looking up from the chart.

"Was he your patient?"

"He *is* my patient, yes. I'm a private-duty nurse." The nurse looked up from the chart at Carol, and said, "They'd better not blame *me* for this. I was only following doctor's orders."

"Blame you?"

The private-duty nurse took note of the blue pinafore over Carol's white uniform, the uniform of the student nurse, and turned her mouth down in tentative derision. "Haven't you studied T.U.R.'s yet?"

Feeling only slightly intimidated, Carol said, "Yes, but T.U.R.'s a very simple prostatectomy. It isn't even major surgery."

11

"Tell me about it, kid," the nurse said and bent over the chart again. Her straight dark hair swung forward to cover her face as she began to write. "I came on at eleven last night and found out the three-to-eleven nurse forgot to record his IV intake. Then I checked Proctor's abdomen and it was tight, but not hard. But how can you tell about abdominal distention on fat people? Anyway—" The nurse fluttered her hand. "Anyway I've got to finish these notes."

Carol tried to see what the nurse was writing, but heard the thud of the defibrillator again and turned just in time to see the resident doctor shake his head as he studied the monitor screen. At the same moment a young man entered the room and paused just inside the door. His face registering a horror Carol would never forget, he stared until a nurse took his arm and ushered him outside the room. A coldness settled over Carol as she realized that the young man was probably a member of the family and had happened upon the scene. How awful it must be for him, she thought. How terrible and how—unexpected.

She continued to watch the resuscitation attempts, repeated over and over again, unable to really see much, until at last, as the people turned around one by one and left the room, she was able to get a closer look at the patient. He was ashen, an obese man lying half-naked upon a urine-soaked bed. His IVs were no longer dripping. The blip on the monitor was only a straight line with an occasional wave. And CPR had ceased.

The resident doctor looked like a sleepless young Raymond Burr. Gloomily he was shaking his head saying, "It shouldn't have happened. God, this shouldn't have happened."

12

Carol remembered that it was past time for her to check on her own patient and sign her chart, so reluctantly she left and went back to room 323. She told Lanelle Godsby good-by, went to the nurses' station, and signed off her chart.

It shouldn't have happened.

They'd better not blame me.

What was the resident insinuating? Who was at fault? A patient was dead. Because somebody somewhere goofed?

The private-duty nurse dropped Mr. Proctor's chart on the desk just as Carol was sliding Lanelle's chart back into the revolving chart holder. Carol watched furtively as the nurse went into the coffee room behind the nurses' station and came out again with her handbag. The nurse's mind was preoccupied at the moment, her forehead was furrowed with . . . concern? Worry? And she disappeared down the corridor.

Only two nurses were occupying the nurses' station now; one was on the telephone, the other was filling out lab requisition slips. Carol scooted her chair from the revolving chart holder to where the private-duty nurse had dropped the chart on the desk. She glanced at the nurses at the desk; nobody was paying her any attention so she drew Proctor's chart in front of her. And opened it.

According to his history and physical sheet, Mr. Proctor was admitted to Bennet Memorial for a transurethral resection of the prostate. His history showed that he suffered from gout, asthma, fluid retention, and hypertension for which he was taking a diuretic. Recent history showed that urination had become gradually more painful until it had become almost impossible. The prostate gland—located posterior to the bladder—had enlarged, pressing upward, obstructing the urethra and bladder orifice.

Mr. Proctor had requested a private suite in the Jenson wing and was admitted to room 308.

On February 19th, which was yesterday, Proctor had been taken to surgery at 7:30 A.M. and had agreed to spinal analgesia.

Carol turned to the doctor's progress report which showed that the operation had been a success and that there was a slight trabiculation of the bladder.

Carol thought a moment. Trabiculation of the bladder would mean that fibrous bands of tissue had formed and extended from the prostate into the bladder.

A T.U.R. had been done, using a cystoscope fitted with an ocular and operating system through which pieces of the prostate had been removed one by one. The cystoscope had been inserted into the urethra of the penis and the pieces of gland removed, under direct vision, by a loop of wire inserted through the cystoscope. Carol remembered that this particular procedure, instead of the abdominal incision procedure, is preferred in poor-risk patients because there is less trauma involved and the hospital stay was usually shorter.

After the surgery, a three-way urinary catheter had been installed into the bladder by Proctor's surgeon, Dr. Tyree, and it had been hooked up to a Murphy drip system.

Once Carol had had a patient who had had a Murphy drip. It consisted of two bags of normal saline hung on an IV pole with the triple lumen catheter

14

running saline, via a Y in the tubing, into the patient's bladder and out again into a collection bag. In Proctor's case, the saline was allowed to drip at a rate of thirty to one hundred drops per minute in a continuous flow, irrigating the bladder.

After the installation of the catheter, Proctor had been returned to his room.

Carol flipped to the front of the chart to the nurses' notes sheet. 11:55 A.M., the nurse in charge of the floor reported that the Murphy drip was running at sixty drops a minute and drainage from the catheter into the catheter bag was clear.

Throughout the rest of the shift the patient had rested quietly and had taken sips of water at frequent intervals.

At 3:00 P.M., the three-to-eleven private-duty nurse had reported that the patient had become nauseated and vomited about 100 cc of dark green fluid. She noted at that time that drainage into the bag from the catheter was bloody. Dr. Tyree had been notified and had ordered hydrocortizone, one hundred milligrams intramuscularly, and the private-duty nurse had administered the injection.

Perspiring with excitement, Carol reached for the *Physician's Desk Reference* on the desk and looked up hydrocortizone. It was a steroid, an anti-inflammatory drug which was used occasionally to combat shock, especially gram negative bacteremia, as well as to reduce inflammation. It was used with caution in patients with hypertension, congestive heart failure, and renal insufficiency. *Proctor had hypertension.* Side effects included water retention and excessive excretion of potassium; therefore, the patient's electrolytes had to be watched closely. Carol flipped to the lab reports in Proctor's chart. There were no reports on his electrolytes, and upon checking through the doctor's orders, she saw no order for electrolyte studies.

At 4:00 P.M., the private-duty nurse reported Proctor's intake and output. Eight hundred cc's of Ringer's lactate had been given intravenously since surgery, and six thousand cc's normal saline via the Murphy drip. There were five thousand cc's urine and saline in the catheter bag.

Six thousand eight hundred cc's fluid in; only 5,000 cc's fluid out.

At 5:00 P.M. the patient had complained of abdominal pain and the private-duty nurse had given Demerol seventy-five milligrams intramuscularly.

At 7:00 P.M., the patient had complained of being cold. Hydrocortizone fifty mg. had been given by the nurse.

8:30 P.M. Proctor's IV had infiltrated and a floor nurse had restarted it.

9:30 P.M. Proctor had became nauseated, but had not vomited.

11:00 P.M. The nurse had reported the amount of Murphy drip given since 4:00 P.M. and it was six thousand cc's. There were two thousand seven hundred and fifty cc's in the catheter bag. *Six thousand cc's in, only 2,750 out.* To Carol's dismay the three-to-eleven nurse had failed to report the patient's IV intake.

At 12:00 midnight, the eleven-to-seven private-duty nurse, the one to whom Carol had spoken, had made her entry on the nurses' notes. She had stated that the patient was complaining of nausea, chills, and "sweating." Carol shook her head wondering if the nurse knew that the technical word for sweating was "diaphoresing." The nurse had given hydrocortizone, fifty milligrams.

At 12:30, the nurse had noted that the patient's face was "puffy" and pale, his abdomen firm but not tense. He had become restless and could not sleep. She administered Vistaril, fifty milligrams for sleep. At that time his pulse had been eighty beats per minute and faint but regular.

3:10 A.M. Proctor had become "breathless." *Didn't the nurse know the proper term was "short of breath"?*

4:00 A.M. The nurse had estimated that six thousand cc's of saline had been given via the Murphy drip and four hundred cc's Ringer's IV. Only one thousand cc's had been emptied from the catheter bag.

Carol bit her lip, took out her pen and notebook and began to add up the amount of fluid Proctor had been given since surgery and the amount returned. His intake had been nineteen thousand two hundred cc's at least—more than that because the day nurse hadn't recorded her IV intake. Eight thousand, seven hundred fifty had been collected in the drainage bag and one hundred cc's had been vomited, bringing the total of his output to eight thousand eight hundred and fifty cc's. Where had the other ten thousand three hundred and fifty cc's of fluid gone, for Pete's sake? That was over ten liters of fluid, almost ten quarts. *Or two and a half gallons unaccounted for.*

Carol glanced at her wrist watch. Past time for post-clinical. To hell with postclinical. She read on.

At 4:10 the private-duty nurse had reported the

17

patient's vital signs. All vitals had been up; pulse eighty, respirations eighteen, blood pressure one hundred and seventy over one hundred and ten. Proctor had become "breathless" when he had changed position. *Why hadn't the nurse called the doctor to report the vital signs and the intake and output? Why hadn't the floor nurses checked on the patient? Why had the doctor ordered hydrocortizone?*

4:30 A.M. Proctor had become restless. Slightly cyanosed? the nurse had wondered in her notes. A reaction to hydrocortizone? she had queried.

She had been still puzzling at 5:00 A.M. when Proctor's IV had infiltrated again. The floor nurse had been called in to restart the IV and evidently hadn't been puzzled at all. When she had been unable to restart the IV, she had called in a resident. Meantime the private-duty nurse had recorded Proctor's vital signs. Temperature ninety-seven, pulse one hundred, respirations thirty-two, blood pressure one hundred thirty over eighty-five.

5:15 A.M. The resident doctor had appeared to restart the IV. Patient immediately had been placed in Trendelenburg position. *The shock position.* An EKG had been done at 5:30. Proctor's blood pressure had been—*ninety?* the nurse wondered? No dyastolic pressure at all.

6:00 A.M. Proctor's blood pressure had become unrecordable.

6:30 Proctor had become unconscious. The resident had done a bilateral suprapubic tap. Carol knew this was a type of paracentesis or drainage of fluid from the peritoneal cavity. The resident had been able to drain only a small amount of fluid from the abdomen.

Two hundred cc's. *Where were the other ten thousand one hundred and fifty cc's of fluid?*

At 6:45, Proctor's blood pressure had still been unrecordable.

At 7:00 the resident had given one ampule of sodium bicarbonate.

At 7:15 Proctor had arrested. The private-duty nurse, using the patient's bedside telephone called the operator for a Dr. Heart. Cardiac massage had been begun by the resident and mouth-to-mouth resuscitation had been instituted by a male nurse until the crash cart could be brought to the bedside and the ambu or breathing bag used. CPR had begun and this had been where Carol had entered the picture.

She scanned the nurses' notes noting the treatments and medications given during CPR, then flipped to the doctors' progress report and read the attending resident's report.

The resident had recorded the CPR efforts, and noted that the patient had been pronounced dead at 8:10 A.M. He had ended by stating in his notes a tentative diagnosis; extravasation of the bladder. Cause of death; gram negative sepsis shock leading to cardiac arrest. He had requested an autopsy to rule out pulmonary embolism and to determine the cause of death.

Carol glanced at her wrist watch again. Being late to postclinical suggested that you were unable to finish your work in the allotted amount of time. She jumped up from the desk and hurried away down the corridor toward the elevator which would take her to the small conference room on the fourth floor. As she went, she was wondering what extravasation of the bladder meant. What was gram negative sepsis shock?

It shouldn't have happened.

They'd better not blame me.

What was the resident implying in his diagnosis? What did the nurse mean in her statement about blame?

Carol's curiosity mushroomed out of control. She *had* to find out why Mr. Proctor had died. Somehow, someway, she *had* to find out what event or series of events had allowed—or caused—such a death. . . . And what could have been done to prevent it? She *must* find out. For wasn't that, after all, one of the reasons she and the others had gone into nurse's training, to learn to prevent disease and death, to give comfort to the sick, and to help people regain their health? These were ideals she and the others had aspired to in the beginning, and in Carol's two years of training, the ideals hadn't changed.

Was it only two years ago that she had been sitting in UTE's main auditorium asking that stupid question? How naive she'd been then. How naive all the students were, just two short years ago.

Chapter One

Fundamentals

"Do we have to give our patients the bedpan our very first day?" Carol still couldn't believe she had blurted out that question. Normally she sorted through the zillions of questions that peppered her mind like scatter shot and asked only the most intelligent ones in class. She found the answers to the dumber ones in her books, or buttonholed the instructors after class and asked them in private. But all reason had abandoned her the instant the director of the nursing curriculum had announced that today the class of two hundred and fifty-six students would be divided into groups of eleven or twelve and that tomorrow they would go in their various groups to the nine hospitals within the city and its suburbs for their first day of clinical experience. The announcement, which had been long anticipated, now blew her mind.

There was a quiet in the auditorium and Carol could feel two hundred and fifty-five pairs of eyes fixed on her burning face. The instructor stared at her. Carol decided that Ms. Black couldn't believe what she had just heard. But the instructor smiled condescendingly. "Only if your patients *ask* for the bedpan," she replied.

Thank God nobody laughed. There was a collective sigh instead, and only when another student asked another stupid question of the director did Carol dare look to the side at her friend, Charlotte. Charlotte smiled at her reassuringly. Carol could almost read her mind. Gosh, Carol, we all have hang-ups, and that really wasn't *too* dumb a question, her look seemed to say.

But Carol didn't miss the line of perspiration that had beaded on her friend's upper lip, or fail to notice that her face was fading from crimson to its normal, almost-jaundiced pallor, or that she took two Life Savers from the roll and popped them into her mouth.

They had sailed through one and a half semesters of college together, she and Charlotte. Rather, Charlotte had sailed and Carol had swum. Academics came easy to Charlotte and Carol could never understand how her diabetic friend could maintain a four point zero grade average so easily, while she herself studied, worried, and wept for her own four point zero.

English, psych, and Latin were the easiest. All four English and lit teachers were super; their psych professor had been a creepy spinster who only last month had been committed to a city psychiatric ward because she'd locked up six dogs in a vacant house and when the authorities had finally broken into the house, they had found dissected dogs on the tables and dog meat in the refrigerator.

History and sociology had demanded a little more study. Chemistry hadn't been as difficult as she had anticipated. Biology had been okay, and she'd hardly needed to study for micro for her A. But for the past two years she'd studied so much she had hardly had time to date, while Charlotte had married the first year and hadn't cracked a book except at exam time.

"Ms. Black, exactly how will we be divided into groups? Do we have a choice of hospitals?" That was Bret Harris. He was one of five male student nurses. Three of the five men were med-vets. Med-vets were Vietnam veterans who had served as medics and had taken the entrance exam hoping to by-pass fundamentals by virtue of their past experience, but who had failed. Some sixteen of their med-vet buddies had passed the exam and had been allowed to by-pass fundamentals and would join the rest of the class in pediatrics for the fall semester.

Bret wasn't a med-vet. Carol remembered his telling her and some of the other students at a table in the cafeteria last semester that he'd served in 'Nam, and when he'd been discharged, had taken a job as a bartender. Carol wasn't sure about Bret's character for that reason, but she had to admire him for his fearless pursuit of an unlikely career.

The nursing director admired no such thing. "Mr. Harris," she said tightly. "You'll find out how you'll be divided soon enough. Be patient!"

Carol looked at Bret as he shrugged and settled back in his chair two seats away from her. She was just beginning to perceive the hostility that Black and certain of the other nursing instructors felt toward Bret. For he and the other male nursing students were attempting to intrude into a women's world and the intrusion was looked upon with righteous suspicion.

But Black knew Bret's name and that was unusual. Lena Black had taken the job as director of the nursing division only last month when the then-current director, Lillian Mulhern, had decided to get married and move away from the city. The university had been left without a director for the nursing school and Lena Black had been asked to return to her old position, which she had held four years previously. She had accepted, and now seemed to be enjoying her new-old position.

Carol thought it was just as well that Black was the director now. She might be eccentric, but at least she was interested. When Carol had applied for nursing school in the spring and the counselor had reviewed her grades, the last hurdle had been an interview by the director. When Carol's time came to be interviewed, she found Lillian Mulhern seated at her desk, smoking a cigarette, and swinging her crossed leg in time to the music coming from a transistor radio on her desk. Before Carol was even seated in her office, Mulhern told her, "We're full up."

"I beg your pardon?"

"Full up. All the nursing classes are full and there's sixteen in line ahead of you. You'll have to try again next year."

Full up? After two years of pre-nursing courses the interview was supposed to be just a formality if you passed your courses.

Carol, stunned and tearful, went to her parents' house in Oak Grove and cried out her story. She was sorry she did that, because her mother said, "You must have done something to irritate the teachers."

"Mom, I've been a perfect student. Straight A all the way!"

"Well, maybe they don't think you can stand up to the stress of nursing."

24

"They don't even *care*, Mom. The pre-nursing profs are just university profs. They teach and grade papers. And the nursing instructors don't even know us yet. The reason I was turned down was that my name begins with a W. Everybody after T was turned down."

Her father had offered, "If God means for you to be a nurse, He'll open up the doors for you."

Well, God had opened up the doors for her and some six others, but He had a little help. Carol had gone back to the counselor. One look at her grades and a telephone call to Mulhern had been the key. The counselor not only got Carol into the nursing school, but also reviewed Mulhern's procedures for admitting students and took the matter to the chairman of the board. As a result, everybody after T, including Charlotte whose last name was Worth, was interviewed and accepted into the nursing curriculum.

A week later Mulhern resigned.

Now, two weeks after Mulhern had resigned, all two hundred and fifty-six students were assembled on this, their first day of Fundamentals lecture, in the university auditorium. They had each passed their basic college courses and were now about to get down to the ninty-gritty of their chosen profession. They were all bright-eyed with anticipation, trembling with idealistic excitement, anxious to learn and to practice. The eager hospital authorities were beckoning benevolently for their services; the students were longing to see the mysterious inner-workings of medicine and to work side by side with those magnificent gods of life, the physicians of their fantasies. In short, they were a bunch of innocents.

Today they had gathered eagerly and sat in the hard theater chairs of UTE's main auditorium, their spiral notebooks open and propped on top of their *Fundamentals* and *Bedside Nursing Techniques* textbooks. The ink-and-new-paper fragrance of their new books wafted through the humid air of the university's inadequate air-conditioning system.

The director of nursing curriculum, Lena Black, had a lean and hungry look like Cassius in Shakespeare's *Julius Caesar*, and though the students doubted that it was because she thought too much, like Cassius, they were still in awe of her. They gaped as she paced manlike back and forth across the stage, hands clasped behind her back, lecturing about . . . they *thought* she was lecturing about personal hygiene, but nobody was sure. Only bits and pieces of her lecture reached Carol's consciousness, though she took down pages and pages of indecipherable notes.

Students' uniforms must be immaculate at all times
Shoes freshly polished
No jewelry except a wrist watch with a second hand.
No fingernail polish, no heavy makeup, hair no longer than just below the lower part of the pinna.

Pinna?
Charlotte whispered to Carol, "I think she means the earlobe."

Carol wondered if everybody else's impression of this first lecture in fundamentals was like hers, that

Lena Black fancied she was General Patton. From the way she lectured, Carol decided Black's nursing skills were probably antiquated and that her thought processes were generally uncoordinated, disjointed, and confused. When the lecture was over, Carol looked down at her notes. She had ceased to write anything after the word *pinna*, except to scribble.

Tapes, 1, 2, 3, and 4 by next Monday

Shortly, the students were divided into clinical groups. The process by which they arrived at who would go into what group was unknown. Nursing instructors handed out the students' assignments. Carol drew Ross Street Presbyterian, a small prestigious hospital in the inner city, across the street from the huge Bennet Memorial medical complex to which she had longed to be assigned.

"Could we trade hospital assignments with someone else?" a student ventured to ask Black.

"Certainly not," Black snapped from her place behind the lectern.

"Even though the hospital I'm assigned to is forty miles from where I live and another student's is closer, and—" persisted the intrepid student.

Black leaned swiftly toward the microphone on the lectern. "All assignments are final. Any student approaching a nursing instructor or counselor with a request to transfer to a different clinical area, will be suspended."

Charlotte had been assigned to Preston Community, another small hospital in the suburbs.

Carol looked at her list of names under Ross Street

Presbyterian and the only name she recognized was Bret Harris's.

Finally the instructors passed out Xeroxed handouts and Charlotte and Carol forgot their disappointments momentarily as they accepted theirs eagerly. Now they had tangible evidence, besides their new textbooks, that they were indeed launching into the nursing profession. Handouts—the first nineteen of ten thousand. Carol scanned hers.

> *The Registered Professional Nurse*
> A. *Independent Areas of Nursing Function*
> 1. *Supervision*
> a. *Safety and security of the patient*

Carol felt the fine hairs on the back of her neck stand up, so she shifted her sheets to the second handout.

NURSING 132 ABBREVIATIONS

abd.	*abdomen*
a.c.	*before meals*
ad lib.	*as desired*
b.i.d.	*twice a day*

No sweat there. She could memorize abbreviations. She looked at the next seventeen handouts. "Team Nursing"; "Intravenous Injection"; "Problem Solving Guide for Nurses"; "Abdellan's 21 Nursing Problems"; "Self Pacing—a Concept"; "Nurses' Notes—Making Them More Meaningful"; "Hazards of Bedrest" . . .

There were others, but by then Carol was disconcerted and looked at Charlotte just as Charlotte looked up from her own handouts at Carol. They saw it in each other's eyes; they'd never be able to learn all this, the study load which the instructors expected of them was impossible. Charlotte popped two more Life Savers into her mouth.

The auditorium was quiet. And as Carol looked around, she saw in the faces of the other students the same mixture of delight and despair that she and Charlotte felt. But she swallowed and squared her shoulders a little. After all, the school couldn't fail all two hundred and fifty-six students. Could it?

Preclinical was a thirty-minute period in which the eleven students at Ross Street Presbyterian met in the conference room where they received their daily patient assignments. The first thing they were given on their first day of clinical, however, was a pop quiz. It was a spelling test. And it counted as their first clinical grade. The students found out quickly that words they thought they could spell, they couldn't. There were words on the test such as hemorrhage, pneumonia, hemorrhoid, bronchioles, catheterize, diarrhea, and ophthalmoscope. The test made everybody furious. It wasn't fair!

But their clinical instructor, pretty, young, petite Cheryl Peavyhouse, smilingly took the test papers from their sweaty palms and stacked them in a manila folder on the table before her. Carol wondered if anybody else was contemplating stealing the folder and stuffing it into the hospital incinerator.

They were all crisp in their new white uniforms and blue pinafores; the starched white caps everybody hated were perched on their heads like over-risen, uncooked buns.

"Okay, group," said Miss Peavyhouse. "For the first few clinical days we'll work in pairs. I'll assign two of you to each patient today, and you'll have to study your patients' charts carefully. From now on, I'll assign patients a day ahead so that you will be able to study their charts, their diagnoses, and meds, and be prepared. Jo will work alone since she's an experienced LVN."

"Glunk," said Jo reddening. Although Jo had been an LVN for five years previous to her admission to the university's nursing school, she was just as nervous as everybody else. Carol studied her. She was a short, swarthy girl with a monotonous voice and cynical opinions. The girl next to her was a direct opposite; she was affable, red-headed Mae Jones whom everybody liked on sight. Then there was Nancy, a plump married girl with a huge moist face and a dry wit. Next to her lounged Bret, nice-looking in his crisp blue smock and white trousers. Across from Bret sat Shelly with a bright, giggly wit, and an ileostomy under her uniform which nobody would have known about had she not mentioned it several times already. Shelly was the only student nurse who *admitted* that she wanted to become a nurse in order to catch a doctor. But Shelly wanted to catch a *certain* doctor. She was working part-time now as a flight attendant for TWA.

Miss Peavyhouse was handing out assignments with the same pleasant obliviousness to their anxiety that she had demonstrated when she had handed out the pop quiz. Carol was paired with Nancy with the big face and ready wit.

They all studied their assignments, and it was not

long before they realized that their patients had one thing in common — they were well on their way to recovery, and required nothing more than to have their vital signs taken once, their bedbaths given, and their beds made. Nancy's and Carol's heads came together over their patient assignment sheet.

Room 101-A. Bea Brice. Female. 78 years old
Exploratory laparotomy of June 1st
Vital signs q. 8 hrs.
Bedbath

Miss Peavyhouse was saying, "The patient in the room with Mrs. Brice is going to surgery at eight o'clock this morning so you can practice making her surgical bed while she is gone."

"Oh, goody," Nancy said clapping her hands. She and Carol could not believe their good fortune and the other students regarded them with a torpid envy.

The students had had only one chance at learning to make a hospital bed before their first clinical day. That had come at the end of their first day of lecture in fundamentals. Two hundred fifty-six students had gathered around four hospital beds in the auditorium and practiced making beds. Carol had gotten one try at it. The results had been poor. A surgical bed was even harder to make because you added a draw sheet and fan-folded the top sheet to one side. The students thought they knew how to make a bed, but they didn't. You learned to make a hospital bed one side at a time. You completely made up one side before you went around to make up the other. There was a trick to it and to getting the corners mitered just right.

Their patient, Mrs. Brice, was a pleasant, youngish, seventy-eight-year-old lady who seemed to enjoy having Carol and Nancy fuss over her, which they did eagerly. Nancy's wit kept her and Carol laughing and when the bedbath was over, Nancy informed Mrs. Brice that they kept *all* their patients in stitches. Meanwhile, both students were pleased with their performance. A bedbath was tricky, like the bed-making. You bathed one half of the patient at a time. You placed towels under each part you were to bathe and you began with the face. You worked your way down to their feet, keeping all of their body covered with the top sheet except the part you were bathing. You changed the water in the basin often and when you had completely finished one-half of the body, you went around to the other side and did the same thing all over again. If you did it right, the patient would only have to turn on her side once in order for you to wash her back. The bedbath took skill and planning, and if you were lucky, your patient would be like Mrs. Brice, alert enough to wash her own privates.

After Mrs. Brice, glowing pink from her bath, lay chuckling between her clean white sheets, Carol and Nancy turned with eager anticipation to the vacated bed of the surgical patient.

Carol regarded the bed silently, then looked up at Nancy.

"It's electric!" Nancy exclaimed with delight. "We should *really* get a charge out of this!"

Ross Street Presbyterian was an ancient, highly respected hospital run by a board of patriarchal directors, staffed by inveterate nurses and aging physicians, and patronized by loyal patients. The hospital beds at Presby were the old reliable kind you had to crank. You rolled up the head of the bed laboriously by turning the crank on the right-hand side of the foot of the bed. By turning another crank at the left, you could lower the height of the entire bed. To Presby staff, the four new electric beds in the hospital represented an experiment in innovative medical equipment, and judgment as to their plausibility was still pending; although every other hospital in town had done away with cranked beds years before.

Carol and Nancy fell to stripping off the used sheets of the electric bed enthusiastically. Nancy went to the linen room in the corridor to get clean linen while Carol tidied up the bedside and overbed tables.

"Okay," Nancy announced, "here's the bottom sheet. Here we go!"

They were being studiously careful not to shake the sheet or to expose it unnecessarily to the invisible germs that might be sifting into the air in the room, as *Fundamentals* had warned, when it occurred to Carol that they were bending down too much to reach the bed. Chapter I in *Fundamentals* warned about that, too. "We need to raise the bed," she said feeling smart for remembering.

"You're right," Nancy said, and Carol took the detachable control from its hook on the side of the bed and studied it. It didn't make sense, but she pressed a button gingerly as if it did.

The bed began to rise. Creaking and groaning, it rose as Nancy and Carol beamed at each other across the newly stretched bottom sheet. And it rose and rose until Nancy's happy smile began to dim a little and she said, "Uh . . . that's fine, Carol."

Carol pressed another button to make the bed stop rising, but it didn't.

By then, Nancy's smile was a faint grimace. "You can . . . lower it a little . . . uh . . . Welles," she said.

Carol was beginning to perspire as she pressed the button with an arrow pointing down. Suddenly the foot of the bed creaked and groaned and began to lower. In a mild panic now, Carol pressed a different button and the head of the bed, squeaking and clanking, began to rise. Presby's new electric bed was still ascending and was now roughly in the shape of an N.

Carol gasped and tossed the control to Nancy. "See if you can do anything with this," she cried. In her mind's eye she could picture the bed rising and rising until it pushed slowly through the ceiling into the second floor above, and on and on . . .

Nancy pressed one button after the other, and though the bed changed its configuration from an N to a W, it continued to rise. Nancy panicked. "Hello," she cried into the control as if it were a microphone. "I say stop! Stop! Stop, I tell you. Descend! Hello, hello!"

The bed stopped because it had reached the limit of its mechanism.

They were staring up at the bed wondering how they would go about lowering the damned thing when Miss Peavyhouse materialized in the doorway. Nancy saw Carol's stare and turned to face their instructor.

Nancy grinned and gestured toward the bed. "Er . . . we were just practicing making a bed in its various positions. You know, Trendelenburg, Fowler's . . ."

Carol thought Miss Peavyhouse might have believed her if Mrs. Brice in the next bed hadn't been thrashing about cackling hysterically.

Every day in preclinical or postclinical they practiced taking vital signs on each other and all of it was fun and frolic. But taking vitals of a patient was different. It was terrifying.

Carol and her partner, Nancy, were assigned to Mrs. Brice for two days. The lady amusedly endured the students' studious if bungling vital sign-taking, their puzzling over how to keep the blood-pressure cuff on her arm when they pumped air into it, their forgetting the thermometer and leaving it in her mouth for ten minutes, their being unable to locate her radial pulse. She laughed and endured and by the end of their second morning, when they had finished charting—under Peavyhouse's close scrutiny—and gone in to say good-by to their beloved first patient, Mrs. Brice pronounced both girls experts. Carol decided that at least she and Nancy had been a diversion in their patient's otherwise dull hospital stay.

Miss Peavyhouse must have been satisfied with their progress, for the next day both Carol and Nancy were assigned to different patients, separately.

Miss Peavyhouse sat at the head of the conference table in preclinical and, with her usual apparent obliviousness to their consternation, gave out patient assignments. When she called Carol's name, all eyes fell upon her. They had not forgotten her anxiety over the possibility of being assigned to a male patient so soon. Tales had circulated among the students about patients' propositioning students, of patients' pinching students; and Carol had asked Jo, who was the experienced one in their midst, what she would do if a patient pinched her. Jo had laughed in her monotonous voice and said, "Honey, you just turn the other cheek." That was the kind of help you could expect from Jo.

Now Peavyhouse said, "Carol, your patient for the next three days is Mr. Wolfe."

The students cackled and roared. Carol laughed too, her laugh catching in her throat as Miss Peavyhouse handed her the assignment sheet. She didn't look at it though, until the students were dismissed and she paused in the hospital corridor outside the conference room.

Mr. James M. Wolfe.   Age: 70
Diagnosis: Cholecystitis
Surgery: Cholecystectomy of May 29th
Complete bedbath. Vital signs q. 8 hrs.
Up in bedside chair t.i.d.
General diet

"He's a cinch, Carol."

She looked up at Bret who was looking over her shoulder at the assignment sheet.

"At seventy he shouldn't be dangerous. And you know by now how to give a bedbath without exposing anything. You can do it."

"Of course I can," Carol told him, resenting his intrusion. "I'm not really worried. Two whole bedbaths and I feel like an expert."

"Sure you are. And—but if you do get into any difficulties, I'll be in the room across the hall."

"I'll be fine, Bret, thanks. I don't anticipate any problems."

That was before she met Mr. Wolfe.

At the nurses' station she read his chart. He was an ex-newspaper columnist. She pictured a distinguished, gray-haired gentleman as she checked the info on him carefully. Time was short, though, so she was only able to see that his surgery had been a week earlier and that he had progressed well and would be ready to be discharged from the hospital soon. Carol took a stethoscope from the hook near the nurses' station and strode down the corridor looking for room 106.

Mr. Wolfe lay upon his rumpled bed, sullen, unshaven, and silent.

"Hi, Mr. Wolfe," Carol said brightly. "I'm your nurse for the morning."

Mr. Wolfe turned his face toward her and snarled, "Get the goddamned hell out of here, you bitch."

It felt like somebody had hit her with a plank. Carol's face fell and her pulse began to beat a steady rhythm in her temples. "M—Mr. Wolfe, I've come to take your vitals, sir."

"Like hell you will," he shouted in a deep, commanding voice. "You've taken my gall bladder, you goddamned whore, and you're not about to take anything else from me, much less my vitals!" He clutched his privates protectively with one hand and with the other he gestured toward the door. "Get out!" he shouted and called her an obscene name.

It's got to be a test, Carol thought. The instructor gave him to me to test me. I showed a weakness by being afraid of male patients and she's testing me to see if I can handle difficult situations. She stammered, "I mean I'm supposed to take your temperature, pulse, respiration, and blood pressure."

Wolfe set his jaw defiantly. "What for?"

"Well, because . . . your doctor wants me to."

"Like hell he does. Do it then and get the god-damned hell out of here, you—"

"Don't bite the thermometer, okay?" she said thrusting it between his lips.

Wolfe grumbled obscenities around the thermometer and Carol took his leathery wrist to feel his pulse. Mr. Wolfe's pulse was a normal seventy-four, and his blood pressure a calm one hundred and forty-two over sixty.

Carol jotted the vitals on her small notebook to be recorded in the patient's chart later. She had exactly an hour before the eight o'clock vital signs had to be charted. She was dreading the bedbath and her face burned as she took the basin from under Mr. Wolfe's bedside table.

"Mr. Wolfe?" she said timidly. "It's time for your bedbath, sir. okay?"

Mr. Wolfe loudly gave his advice as to what she should do to herself.

Tearful but undaunted, Carol proceeded. She filled the basin, found the soap, fetched clean linen from the linen room, and approached him. "I'm going to help you with your bath now. I'll just s-slip your arm out of your gown—"

He refused to let her do any such thing and told her what she could do with the bath.

"But, sir, your doctor wants you to have your bed-bath," she offered feebly.

At first Wolfe resisted, but as Carol persisted authoritatively, Wolfe's resistance diminished to offering mild obscenities. It was a struggle of wills. Carol was determined to succeed because she wanted to be a nurse. She wanted to be a nurse more than anything in the world and this test she was being put through—it was a crisis. It meant whether or not she had what it took to be a nurse. Wolfe allowed her to remove his hospital gown while she kept the top sheet covering his body. She bathed and he cursed under his breath, as dedicated to voicing his vulgarities as she was to doing her duty. Carol was determined not to weaken. She bathed his gaunt, dark, leathery body and prayed as he cursed.

When the bath was over, she felt a brief, mild triumph, and as she poured the last basinful of bath water into the sink, she asked, "How would you like to get up in your chair, Mr. Wolfe?"

He said, "How'd ya like to kiss my ass, you son of a bitch?"

Carol helped him out of the bed carefully. He was a little wobbly on his feet, but she managed to get him to his chair. It occurred to her once to ask for Bret's help, but her former stubborn resolution to handle the situation all by herself caused her to abandon the idea almost as quickly as it had occurred to her. Meanwhile, Wolfe was shouting oaths and referring to her by various colorful nicknames.

By then, Carol was certain there was something very wrong with Mr. Wolfe, something worse than gallstones or surgery. Though he shouted obscenities, he never once answered her questions appropriately. He never once looked at her, and his eyes were glazed and unfocused.

But she had managed. She had taken his vital signs, bathed him, got him up in a chair. All in a matter of one hour, and *all by herself*.

Then Peavyhouse appeared in the doorway just as Carol was tucking a draw sheet around Mr. Wolfe's legs.

While Carol stood smiling behind Wolfe's chair, Miss Peavyhouse surveyed the room.

It was tidy. The linen on the old bed was crisp and tight. The bedside table had been cleared of everything but Mr. Wolfe's thermometer, water pitcher, and water glass. His overbed table had been cleaned with alcohol. His sink was shining and immaculate. Even the private bathroom was neat with a fresh supply of clean towels. The bedpan and toilet paper were out of sight. The dull, green walls of the room were a bit chipped and the venetian blinds at the window were a little bent, but Carol had opened them to admit the morning sun and the room had a cheerful appearance.

Wolfe himself sat like an Apache in his bedside chair, scrubbed, hair combed, a clean draw sheet over his bony knees.

Peavyhouse drawled, "Well, it all looks fine, Carol, but you didn't get him shaved, did you?"

Carol stood aghast, but even as Mr. Wolfe offered Peavyhouse a list of nicknames, informing her of her canine ancestry, Carol was certain she saw a gleam of amusement in the serene instructor's face. At that moment, Bret entered the room pushing a wheelchair before him. He winked at Carol and said to Wolfe, "Hey, there, James. They say you're ready to move, fella. You ready?"

Move? Carol folded her arms and awaited Wolfe's nickname for Bret.

It didn't happen.

Wolfe's stoic scowl faded, his eyes brightened, and he looked directly into Bret's eyes. His face lit up and he said cheerfully, "Yes, *sir!*"

"Okay Let's get you into this wheelchair. Up we go. That's it," Bret coaxed as it occurred to Carol to help with the sheet over Wolfe's knees or something.

"Yes, *sir!*" Wolfe said.

As Bret helped him into the chair, Wolfe beamed worshipfully upon him and sat obediently in the wheelchair. "Okay, fellow. Here we go. To Charleston wing. Ready?"

"Ready!" Wolfe shouted jauntily.

And they were off while Carol stood agape and Peavyhouse stood aside smiling gently.

"Charleston wing," Carol murmured to her instructor. "Isn't that the—"

Peavyhouse nodded. "The psychiatric wing over at Bennet," she said calmly. And while Carol's mouth dropped open, Peavyhouse drawled, "I must apologize. I made a mistake when I assigned you to Mr. Wolfe. I didn't read his chart thoroughly enough and I guess you didn't have time to note that just before his surgery he'd had a stroke of some kind and he's been rather belligerent ever since. The staff nurses didn't warn me. I guess because they saw an opportunity to let somebody else take care of him for a change."

Carol was speechless. She was frightened and angry and just beginning to feel sorry for herself when

Peavyhouse smiled and said, "Anyway, you can rest assured that today you earned an A in clinical, because Mr. Wolfe is the most difficult patient any of us nurses have ever seen."

In preclinical that day Carol shared her "patient experience" with the other students. She had learned that the nurses on the first floor had asked Bret, the only male student in the hospital, to wheel Wolfe to Bennet's Charleston wing. It had become apparent to Carol by then that the nurses liked to use Bret as a handyman, to do odd chores for them. Bret always complied cheerfully, running errands and doing "heavy" work in addition to his patient care. After Carol told the other students about her experience with Wolfe, she concluded by asking, "Why was Mr. Wolfe's attitude toward Bret different from his attitude toward me and Miss Peavyhouse and the other nurses?"

The students puzzled about that. Nobody knew why and nobody came up with any good theories; but Bret said that Wolfe had called him "Jimmy" and that Jim Wolfe was the patient's son. But why had Wolfe called Bret "sir?" Nobody could figure it out and nobody ever would.

Chapter Two

Math

Unfortunately, fundamentals included math. As a nurse you would have to know how to convert apothecary to metric, and vice versa, because doctors often ordered dosages in apothecary when the medication was packaged in metric—and vice versa.

The students' math book was a thin, innocent-looking paperback workbook. A first glance through its neat pages allayed any fears that Carol had had of learning to work the problems. But after their fourth assignment, which was given to them during their fifth week of fundamentals lectures, she knew she was doomed.

The first assignment was Chapter I entitled, "Apothecary System":

> *Units of weight of the Apothecary system used to measure drugs are the grain, the dram, and the ounce.*

The second assignment was entitled, "Household Measurements":

> *Fluid measurements in the household system*

are the pint, the quart, the ounce . . .

The third assignment was entitled, "Metric System":

Units of weight of the metric system are the kilogram, gram, milligram. By volume—the liter, millimeter, or cubic centimeter.

Carol sailed through those first three assignments and blithely accepted the fourth, "Equivalents":

Practice Problem: How many grains are in 2.0 grams?

Well, since there were fifteen grains in one gram, you multiply one gram by fifteen. Only thing was, you had to deal with decimals—and later on in the chapter you had to deal with fractions, and still later with the weird symbols that expressed each system. For instance, thirty grams was expressed as 30.0 gm, the symbol for dram looked like a fancy number three and placed *before* the number it represented—hence one dram was expressed, ß 1. But things really started getting sticky when, toward the end of the assignment, the programmed test included problems like:

From terramycin 100.0 mg. per ml, give 0.02 gm.

In July, Peavyhouse gave them their first test in math. Carol got every problem wrong. So did Mae Jones and Jo Stephens and Nancy. Bret and Shelly missed all but two. Nobody in Peavyhouse's clinical group had passed the test, but that was no comfort whatever to Carol; for *she* had failed and the quiz counted as a grade.

As always, Jo walked with Carol out to the hospital parking lot after the test. Each had become the other's confidante, somebody to whom to complain about clinical, somebody with whom to worry and trade views, and somebody from whom to seek moral support. Carol suspected that Jo sought her company because she made good grades, whereas Jo failed or barely passed every test. She guessed that Jo figured some of Carol's "brains" might rub off on her or something.

And Carol needed Jo's moral support, dubious as it was. She had observed that the stress of nursing school had caused the emotional fusion of strange pairs and groups of personalities. Bright students found their lagging self-confidence boosted when frightened mediocre ones suddenly sought their everlasting friendship. Mediocre or poor students counted themselves lucky if the bright students allowed them to tag along to lunch with them and to let them sneak a peek at their notes in lecture.

After the first math test, on her way to the parking lot, Carol had wept tears of fury and frustration, but Jo was taking her own defeat well and offered, "Oh well, I guess I can always just stay an LVN. I don't mind doing the dirty work while the R.N.'s sit at the desk and do paperwork and draw bigger salaries."

Carol was thinking, *Mom was right, Mom was right.* When she had told her mother three years ago that she wanted to go to nursing school, her mother had said, "Not nursing, Carol. You don't have the stamina for it."

Well, maybe she also didn't have the brains.

"I don't know why *you're* upset," Jo said now. "You've got all A's so far and you can't fail because of one zero."

Furiously Carol turned on her. "One zero! Jo, if I can't pass this test I can't pass the other math tests either!"

"Trouble is, you aren't satisfied with B's or C's or D's. You have to make all A's."

"I've *never* been good in math," Carol groaned.

"Well, it would be a shame to fail nursing because you can't do the math."

"A nurse has to know how to convert from one kind of system to the other."

"I never saw any nurse run into such problems myself."

"It makes no difference. Passing the math is a requirement in all nursing schools."

They saw Bret Harris just as he was fitting his key into the lock of his car door.

Jo, the unflappable pessimist, called to him in her flat, low voice, "What'd you think of that math test, Bret?"

He shook his head grinning and gave the test a thumbs-down. "But I've been working on it and I think I've figured out a formula that'll work on all conversions if you know the equivalents."

Jo stopped abruptly in her tracks at the words "I think I've figured out . . ." "Well," she said, "maybe you shoulda gone to medical school."

Bret shrugged and opened up the car door. "I

didn't want to go to medical school." Then his eyes fell upon Carol's face and stayed there. She was suddenly ashamed of her red, swollen eyes, and started to walk away.

"Hey, Welles?"

She turned back toward him.

"Wanna know the formula?"

In a moment of insanity that had a lot to do with pride, Carol replied, "No, thanks. If I can't figure it out on my own, I don't deserve to know."

Jo said, "Well *I* do." And Carol left them both, Bret, with notebook and pen, leaning on the hood of his car and showing Jo the formula.

She had made "flash cards" using index cards and a marks-a-lot like the ones her father had made for her when he had taught her the multiplication tables when she was in third grade. Only these cards were the metric-apothecary equivalents. She had taped them to the walls of her apartment, to the pleated lampshade on her bedside table, to the headboard of her bed, the dresser mirror, the mirror in her bathroom, and the wall in front of the toilet.

$$1cc = 1 \; milliliter$$
$$(1.0cc = 1.0 \; ml)$$

$$60 \; mg = 1 \; grain$$
$$(60.0 \; mg = gr. \; i)$$

The cards were everywhere, thirty-seven of them. Carol knew she could eventually memorize the equivalents, but then what? Suppose a doctor ordered thirty cc's of a medication and it was packaged in a one-and-a-half-ounce package?

She wept again and didn't eat dinner. At seven P.M. she finally gave up and called Jo. Timidly Carol said, "Jo, did Bret give you the math formula he was so proud of?"

"Yeah," Jo said in a monosyllable, "but I don't understand a thing about it. All those dots that mean 'is to this and is to that . . .' "

At eight Carol gave up nursing. She'd go back to being a secretary for the insurance company. She'd get married, have kids, be a housewife. She'd—

The telephone on her bedside table rang and she got up from the floor where she had been surrounded by flash cards, notepaper, pens, and pencils, and she answered it. "Carol speaking."

"Carol? Bret Harris."

She was shocked to hear his voice. She liked Bret, and some of the other students thought he was good-looking, but she hadn't expected him to notice her, much less to telephone.

"Hi, Bret. I guess you got my number from the student directory."

"I did. Have you mastered the math?"

She sat down on her bed and shut her eyes. "No."

"The formula is; whatever is to that as this is to x."

"*What?*"

"Get your math book, Carol, and look at problem number four on page sixty."

She had only to bend over, pick the book up off the floor, and find the page. "Okay, I have it."

"It says, 'From streptomycin solution containing five hundred milligrams in one cc, give four hundred milligrams.' The formula is: five hundred is to one as four hundred is to x. You multiply the two outside numbers, five hundred and x and you get 500x . . ."

She jotted down his instructions disinterestedly. It was as much "Greek" to her as the rest of it, but she said, "Thanks, Bret. I'll try it."

"Okay, Welles. Just thought I'd pass it on."

"Sure, thanks." She detected a pause as Bret considered further conversation, thought better of it, told her good-by, and hung up.

Carol dropped onto the floor against amidst the litter of papers and tried Bret's formula. She got the problem wrong. She checked the problem and discovered that she had divided wrong. She bent back over the problem.

Five hundred is to one as four hundred is to x. Five hundred multiplied by x equals 500x. One multiplied by four hundred is four hundred. Five hundred divided into four hundred equals point eight. She looked up the answer in the back of the math book. It was correct.

After that she had an orgy that lasted two hours, using Bret's formula for every problem she could find. And she never got another equivalent problem wrong again—ever.

Chapter Three

Anatomy & Physiology I

Up until that summer, A&P had always meant Atlantic and Pacific Tea Company, the old A&P grocery store chain, but now A&P meant anatomy and physiology.

Carol stood looking at the jar of mice. There were thirty of the tiny creatures, tinier than any mice she had ever seen, and they were either white or black. Out of thirty little live mice climbing, crawling, sitting up on hind legs with noses twitching, she wondered how one chose which one to kill.

Jason had ordered her to select the mouse. He had told Charlotte to get the test tube of chloroform from Murphy's desk. He had instructed Mae to check out and bring a kit of instruments to their table, while he perused the lab manual and studied the dissecting procedure.

She shut her eyes and dipped her hand into the cage, certain she would be bitten even though Professor Murphy had said they were lab mice and used to being handled and would not bite. Furry creatures scurried squeaking as her fingers found a tail. She lifted the tail and brought the creature up out of the cage. Then she opened her eyes and looked at him.

He was black. It didn't make sense at all—to slay a creature so one could become a nurse. When she and some of the other female students had protested earlier about dissecting live mice, Murphy had smiled strangely. "You have to dissect a live animal in order to see the organs functioning."

Why must they observe the organs functioning? Murphy's popularity was at an all-time low with the female students at the moment.

Jason, the med-vet who shared the lab table with Carol, Mae, and Charlotte, had scoffed at their protests. Carol thought that Jason's face was an exact likeness to famous paintings of Christ in that he had a perfect, flawless complexion, straight nose, solemn blue eyes, ash brown beard, and almost shoulder-length hair. Nobody could understand how Jason got by with such long hair since the rules were, "No hair below the *pinna.*" There had been some crude observations made about it though.

Jason was one of the med-vets who'd failed the entrance exam. Vietnam, or something before Vietnam, had caused his personality to change, someone had said, and had rendered him remote and strange.

Carol dropped the little mouse quickly into a jar while other students gathered around the cage to select their victims.

A&P classes met three times a week for lecture and twice for lab. The most interesting facet of A&P to Carol was that the human body was divided up into systems: skeletal system, muscular system, nervous system, integumentary system, reproductive system, and so on. It made learning about the human body easier.

Lab had met five times. They had taken pop quizzes on the muscular system and skeletal system. During the quiz on the skeletal system, Murphy had carried the class skeleton, Clarence, around the lab among the tables, pointing to various bones; and the students had had to write down the names of the bones. The more the students learned about the human body and its functions, the more they realized they didn't know, and the more in awe of it they became. "That," said Lena Black in lecture, "is the beginning of wisdom!"

Just last week they had dissected a fetal pig. Why fetal pigs were favorite dissecting material in college labs, nobody seemed to know. It was the first time many of the students had smelled formaldehyde—a stench that had no equal, a chemical odor totally uncompromising in its assault on the olfactory senses.

Charlotte grimaced when Carol brought the jar with its single black mouse to the table. "Oh, Carol, he's so tiny," she said sympathetically. Charlotte had a child's voice, and large black sympathetic eyes. Her hair was very dark brown, almost black. She was attractive but not much interested in men, and because sometimes her attitude was surly, men didn't seem much interested in her. Or maybe her intelligence scared them. At the moment she was clutching a wad of cotton balls in one hand and a test tube of chloroform in the other.

Jason looked from Carol to Charlotte and smiled mockingly. "So he's going to get high on chloroform, ladies, and after that, he'll never feel a thing." He looked from Charlotte to Carol. "Well, soak the cotton in the chloroform and drop it into the jar." He glanced at his wrist watch. "We've got thirty minutes to get this assignment over with."

But Charlotte stood frozen to the spot and Carol couldn't take her eyes off the little animal in the jar.

Disgustedly, Jason took the test tube from Charlotte and held out his hand to her, palm up. "Gimme the cotton, Charlotte," he said wearily.

Mae returned with the dissecting kit just as Jason dropped the chloroform-saturated cotton ball into the jar with the mouse and screwed the lid on. The four students watched as the little mouse went berserk, spinning around and around the jar crazily, then slowing, then stumbling, falling, closing his eyes, lying still. They waited.

When Jason took the unconscious mouse from the jar, the girls stared in mute aversion. Jason sat down in his chair at the table and placed the mouse on a paper towel. Then he looked up at the girls still standing silently, mesmerized by the mouse, and said, "I suppose I'm elected to do the dissecting."

Nobody answered at first; then Carol said, "I'll help keep him anesthetized. I don't want him to wake up with his—his abdomen slit open."

"Okay, but don't kill him till we're through with him," Jason snarled. He smiled at Mae. "Scalpel," he said and held out his palm toward her.

She handed him the knife slowly. Charlotte popped a couple of Life Savers into her mouth, and Carol shut her eyes.

When Carol opened her eyes again, Jason had the creature's abdomen slit from the base of his neck to his tiny genitals. She pressed the saturated cotton ball to the mouse's nose, watching as the little back feet twitched and the miniature heart beat rapidly.

It was all there; rapidly beating heart, tiny worm-like intestines, miniature stomach, spleen, bladder, all wet and pink and alive. Very little blood issued from the wound. Carol ducked her head thinking she might faint. She mustn't faint. This mouse represented a human being. Someday she'd witness surgery and if she was lucky, she might even get to assist. Nursing students were exposed very little to surgery these days. Anyone who wanted training as a surgical nurse had to apply to a hospital for in-service training as an OR nurse, or had to take a year of training at a university hospital as an OR technician.

"Notice the peristalsis of his intestines," Professor Murphy said suddenly over her shoulder. His finger pushed at the small intestine, no larger in diameter than a piece of string.

"I still can't see how this is any better than a picture," Charlotte snapped.

"Nor I," Carol murmured.

Murphy looked at Charlotte. "What would really teach you anatomy is an autopsy. Unfortunately, you'll probably never have an opportunity to see one. The real thing is better than any picture." He looked at Carol. She saw sympathy in his eyes for *them,* not the mouse.

"We can see this in surgery," Carol said.

"Only glimpses of certain areas. My guess is that as students you'll be lucky to see more than a hysterectomy and an appendectomy. With this live mouse, you can observe his heart beat, the peristalsis of his intestines, his stomach, and the constriction of his muscles. There's the spleen, and the bladder."

"We could have learned from a film," Charlotte insisted softly.

Mae, who hated the dissection as much as the rest of them, but who didn't want them to seem unprofessional, said apologetically to the instructor, "I guess we won't make very good nurses if we keep this kind of attitude, will we?"

Murphy smiled and said, "On the contrary, that's exactly the kind of attitude you *should* have as a nurse. I only hope you *can* keep it." And he moved away to another table.

Jason told Carol, "You can put him on out if you girls think you can label the organs in your manuals now."

"I could have done that before this absurdity," Charlotte said.

Carol poured more chloroform onto the cotton ball, hoping the little mouse would die quickly. He didn't. The tiny heart, smaller than the eraser on her pencil, kept beating and beating.

Jason glanced at his watch. "Five minutes. We've got only five minutes to clean up."

Carol shut her eyes just in time. When she opened them, Jason was tossing the heart onto the paper towel. Charlotte was pale, and Mae had turned away to wash her hands.

How would they ever be able to observe surgery if they were squeamish about dissecting a mere mouse? Maybe they weren't so much squeamish as they were sympathetic. Maybe that's what Murphy had meant. But was it really necessary that dozens of little mice die that day just so nursing students could observe a beating heart and peristalsis?

"You must learn to be objective," Murphy had said when they first began to dissect the fetal pig.

But would they ever?

Chapter Four

Fundamentals— The Last Days

In their first days of clinical experience, the students learned to give bedbaths. Over and over. They also learned to make beds. Over and over. They had anticipated learning many things quickly, and they had. But as the middle of the semester approached, they realized that staff nurses considered first-year nursing students useful for only two things; giving bedbaths and making beds. These two time-consuming occupations, when taken over by students, relieved the staff workload. Also, the students learned that hospital staff nurses wanted no part in teaching them anything; they were overworked and under-staffed and didn't have time and it wasn't their job anyway.

Once, when Carol realized she had been giving bedbaths and making beds for two months and hadn't given an enema yet or catheterized anyone or witnessed any treatments like spinal taps or a thoracenteses, she and Nancy approached the nurses' station where the nurses were jotting hurriedly in charts, answering the telephone, and flinging lab request slips around. Carol approached the charge nurse timidly and asked, "Is there anybody at all that I can catheterize? I haven't done it yet."

The nurses at the desk all paused and smiled amusedly at her. Then the charge nurse said, "Well, honey, if I don't get a break soon so that I can go to the bathroom, you can catheterize *me!*"

The nurses laughed hilariously at that and Carol and Nancy crept away from the station red-faced.

Nobody in the clinical group at Ross Street Presby had catheterized a patient yet except Bret. Since staff nurses didn't like to catheterize alert male patients, Bret was called on occasionally to do the job. The other students longed for such an opportunity, be it male or female. Since Presby's census was low and only a small percentage of patients needed to be catheterized when the students were there, the chances of a student getting to catheterize somebody were almost nil.

But one day when they were well into their fundamentals semester, Carol's patient's doctor ordered the patient to be catheterized sometime that morning, and Peavyhouse announced it in preclinical, saying that everybody could watch, because Carol's patient had agreed to it.

All the other students except Bret burned with envy as Carol, trembling, went to the supply room near the nurses' station to secure the catheter tray, and marched ahead of them down the corridor to room 110.

The patient was Mrs. Calpurnia Oglesby, age sixty-two, and she had been hospitalized the day before in order for her doctor to do a work-up on her to try to discover why she suffered constant abdominal pain. Mrs. Oglesby was a cheerful, raucous-voiced patient who wore red fingernail polish, smoked like a locomotive, and talked a lot about her favorite cocktails. Carol had introduced herself to her earlier and had explained in detail what catheterization meant and that she would catheterize her before she helped her with her bedbath and made her bed. Mrs. Oglesby was amusedly agreeable, but she put her wrinkled bejeweled fingers on Carol's arm and said, "Go ahead, sweetheart, and try. But you won't find the pee hole."

Carol had blushed furiously. "It's called a urethra, Mrs. Oglesby," she had told her. Medical terminology was something new and sacred to the students and anybody who didn't speak it was simply—simple. Gallbladder surgery was a cholecystectomy. You didn't give shots, you gave injections. The jawbone was a mandible, and you didn't chew, you masticated. If a patient lay flat, he was recumbent, and nobody had problems breathing, he experienced respiratory difficulty instead. And people didn't pee anymore, they urinated.

Besides, Carol knew she *could* find the urethra. She'd studied her *Bedside Nursing Techniques* book well and the diagrams on catheterization were very clear in her mind.

First she washed her hands as her fellow students watched enviously. Then she opened the sterile pack. The contents were impressive. There were disposable sterile drapes, a long clear plastic tube attached to the rubber catheter on one end and a clear plastic collection bag on the other; a packet of Betadine solution, cotton balls, a plastic forceps, a prefilled syringe of saline, and surgical gloves. After Carol placed the drapes, one beneath the patient's buttocks, the one with the little window over the patient's pubic area, she shakily pulled on the gloves. It took four tries on each hand to get her fingers into their proper glove fingers, but she sensed that the other students were impressed, nevertheless.

Next, she poured Betadine solution onto the sterile cotton balls. Although she felt herself begin to perspire, Carol then separated the patient's labia minora with the thumb and forefinger of her left hand; and with her right hand, she took the little plastic forceps, picked up a cotton ball, and cleansed the area—from the top to the bottom, one stroke. Another cotton ball, top to bottom, one stroke. She proceeded with the cleansing exactly as *Beside Nursing Techniques* had directed, from the inside toward the outside, left and right.

After all the cotton balls had been used, Carol picked up the prelubricated rubber catheter with its preattached syringe of saline. If all went well, she would thread the opaque, rubber catheter into the urethra, urine would appear in the clear tubing, and she would inflate the rubber balloon on the end of the catheter with the syringe of saline—which would keep the catheter from slipping out of the bladder—and the job would be finished.

Her moment of truth had come.

Tension in the room was unbearable. Would Carol contaminate the urethra? Would she be able to *find* the urethra?

She held her breath and bent down to look for the opening where it was supposed to be. *The urethra in the female patient is approximately one and one half inches long and is located posterior to the clitoris.*

But it wasn't there. Carol bit her lip and stuck the catheter where it ought to be. Nothing happened. After a gentle probe or two, somebody snickered.

"In the elderly patient the urethra is often inside farther," offered Miss Peavyhouse.

"You won't find it," Mrs. Oglesby said.

Carol steadfastly inserted the catheter farther inside, but since no urine appeared in the tubing, it became apparent that she wasn't in the right place.

Eyes tearing now, she looked at Nancy. Nancy's smile was frozen. Jo, the LVN, had done this procedure dozens—*hundreds* of times and she smirked. Another gentle probe or two was to no avail.

"Well, Jo," said Peavyhouse at last, "go get another catheter tray and demonstrate to us how it's done, will you?"

Carol's face burned with embarrassment and humiliation as she peeled off the Betadine-stained gloves and received secretly gleeful sympathetic remarks from some of the other students.

Jo reappeared still smirking. Nobody could smirk like Jo. She washed her hands, opened the sterile pack, snapped on the gloves, opened the patient's labia—and couldn't find the urethra.

Irritably, Peavyhouse decided not to put the patient through any more of this ordeal so she sent for another pair of sterile gloves and proceeded with the catheterization herself. But she couldn't find the urethra either.

Blushing and furious, she trailed with all ten female students to the nurses' desk and confessed. The charge nurse laughed, threw down her pencil, and shook her head incredulously. The students followed her as she took another catheter tray from the supply room and set off down the corridor to Mrs. Oglesby's room. They grouped around the bed once more as Mrs. Oglesby looked up at the charge nurse and said, "You won't find it."

"Now, now, Oglesby. Everybody's got one; otherwise how would you ever be able to urinate?" The charge nurse laughed as she snapped on her gloves.

"I don't know," Mrs. Oglesby said. "All I know is, nobody's *ever* been able to find it."

"Well, I've done a few thousand of these in my day, lady, and *I'll* find it."

She did not.

After ten minutes of probing and prodding, the charge nurse, embarrassed and furious, gathered up the catheter kit and dropped it into the wastebasket with the other two kits. "This is a job for the doctor," she announced.

Carol was sure her image had improved a little since her failure, but she was still disappointed. Luckily, she and Peavyhouse were at the desk when Mrs. Oglesby's doctor appeared. He laughed uproariously when the charge nurse explained their failure to catheterize the patient.

"Catheter tray," he commanded of the charge nurse as he took out his reading glasses and adjusted them on his nose. "Get me some number eight gloves, too. The ones in the tray are too small."

"May the students watch?" Mrs. Peavyhouse asked meekly.

He laughed. "Of course, of course," he roared. His name was Dr. Charles and he was tall, gray, fiftyish, and thoroughly self-confident.

Peavyhouse rounded up the other students and they trooped behind Dr. Charles down the corridor and into Mrs. Oglesby's room.

"You won't find it either," Mrs. Oglesby informed the doctor.

He roared and snapped on the gloves in two fluid motions. The charge nurse snapped open the catheter set.

"Tum-tum-tum-de-dum," hummed the doctor as he proceeded, and the ten students and two nurses moved closer around the bed to watch. The doctor glanced up as he picked up the Betadine-soaked cotton ball with the forceps. "Any of you happen to see *Manon* last week? Our civic opera is every bit as excellent as the Met in my opinion," he said. And not waiting for an answer, he bent his gaze back to the work at hand. "Rrrrrum-tum-diddy-dum-dum-dum. Rrrrrum-tum-diddy-diddy-diddy-dum. Tum-tum-tum—Turn that goddamned overhead light on, nurse," he commanded. The charge nurse obeyed and the doctor bent back to his work again. "Tum-tum-diddy-diddy-dum-dum-dum. Rrrrum-tum . . . diddy . . . dum . . . dum . . . dum . . ."

Ten minutes later the doctor paced furiously from the room followed by Mrs. Oglesby's "I told ya you wouldn't find it," and trailed by ten students and two nurses.

At the nurses' station he sat down and ran his hands through his hair. "I don't understand it," he told the charge nurse as he removed his glasses. "It's impossible. I've never encountered this problem before. I couldn't *see* it, I couldn't *feel* it. The damned thing just wasn't *there*."

As the students glanced at each other, he went on, "This is a medical first. It's got to be. I've never even *heard* of it before." He pondered about it and the more he thought about it the angrier he became. Finally he flung the patient's chart on the desk and said, "Hell, nurse. Everybody's got to have a pee hole!"

Carol wasn't sure, but she thought that Miss Peavyhouse's group at Ross Street Presbyterian were the only students who managed to get through fundamentals without giving an enema, passing a nasogastric tube, giving a surgical douche, or catheterizing anybody.

PART TWO

Chapter Five

Pediatrics

"Strawberry blonde."

Carol and Mae, riding the elevator down to the first floor, were standing with their backs to five young men in white lab coats, who they guessed were medical students from Bennet.

"What color do you reckon her eyes are, Duane?"

"Mmmmm, I'd say green."

"Naw. Brown."

Mae, the affable, laughed and turned toward the med students. Since she was happily married and safely maternal, she was as unself-conscious as a marigold. "You're both right." She laughed, glancing at Carol. Mae never saw a stranger and, consequently, was never regarded as one.

"No," said the voice called Duane wonderingly. "This I gotta see. Hey, student nurse with the strawberry blonde hair, turn around and let us see your eyes."

Carol turned toward the students. Most med students were either carefully polite to student nurses or they ignored them completely. Three of the medical students in the elevator were smiling embarrassedly at Carol while the other two grinned unabashedly.

The one called Duane had eyes the color of cocoa, extra shiny under bushy brows. Carol thought he looked a little like the late actor, Tyrone Power, as he peered into her face. "Yep, you're right. They're both colors."

Carol turned back smiling, her face flaming with embarrassment and delight.

"Explain *that* mixture of genes, Duane."

"You explain it, Pearson. You're the one who thinks he's going into ophthalmology."

"Don't show your ignorance. What's ophthalmology got to do with genealogy?"

"Ask Baker."

The elevator door slid open and Carol and Mae paced down the corridor and through the swinging doors of the cafeteria. Carol was sort of hoping the med students would follow them, but they didn't.

Anyway, a fifteen-minute break wasn't long enough for much conversation, but it was sufficient time to drink a cup of coffee or a Coke. At this hour of the day, 10:00 A.M., there wasn't much of a choice of snacks, just some Danish, donuts, packaged peanut butter and crackers, potato chips, a few bowls of solidified Jell-o, soft drinks on tap, and strong coffee from an overheated carafe.

Carol selected a Danish and a Coke, Mae a cup of coffee, and they went to a table and sat down.

All hospital cafeterias looked and smelled alike to Carol, their only differences being in size and the amount spent on decoration. The cafeteria at Children's Medical was decorated with Disney characters scampering about on the walls. No children ever ate here, but still the cafeteria was decorated with Disney characters. It may not have made much sense, but at least it broke the monotony.

Carol wasn't feeling well that morning, and the reason was her former patient, Willy Fry.

Willy Fry had been a four-year-old with straight dark brown hair. His face was pale and the tissue around his eyes was discolored. Carol had never seen the color of Willy's eyes.

Willy had lain in an oversized metal crib, sometimes very still, sometimes convulsing. When Carol had taken his vital signs he often had convulsed, which had been startling. His arms had drawn inward toward his chest and his knees had drawn up toward his abdomen, and he had held that position for several seconds before he had relaxed with four spasmodic jerkings. The crib had rattled. A stuffed Winnie the Pooh had sat in the corner of Willy's crib regarding him hopefully.

Willy was an abused child. That was all Carol had known at first, that and the fact that she must take his vital signs and intake and output hourly, and watch for signs of increased intracranial pressure. Nobody ever visited Willy.

Carol's anger at whoever had abused Willy was eclipsed at first by her horror at the little boy's condition, and her awareness that Mrs. Patterson had assigned *her* to the most talked-about child at Children's Medical.

Not that battered children were rare at Children's. They weren't. The charge nurse at the nurses' station told Carol that there was almost always a battered child or two convalescing in the hospital. But Willy wasn't convalescing; he was dying when Patterson had assigned Carol to his care.

That first day, Willy's vitals were below normal, as was expected. So was his output. As she touched the soft skin of his arms and bathed him gently, her anger grew. There were two old bruises on Willy's back and two burn scars on his chest.

After she had finished the bath, it was time to take his vitals again and it was nearly ten o'clock before she was able to hurry to the nurses' station to chart his vital signs and her own initial observations. It was then that she read Willy's chart thoroughly.

The first sheet in the chart was his admissions sheet. His name was William Bradford Fry. He would be five years old in December. He was the younger of two children, the son of a brickmason. His mother did not work outside the home.

Carol turned to the history and physical sheet.

This four-year-old white male was admitted at ten A.M. October 2nd directly from Bennet Memorial's ER via ambulance. At that time he was comatose. There were two contusions over the right scapula and two apparent burned lesions over his sternum, both in an advanced state of resolution.

Routine exam by me, abdominal tap, and x-rays showed no pathology. (See emergency admit sheet.) Pneumoencephalography done to determine source of intracranial pressure. (See x-ray report.) Lumbar puncture revealed increased pressure. (See progress notes), but no erythrocytes in spinal fluid. There were no objective signs of a blow to the skull.

I questioned the mother who said the father had only "shaken" the patient.

Diagnosis: advanced cerebral edema, due to multiple contusions to frontal and occipital lobes of the cerebrum, resulting in damage to as-yet-undetermined areas of brain.

Admitted to first-floor ward via stretcher.

Archibald Ruskin, M.D.

How cold and impersonal the history and physical was, the clinical evaluation of a child abused so severely that he was in coma, with a prognosis that was grave. It was evident that Willy had been abused before, but the act which had resulted in coma was unbelievably mild. The father had only shaken Willy.

Carol had never approached a doctor with a question before. She, like the rest of the students, was in awe of the doctors, a little afraid of them, and considerate enough not to intrude on their valuable time. And students were, without exception, ignored by the doctors.

In Willy Fry's chart, the physician in charge of his care, Dr. Ruskin, had not in any of his progress notes or in the history and physical, explained how shaking the child had caused coma. Luckily, Ruskin came into Willy's room to check on him while Carol was changing his diaper during her second day of his care.

Ruskin was short, dark, easy-going, and stood with his hands in his pockets looking down at the unconscious child in the crib.

"I read the history and physical on Willy, Dr. Ruskin," Carol ventured timidly. "But I don't understand how shaking a child can result in his becoming comatose."

However nebulous Dr. Ruskin had been at writing the history and physical on Willy, he was nevertheless one of those rare doctors who didn't mind teaching nurses, nursing students, or medical students; so he leaned against the wall, hands in his pockets and explained.

"The brain is suspended in the cranial vault in cerebral fluid. When Willy's father shook him, Willy's brain literally sloshed back and forth in his skull, slamming against the inside of the skull, bruising both the frontal and occipital lobes of his brain."

"Oh God," Carol breathed.

Ruskin went on. "The bruising caused swelling of brain tissue, cerebral edema, which cut off cerebral circulation. Very little blood was able to get through to the various parts of his brain because of the edema and those parts simply died." The doctor's eyes narrowed and his lips tightened over his teeth, turning white. "If the parents had brought Willy in when he first became lethargic, we could have given him a steriod to reduce the swelling and we *might*—I say we *might*—have been able to save his brain. Instead, they waited until he was unconscious. By then, it was too late."

After the doctor had left and Carol had finished with Willy's care, she went back to the nurses' station, charted his vital signs, and her observations in the nurses' notes:

Vital signs stable. Skin cool and dry, color good. Convulsions q. ten to fifteen minutes. Appears to be resting between convulsions.

(Patterson said even comatose patients were either restless or resting.) Carol signed her entry, *Carol W., S.N.*

Carol W., S.N. — student nurse — with a hell of a lot yet to learn about everything.

Today, Patterson had assigned her to ten-month-old Ricky Davis, and when she had finished taking Ricky's vital signs, she had stopped by room 101 to see Willy. The crib was empty.

Then she had gone to the nurses' station and asked the charge nurse about him.

"Willy?" the nurse said loudly as she looked up from a patient's chart. "Honey, Willy died yesterday."

Stunned, Carol couldn't speak.

Nodding, the nurse went back to writing her nurses' notes saying, "That's right. Willy died. Cerebral hemorrhage. Musta had a bruised vessel or something." She looked up again at Carol. "Don't fret, though, honey. You can bet there'll be charges filed against them parents. Not that it'll do any good. The doctor doesn't think they can convict somebody of shaking his kid to death."

Carol did not cry for Willy. But for the rest of the morning she felt like throwing up — or murdering a couple of parents. She hated pediatrics so far, but she was intensely glad they were through with fundamentals.

One of the worst things about fundamentals was that the students had been required to listen to from four to eight tapes a week up in the audio lab of the university library. For eleven weeks they had ridden the elevator up to the third floor, checked out tapes from a bored secretary, retired to private cubicles, placed the tapes on tape players, put on headphones, and hoped the damned things worked. Most of the time they did and the students would take notes furiously.

The ingenious device of putting lectures on tapes had saved Lena Black a lot of time and a lot of repetitious preparation. The only thing wrong with it was that the tapes had been made six years earlier and no longer coordinated with textbook assignments. The students might be studying chapters on the respiratory system, and Lena Black's taped lectures would be concerned with sickle cell anemia, herpes, and venereal disease.

It did not take the students long to discover that Black liked to say the word, acetylsalicylic acid instead of aspirin and that her favorite nerve was the vagus. Other than learning to pronounce the generic name for aspirin and that the vagus was the body's most important nerve, they learned nothing from the tapes. Some students tried skipping tapes, but that didn't last long because they discovered the hard way that the multiple-choice tests were based on the tapes, not on the reading assignments. The tests were six years old, too. Everybody complained, but it was like beating the Statue of Liberty with their fists.

Once they had finished fundamentals, they sighed with relief. Tapes were a thing of the past. But after their first pediatrics lecture, they found that something had taken the place of the tapes—nursing care plans.

The students complained again to each other. In this, the fall semester, they had three Pedi lectures a week to attend, three clinical days, six hours long;

A&P II with lecture three times a week and lab twice a week, plus three lectures in child development. It was too much to do in too little time. They often did not have time to eat lunch. Driving in noon traffic from clinical to school for a lecture took thirty to forty-five minutes, depending on the hospitals where they had their clinicals, and that was all the time they were allowed. Eating and drinking were not allowed in the classroom.

Every evening Carol sprawled on the bed in her room and studied her assignments. Then she did the nursing care plans. In Pedi, Mrs. Patterson, her pleasant but hard-to-please instructor, gave the students in her group their patient assignments a day ahead so that they could draw up their nursing care plans, but for some reason, their nursing care plans never pleased the instructor. It was never clear to anybody why this was the case. Carol had been assigned to Children's Medical along with a completely different group of students from those in her group at Ross Street Presbyterian, and the only classmate from fundamentals clinical assigned to Children's was Mae. By the second week of Pedi, Carol knew she hated it. This feeling was intensified by her failure to receive A's on her nursing care plans. She couldn't understand why nobody, *nobody,* made an A on a care plan; their format was simple.

You wrote a page or so of the patient's medical history, and your own assessment of his needs. You wrote another page about what research you had done in order to plan your "nursing action" to meet those needs. Then, step three, you developed a plan of care:

PROBLEM	NURSING GOAL
Diaper rash	To help cure rash and prevent further breaking out of rash

NURSING ACTION	SCIENTIFIC PRINCIPLE
Change diapers immediately after wetting	Ammonia from stale urine causes allergic reaction

Then sometimes the care plans went on for pages and pages. In the cafeteria on her break, Carol was now showing Mae a particular care plan, for which she had received a disgusting eighty-six. Mae hadn't received a passing mark in Pedi yet. Her two test scores had been below seventy-five—which in nursing school was a D—and her care plans were a daily disaster. Mae just couldn't get the hang of the care plans.

Mae always maintained a smile on her face, but lately the smile was beginning to look a bit strained and Carol was determined to help her. She opened up her ten-page care plan, written in longhand on notebook paper.

"It's a matter organization," she told Mae. "The instant you walk into a patient's room, you make an initial assessment; his position, coloring, clearness of eyes, feel of his skin, mental status, and so on. Then you think, 'what is my goal to help this patient?' You think long-term goal, short-term goal . . ."

"But that sounds so cold and impersonal," Mae said. "When I walk into a room, I see a sick kid. I go and talk to him, hold him. I don't think about long-term goals and short-term goals. I don't assess all the things that aren't right with him."

Carol knew this was so. Mae loved her patients, but . . . "Mae, assessing and planning care is part of the objectivity we have to develop in order to be nurses. Besides, you do some assessing while you're holding him. Are his eyes clear? Is he lethargic or listless . . . ?"

Mae shook her head and looked down into her cup of coffee.

"Mae, look. You can be a warm, feeling person, and make an objective assessment at the same time. It's just a matter of developing a *therapeutic* objectivity."

While Shelly and Charlotte vied for top scores on every test in every subject, Mae's and Jo's scores hovered just above or below passing. Mae had become another of Carol's school buddies. Mae needed moral support and Carol guessed that Mae hoped to absorb some of her knowledge, maybe by the process of osmosis. In lecture now, it was always Charlotte on the aisle seat, then Carol, then Mae, then Jo. Or Jo and Mae might occasionally swap seats, but Carol and Charlotte never changed. Jo liked Mae, but she didn't like Charlotte. Mae liked everybody. Charlotte tolerated both Mae and Jo because they were Carol's clinical buddies. In every lecture, the four sat together no matter what, like crows on a fence, set in their ways.

"There's a June bug in my Jell-O!"

Carol and Mae looked up from the care plan. Neither of them had noticed the two medical students when they'd entered the cafeteria.

"I swear to God!" the student named Duane said incredulously as he stood beside their table with a bowl of lime-flavored Jell-O in one hand and a cup of coffee in the other. "It's a damned June bug!"

The student named Charley said, "Aw c'mon, Duren. Stop trying to grandstand to get attention."

"No!" Duane exclaimed. "Look! I swear! It's a damned June bug!" He set the bowl down on the table beside Carol and pointed. "It's a June bug," he said softly. "I don't believe it, but there it is."

"It can't be," said Charley. "Not in October."

Carol's mouth flew open as she looked at the Jell-O. There were a couple of small grapes in it, a few pieces of diced fruit, and a June bug — big as life, suspended like a museum exhibit, legs and all.

"Oh my God!" she said.

Duane said, "There, you see?" to Charley. "I always suspected some of their food was six months old."

Charley bent down his brown, tousled head and

peered closely at the Jell-O. "I'll be damned," he breathed, and straightening said to Duane, "I'd go get my money back if I were you."

Oblivious to the stares of a few lab techs and nurses sitting around at the tables, Duane stood a moment looking across the cafeteria to the far wall, then said thoughtfully, "No. No, I think I'll take this up with the hospital administrator."

"Oh c'mon, Duren."

Duane looked at his friend. "Do you realize, Charley, that if we let this go nothing will ever be done about it? Somebody let down on their job and it ought to be called to the attention of the authorities. If this is the kind of quality control the dietary department has, I wonder how many little kids have eaten worms and bugs and—no telling what else."

Charley looked sheepishly wide-eyed. "Yeah. Maybe you're right."

Carol smiled. Suddenly she really liked Duane and she looked up at him. He saw her smile and his half-thoughtful indignant expression changed, his face softened as he returned her smile.

"But should you rock the boat, Duane?" said Charley.

Duane looked at him. "If it means some little kid won't have to eat June bugs with his Jell-O, I'll risk it," said he gallantly.

Charley crept away to another table with his cup of coffee and Duane sat down in the chair beside Carol. She sipped her Coke, aware that he was staring at her, and when he said nothing, she looked back at him.

"Your mother must have green eyes and your father brown."

She shook her head. "Nope."

He was magnificent: tall, broad-shouldered, small through the hips; he had black curly hair and cocoa eyes. "Are you a senior?" he asked.

"Junior."

"I'm a third-year med student. Bennet."

"And you're on pediatrics rotation?"

"Right."

They looked at each other for a moment and when it became apparent that neither of them had anything else to say, Carol went back to drinking her Coke and Duane to his coffee.

Presently Duane said, "Your mother has brown eyes and your father green."

She laughed at him. "No. Both blue."

"Both blue," he said thoughtfully. And when neither of them could think of anything else to say, they went back to sipping their drinks.

Mae said, "Are you really going to take that Jell-O to the administrator?"

"Oh, indeed I am. I'm a firm believer that unless we as consumers complain about such things as defective merchandise and contaminated foodstuffs, things are going to get a lot worse. I once mailed a worm I found in my broccoli to Kildaire Corporation in California. It was frozen broccoli which I cooked myself. Ate half of it, then found a big fat worm in it. So I mailed the worm to them in a match box with a note that said, 'I won't tell if you won't.' Do you know what I got in return?"

Mae was laughing. "No."

"A letter from the manager of quality control at Kildaire Corporation thanking me for my 'interest' and a fifty-nine-cent coupon for another package of frozen broccoli."

They laughed.

Duane, still grinning, looked at Carol. "I'll bet you're a natural with kids and love pediatrics."

"I hate pediatrics."

Duane nodded. "I do, too. I like kids, but I hate pediatrics."

Suddenly the paging operator's voice sounded over the system overhead. "Duane Duren, please call the operator. Duane Duren, call the operator please."

Duane stood up. "That'll be Leventhal," he said. "He's a chief of pediatrics at Bennet and I'm supposed to meet with him and a couple of others to examine a little kid with Down's syndrome."

"Going to take your Jell-O?" Mae asked.

Duane picked up the bowl. "It's my duty as a committed student of medicine. Do I have a choice?"

Carol laughed and Duane looked at her again. "Besides," he said, "I hate June bugs. You know why?"

"No." She laughed.

"Because they're stupid. And they're useless. Tell me one thing they're good for. One."

"Sparrow food," Carol offered.

He grinned. "You're right. Will I be seeing you around?"

"In the mornings."

"I'll keep an eye out for you."

"Duane Duren, please call the operator. Duane Duren, call the operator, please," the operator paged again.

Duane turned to leave, stopped, turned back. "Your name," he said.

"Carol."

"Carol," he said softly, then again "Carol", as if to memorize the name, and left through the swinging doors of the cafeteria carrying his Jell-O.

The rest of the morning Carol kept an eye out for Duane, but didn't see him. Going to the parking lot of Children's Medical Hospital, which was an extension of Bennet's pediatrics department, she decided that maybe she'd get to like pediatrics after all.

The students were in their third week of pediatrics and had encountered some really interesting but heartrending cases. But so far everybody hated pediatrics. Sick kids bothered them. The kids' parents weren't particularly happy to have students "practicing" on their children—until they noticed that the students were more available than the hospital staff nurses and gave their kids more attention. The nursing care plans were hard to do, the schedule impossible to meet. And to make everything worse, their pediatrics lecture instructor was a queer.

Mario Manticello had never been married, had never had a child, always wore pink oxford cloth shirts, navy slacks, and loafers decorated with gold coins and tassles. He maintained a healthy dislike for the students, sneering at their answers when he asked questions in lecture, and he was immensely fond of telling them, "You must learn to do more than give bedbaths. Apes can be trained to give bedbaths. Use your *brains*, people. You're not using your *brains*." But worse than anything else he did, he liked to give pop quizzes with trick questions:

> *Your five-month-old patient has just had surgery to repair his cleft lip. His mother brings him a rattle to play with. You would:*
> 1. *Tie the rattle to the side of the crib out of his reach.*
> 2. *Let him have the rattle.*
> 3. *Tie the rattle over his head so that he can reach toward it, but not grasp it.*
> 4. *None of the above.*

Most everybody in lecture circled number three. They were wrong, Manticello informed them triumphantly. The students protested.

Manticello raised his brows and pointed to Carol. "You. What's your name? Welles? Why did you circle number three?"

"Because you can't let a five-month-old with a

repaired cleft lip have the rattle because he'll put it in his mouth which could cause him to injure his lip," Carol said.

"Ah," said Manticello cheerfully as he tapped his pen on the lectern. "But the question stated that he had a repaired cleft *lip* not palate! He couldn't hurt his lip so he should have the rattle."

The logic was obvious to Manticello but not to everybody else.

"Brains," he said pointing to his head. "Learn to use your *brains,* people. Learn to do something besides give bedbaths. Apes . . ."

Another characteristic of Manticello's that annoyed the students was his obsession with cleaning the earpieces of stethoscopes with alcohol-soaked pledgets. Everybody did it except full-fledged nurses and doctors; but occasionally some preoccupied student would forget and Manticello liked to swoop down upon students in clinical and demand to see their alcohol pledgets which they were supposed to keep in their pockets.

But, in spite of hating pediatrics and care plans, Carol was still maintaining an A, and her two constant companions, Jo and Mae, never left her wanting for somebody close with whom to bitch.

Chapter 6

Child Development

Ronald Conklemeyer was a bachelor, had never been married, did not have a child, and taught child development. His theories of child development were patterned closely after Freud's. Infants went through the oral stage, anal stage, Oedipal stage. Every male child, he was convinced, played in his own feces during the anal stage, and later fantasized about having sex with his mother.

The students knew there was something odd about Conklemeyer the first day of lecture when he came into the classroom pulling a rolling, quacking, toy duck. Nobody ever got the point of it, and he never explained. It wasn't long before the students were *certain* there was something odd about Conklemeyer because he talked excessively about the anal stage of child development. With an expressionless face and cool manner, he discussed feces, rectums, anuses, hemorrhoids, and constipation, over and over. After Conklemeyer's class all the students felt like washing their hands.

It was mid-semester when Conklemeyer asserted for the hundredth time that every male child played in his feces and fantasized about having sex with his mother.

The class groaned as a unit and Carol, who had a younger brother who never did any such thing, asserted herself.

"How can you say that *every* child does such things?" she asked, her voice ringing clear and high in the classroom. "Every child is different and besides, everybody knows Freud was screwed up on some of his theories."

The class roared.

Conklemeyer eyed her unperturbed. "*Every* child," he said. "And every theory, as you call it, of Freud's is not theory. It's *fact.*"

Married students with children protested, and the classroom became an uproar.

Easygoing Bret Harris, who never spoke up much in class, was red-faced when the students turned to see why he had guffawed so loudly. Bret was tapping his pen on his desk, and leveling a disgusted gaze at the child development instructor. "You may have played in feces when you were a kid, Mr. Conklemeyer, maybe you still do, but that doesn't mean *every* kid does it."

The students wanted to roar, but instantly they swung their faces around to look at the instructor.

Conklemeyer was pale and said in a steady, cool voice, "What's your name? Harris? Well, Harris, please leave this classroom immediately and consider yourself dismissed from lecture for the rest of the semester."

After class Carol met Bret in the corridor. "I've taken good notes in child development today, Bret. Why don't you copy mine."

Bret had been friendly to her, but had not

telephoned her again after the time he had given her the math formula. He smiled. "Thanks Carol, I'd like that." He walked along beside her to the elevator. "That instructor, Conklemeyer, irritates me. Manticello irritates me. I guess I'm just generally irritated because they've gotten bachelors to lecture in pediatrics and child development."

They stopped in front of the elevators. "Bret, why did you choose to go into nursing?"

The door opened and they stepped inside with seven other students. "I like the hospital atmosphere, the drama, the tension, even the routine. I like people. I don't have the money to go to med school — and no initiative. For one thing, I spent four years in the navy and I'm too old now to start thinking about four years of college, plus four years of med school, plus four or five years' residency."

Carol watched him, saw the light in his eyes flicker and go out, then return. As the elevator door opened out onto the university lobby and they began to walk through it, she said, "You didn't really answer me, Bret."

"I know. It's painful. I was a patient in a veterans' hospital for a while after 'Nam and saw a lot of . . . crap . . . doctors doing a lousy job on the servicemen, nurses' neglect—"

"So you figured somebody needed to step in and do something?"

He smiled quickly. "Yeah. I'd like to go on for my master's in nursing, and on and on to the top. Get some . . . crap . . . straightened out in that particular veterans' hospital— Sorry, Carol, but you asked."

"I'm glad I did," she said.

In the school parking lot, Bret came to his car before she came to hers and he turned to her smiling. She looked at him closely for the first time.

He wasn't tall, only just under six feet, had blue eyes, brown hair, wide shoulders, and a boyish face that was sprinkled with the same fading freckles across the bridge of his nose and his cheeks that she had on her own. Bret never seemed to get flustered or frustrated. He was "laid back," as Jo put it — easygoing, shrugging his way through nursing school and making B's without much effort.

In fundamentals he'd been assigned to male patients only, in Pedi to male children. Bret's nursing experience so far had been strictly male-oriented, and Carol wondered what would become of him next semester in obstetrics. For the same objectives that applied to female nurses did not apply to male nurses. Bret and the other male students were a threat to everybody; to female patients because they were male, to male patients because they were suspect, to female nurses because male nurses were often better organized and calmer under stress, and to doctors because they weren't easily intimidated. That's why Carol asked him why he had become a nurse.

"Thanks for the notes," he said smiling. "Need any help with the pediatrics solutions, call me. My name's in the student directory, too."

"Thanks," Carol said and went on to her car. Pediatrics math problems weren't too different from the ones for adults. All you had to do was learn Young's rule — age in years divided by age plus twelve, times the adult dose equals the child's dose — for kids two to twelve years old. And Cowling's rule and Fried's rule, and Clark's rule. No problem. All that was required was that you be a mathematical genius and have the memory of an elephant.

Going home, Carol counted on her fingers just how many days they had left of Pedi. Twenty-two. Twelve clinical lectures. She'd never make it. Bret would never make it. Neither would Mae, or Jo.

As it turned out, she was wrong about everybody.

Chapter 7

Anatomy & Physiology II

Dissections of fetal pigs and live mice were over. Crucifying frogs on crosses of wire for the purpose of observing muscular and tendon reflexes was over too. The second semester of A&P focused on physiology and the disease process. Out had come the lab's microscopes and the various dyes for staining the different types of tissues for study.

Midway through the fall semester, the enrollment in nursing school had dropped from two hundred seventy-two to two hundred thirty. Everybody knew that, because all those remaining had to do was count the number of social security numbers that were posted with the test scores. Lecture profs made no attempt to know individual students. Grades were posted by the professors' office doors, not by name but by the last four digits of the students' social security numbers.

After every A&P test, Carol began looking for her score down near the bottom of the sheet, but invariably, to her surprise and delight, followed the numbers up until she found hers near the top. Charlotte and Shelly jockeyed for the very top score. They had never officially met, but each knew the other's social security number. Bret's grades hovered near Carol's, and Mae's and Jo's scores hovered somewhere just above or below the last passing grade. Competition for good test scores was fierce. Shelly and Charlotte were often accused of cheating. Rumors flew, especially those about the two highest scoring students because their scores were consistently high and it didn't make sense to those who studied and worked and never made a top score. One rumor was that Charlotte was having an affair with somebody (nobody knew who) in the university's office where the test sheets were Xeroxed. Rumors flew that Shelly had an "in" with every instructor she had. Nobody actually believed the rumors, but it helped to lessen the tension to mouth them. Students eyed each other with suspicion just before and immediately after every test. Then forgot their suspicions and forgave everybody afterward. The rest of the time, between tests, they were Florence Nightingales carrying the lamp of idealism that never went out. They were eager to aid the omnipotent physicians in their struggles to fight sickness, and to save their future patients single-handedly from death. After a semester and a half they were still naive.

LVNs like Jo—who shared the lab table with Carol and Charlotte—were not naïve. One med-vet who had failed the entrance exam even though he was an LVN and worked in a hospital ICU, was not naïve either. He was of Mexican descent and his name was Rio. It irritated Charlotte that Rio did his lab tests sloppily. She and Carol and Jo took great pains to do their CBCs carefully. After having drawn blood from each other's fingers and smeared the blood on slides, they placed the slides under the microscope and counted every single blood cell; the red blood cells, called erythrocytes, that looked like fat frisbees; the white blood cells, each type with different characteristics. They recorded everything precisely in their lab manuals. Rio couldn't see how counting blood cells made you an R.N. so he wrote down erroneous numbers in his lab manual. When the girls studied hemoglobin and hematocrit values and learned how to do the lab tests that resulted in such values, Rio faked that too.

One day Charlotte was washing her hands and Rio said, "You wash hands, all of you girls, alla time. You wash your hands. Are you going to a tea party?"

Charlotte was a perfectionist and an idealist and that irritated Rio almost as much as his disinterest and sloppy work irritated her. "We wash our hands, Rio, to reduce the possibility of transmitting germs. Don't tell me you don't wash your hands at the hospital."

"Rarely."

Charlotte gasped. "Are you kidding? You work in ICU and never wash your hands?"

"You'll see," Rio said. "Real nurses don't have time. And what do you wash your hands for? Washing doesn't kill germs. If you took microbiology you'd know nothing kills germs but sterilization."

Charlotte and Carol exploded at once. "Washing reduces the number of germs on your hands—"

"Reduces. It doesn't do away with them completely. In five minutes after you wash, the germs have multiplied back to their original number."

It was absurd, of course, and anyone but Charlotte would have shrugged and let it go, thinking Rio was nuts so why bother with him. But Charlotte said, "Reduction is better than nothing, fool. You accumulate bacteria all day and carry them from patient to patient. How could you!"

Rio shrugged. "You're telling me, Charlotte. I've been in the clinical situation for years; you haven't. You'll see. You girls are all perfectionists. Nobody that's been a nurse for years is a perfectionist anymore."

His statement was disconcerting and Jo did not deny it. All she said was, "Rio's right in a way. Don't get me wrong, though. I wash my hands. But you and Carol are a little extreme about it."

Disconcerting. Were there really nurses who did not wash their hands?

Carol refused to let her idealism die. A tough grading system, complaints, pessimism, suspicion, disappointment with instructors; it was all a part of nursing school. It was a rendering-out process in which all the excess fat was removed from the students, such as sentimentalism, carelessness, fantasies about medicine and medical personnel. It was all a part of toughening, a survival of the fittest. Students who couldn't take it dropped out of school. Those who didn't pass dropped out forever; or if they were determined, reenrolled for the next year. Most, like Carol, wouldn't have dropped nursing school for the world, because in spite of all the unpleasant things about it, it was still the most fascinating and rewarding experience in the world.

"Carol."

She was walking down the corridor of Children's

Medical toward the conference room when Duane Duren called to her and galloped up to her side.

"Hi," she said. "Where have you been?"

"Here, there, everywhere," he told her as they paused in the corridor. "Med school's not like nursing school. We hop around a lot. You leaving?"

"Not yet."

Duane glanced down the corridor. "I don't want to be seen talking to you because I'm supposed to be making rounds, practicing to be an intern, you see." He grinned. "So if you see Leventhal, tell me."

"I don't know Dr. Leventhal when I see him. He's chief of pedi over at Bennet and I've never been to Bennet."

"He's chief here, too, but he's a busy man. I'm flattered that I'm one of the few whom he takes around with him. Say, listen, meet me for coffee in the cafeteria in—" He glanced at his watch. "In about an hour."

She laughed. "In an hour I'll be taking a test in child development."

"Oh. Well—tell you what. Give me your phone number."

Carol didn't move for a moment. Let something get started with this energetic med student? Could she handle that and nursing school, too? She smiled, took out the little notebook from her pocket, wrote down her number, tore off the page, and handed it to him.

"Thanks." He grinned, looking down at the piece of paper. "Carol Welles, eh? Sounds like Christmas." He glanced up, his smile faded, he whispered, "Leventhal," and walked away from her casually, stuffing her telephone number into his pocket as he went.

Carol Welles, eh? Sounds like Christmas. The rest of the semester she smiled when she remembered that. Every evening after that day she half-expected his call.

But it didn't come until she had altogether quit expecting it.

PART THREE

Chapter 8

Obstetrics
Labor and Delivery

Most Southern Christmases are not snowy and neither was this one. The sun was shining brightly through misty-cool air when Carol returned to her apartment. The small compact car, which she'd purchased while working as a typist for an insurance firm for four years after high school, was laden with useless gifts, mostly clothes—dressy things she'd never wear.

What she really needed was school clothes—skirts, blouses, sweaters, jeans. She could wear the student uniform in clinical, but must change into street clothes after postclinicals, to attend classes. Uniforms were not allowed on campus. Her parents were paying her way through school and paying her rent, though they disapproved of unmarried females living in apartments. Any girl who didn't want to live with her parents while she went to school was suspect, as far as her folks were concerned. They were old-fashioned. When *they* had been young girls had stayed at home until they could catch a fellow at a church picnic or something, and everybody got married soon after high school. During her working days Carol had saved several thousand dollars for spending money and relatives often tried to help her out by buying her clothes for Christmas or sending money on birthdays.

They meant well but as she pulled the car into her own private parking slot outside the apartment complex, she was thinking how glad she was that she had been able to escape from the annual family conclave early. It was Christmas afternoon and she'd gotten her fill of the family's get-together at her parents' house in the suburbs: middle-aged aunts discussing menopause and operations, uncles discussing fishing and politics, weird cousins not her age, and everybody's kids—the noise, the chatter. It was fun for a while and she really had enjoyed everybody, but for a twenty-five-year-old things like family get-togethers get old fast.

Now she was wishing she could carry all the stuff inside at once. She began to pile boxes one on top of the other in her arms. Sleeves and hems hung out of boxes along with tissue and ribbon as she kicked the car door shut. Staggering, she went to her door. A sheet of tissue paper blew from a box in the inevitable wind as she fumbled with her key in the lock of the door. A box fell and a velvet blazer sleeve flopped into a puddle of water left on her porch by a brief winter shower.

"Oh you stupid—" she began and shoved the door open. She bent to pick up the blazer and boxes slid and toppled, half-in, half-out of her door.

The telephone began to ring, and in her hurry and fury she lost patience and began to kick the boxes inside the door, slamming it shut behind her at last, and locking it. Then howling, she limped to the telephone; she had forgotten Aunt Agnes had given her a set of white onyx book ends, of all things—

Her apartment was a one-room efficiency with a sitting room at one end of the room and the bedroom at the other. Her kitchen was but an alcove with cabinets. She ate on a TV tray.

She sat down on her bed holding her foot and moaning, and answered the telephone. "Carol speaking."

"Carol?" It was a male voice, and her heart leaped into her mouth.

"Yes?"

"Bret Harris. Merry Christmas."

For an instant as she held her breath, she hated Bret Harris. Hated him for existing. "Hi, Bret," she said disappointedly. "Merry Christmas to you, too."

There was silence on the other end of the line for a moment. "Uh . . . did I intrude on something? Or something?"

"No. I just kicked Aunt Agnes's book ends."

There was silence again on Bret's end of the line.

Carol laughed. "It's a long story. The book ends are onyx."

"Oh," he said. "That explains everything."

She giggled.

"Just was curious where they assigned you for OB," Bret said.

Carol sighed. "St. John's Episcopal."

"You didn't get Bennet as you'd hoped."

"No. Did you?"

"No. I got St. John's, too. Don't be disappointed," he said. "St. John's has one of the best obstetrics units in the city. Brand-new like the rest of the hospital, in a prestigious part of town."

"I know. It's just that I've looked forward to being assigned to Bennet from the beginning of nursing school. To work at Bennet is my ultimate goal."

"I thought your ultimate goal was to be a nurse."

"It is. You're right. Now, Bret, why did you call?"

"It's Christmas and I'm lonesome. Got no family in town; couldn't afford to go home for Christmas; I'm tired of my friends; and I . . . thought of you."

Carol remained silent. Bret was nice, but—

"I was wondering how you feel about the instructor we were assigned to and our textbook, stuff like that."

"Bret," she said lying back against her pillows. "All of us are looking forward to OB, probably more than any other nursing courses. To see a baby born must be the most wonderful thing in the world. OB's going to be terribly fascinating."

"It'll be the pits for me."

She smiled. "Sorry, Bret. You're probably right. I can't imagine what you'll do while the rest of us—"

"Yeah. That's what I mean," he said. "What will the male students do? It haunts me in the middle of the night. An entire semester of . . . what?"

Poor Bret must have been pretty "down." No family with whom to share Christmas in town and facing a semester of nursing that offered nothing at all for a male nurse. They talked about it. He couldn't observe a woman in labor, no woman or her husband would allow that. He couldn't observe delivery. He couldn't work on the post-partum floor where new mothers were staggering about in filmy gowns, and breast-feeding babies. Again the same privileges to learn which the female nursing students took for granted, were denied the male students. Doctors were male, but somehow that was different. Why?

"It's our society, I guess, Bret."

"Well, I really am not anxious to watch a birth or see a lady in labor. In fact it scares me. But I've got to earn a credit for the course and it bothers me. What *will* we male students do?"

They found out two weeks later during their first day of lecture in obstetrics.

Clinical instructors would take turns lecturing in obstetrics three days a week in the university auditorium as usual, Lena Black told them after she had the instructors pass out seven mimeographed handouts. All male students, she said, would view films of the birth process during clinical, including normal labor and delivery, Caesarean section, and post-partal medical problems. "They will, however, be able to participate with the rest of the students in the newborn nursery experience."

While Lena Black continued to talk, Carol, Charlotte, Jo, and Mae flipped through their handouts.

"Why Some Mothers Reject Their Babies; The Maternal Touch; The First Trimester; A Wife's View; A Husband's View; The Second Trimester; The Third Trimester; Abnormalities of the Placenta; Regional Anesthesia in Obstetrics; Obstetrics Terms (viable, para, gravida—)". . .

Carol was going to like OB. Her instructor was Mabel Hawthorn, a matronly woman of fifty whose jet black hair color was as fake as her dry wit was genuine. St. John's Episcopal Hospital was only four years old "and one thousand beds strong," Hawthorn told her clinical group their first day.

Labor and delivery, which the students learned to call L&D their first day, was in a separate wing of the hospital. In L&D students wouldn't wear their uniforms; they would wear surgical scrub dresses or pantsuits just like real L&D nurses, Hawthorn said.

Carol was not acquainted with anyone in her new clinical group except Bret. During their first preclinical, Carol perceived that Mabel Hawthorn was going to see that Bret did more in clinical than view films, and that the female students would do more than just observe the labor and delivery process. Hawthorn said she believed students should "jump in and get their feet wet," to experience as much and learn as much in the six hours they were under her "wing" as was humanly possible. After the twenty minutes of preclinical, she said, "Okay, people, it's prime time for obstetricians to pit patients, for nursery nurses to bathe the babies, and for the post-partum floor to start buzzing; so you two who have been assigned to L&D first; let's go see who's on the nest."

There were ten students in Hawthorn's clinical group, but they were divided into three areas. There were three in L&D including Bret, four who were assigned to post-partum, and three to the newborn nursery. Bret would view films today of the labor process, Hawthorn said, from which she would rescue him if somebody went into the delivery room to deliver. Minnie Fields was the other student assigned to L&D with Carol.

Labor and Delivery. The mysterious inner sanctum

lay beyond wide, pneumatic doors that sighed open when Carol, Minnie, and their instructor approached. Within, all was quiet. The walls here were painted a no-nonsense beige and the woodwork was trimmed in chocolate brown. On one side of a corridor, seven small private rooms were lined up side by side; across from labor rooms three and four was the nurses' station, a laminated, two-tiered desk where three L&D nurses were sitting, waiting for something to happen. Behind the nurses' station the three delivery rooms remained dark—nothing going on in there.

Hawthorn took her charges by the elbow and propelled them gently toward the nurses' station. The nurses looked up from their charts, their lab slips, and their romance novels, and regarded the trio, their faces remaining expressionless.

As Carol and Minnie stood smiling hopefully, Hawthorn introduced them to the nurses whom she quizzed about who was in labor and who was scheduled to be admitted. A chubby black-headed nurse whose nametag—pinned over one ample breast—announced that her name was Beth Gregory, looked over at the big-breasted red-headed nurse sitting beside her and said, "Well, all we've got at the moment is Jackie O'Hara. One of the students can be assigned to her."

"Don't give them Claiborne," the pretty red-headed nurse said.

Beth smiled almost apologetically at Hawthorn. "Claiborne's a primagrav who's going to give Lamaze a try. Liz here has claimed her for her very own. She's on her way to the hospital now."

"Well, I'm sure Liz won't mind having a little help

with Claiborne once the pit group starts coming in," Hawthorn said. I'd like to assign Minnie to O'Hara and Carol to Claiborne."

The nurses raised their brows simultaneously. A nursing instructor who could speak L&D? They glanced at each other.

Meanwhile, Carol was thinking. Primagrav? Pit group? She looked from Hawthorn to the nurses, then back to Hawthorn.

"No way," red-headed Liz said. "Claiborne's been attending our natural childbirth classes and if she's attended by a student, she may lose confidence."

Since fundamentals clinical, Carol had felt like the seventh teat on a sow with six piglets, and this attitude of the nurses was nothing new. A student had to prove herself a non-nuisance before the staff nurses would even speak to her.

Hawthorn stood her ground, but she had to walk a tightrope too. As an instructor from the university, she had to avoid disagreements with the nurses who were, in effect, the students' hostesses, yet she must see to it that her students extracted every ounce of knowledge they could from their clinical experience. In fundamentals and pediatrics, both Peavyhouse and Patterson had been easily intimidated by busy staff nurses. Since UTE's students were "allowed" to practice in their hospitals, the instructors hadn't wanted to make waves. Hawthorn figured you couldn't make waves on a choppy sea anyway and said, "Carol is a good student, and she is warm and empathetic. She's calm in crisis and knows when to holler for help if she needs to. She's a natural for Claiborne."

Carol stared at Hawthorn, thinking, She's bluffing!

Hawthorn's bluff worked.

Beth said, "Well . . . all right. But if we see that Claiborne is becoming antsy, we'll have to assign Carol to somebody else."

"You gotta deal," the instructor said.

Antsy? Primagrav? Pit group? It was terminology not in the textbook, but to Carol it sounded more intriguing than the terminology that was.

Beth gave them a brief report on Jackie O'Hara who was in labor room two, who was a para three, gravida four. Carol remembered yesterday's reading assignment in *Maternity Nursing* and understood that to mean that O'Hara had had three viable fetuses and that this was her fourth pregnancy. O'Hara had been admitted at 5:10 that morning, and was to have a caudal anesthetic. When she was through giving the report, Beth pointed to what she called the "scoreboard," a chalkboard mounted on the wall behind the nurses' station.

NAME	GRAVIDA	ADMIT	DIL	STATION
O'Hara	IV	5:10A	3 cm	0

Hawthorn tapped on Minnie's shoulder. "Okay, child, what's a para?"

Minnie's freckled face flushed. "Para is the number of past pregnancies that have reached the period of viability."

"Gravida?"

"A pregnancy?"

"Yes. O'Hara is a para three, gravida four because she's now pregnant for the fourth time. How many babies would she have delivered?"

"Three."

"After she delivers this one she'll be a para—"

"Four."

Hawthorn pounded Minnie's plump back. "Good girl." Then she turned to Carol. "What does three centimeters mean?"

"That O'Hara's cervix is dilated three centimeters."

"Station?"

Station. Station. "Uh—the location of the head of the baby in relation to the ischeal spines."

"What if the baby's breech?"

"Well, it's the relation of the *presenting part* in relation to the ischeal spines."

"That's better. And what's the proper term to use instead of baby?"

"Fetus." Dum-dum, Carol thought. Why didn't I use the right terms as Minnie did?

Hawthorn smiled. "Just a bunch of gobbledegook right now, isn't it, girls? Well, hang on to your hats because it's going to all come together for you real quick now. Minnie, you can go to your patient now. Carol, why don't you go with her until your patient arrives?"

If Jackie O'Hara's cervix was dilated three centimeters, it meant that her labor had just begun. When the students walked into Jackie's room she smiled as if she recognized them, held up ten fingers, made a fist, held up five more fingers. "Fifteen minutes apart," she said smiling. It was evident from Jackie's relaxed and cheerful attitude that she had been through this experience before. Her round face was slightly flushed as she told them that her labor pains were only hard contractions of the uterus at the

108

moment, not much pain. Carol knew that a gravida four could dilate more rapidly, though, than a primagravida—ah! A primigrav, as Beth had called it. Suddenly, as the girls stood beside her bed trying to look experienced, Jackie screwed up her face, turned on her side, gripped the bedrail, and said softly, "Damn." Minnie swallowed and glanced at the clock on the wall at the foot of Minnie's bed. At three centimeters, Jackie was in what the textbook called the latent phase of the first stage of labor, but Carol had the feeling that the latent phase was about to phase out into the active phase, when the cervix would begin to dilate quickly. Carol took Jackie's hand and Jackie looked up at her.

"I think you'd better tell the nurse that I need something for pain. Because by the time it takes effect . . ." Jackie began.

Minnie was allowed to give Jackie her injection of Demerol, and as she was in the process of giving it, Hawthorn came into the room and motioned Carol out into the corridor. "Your patient's here," she said. Luckily Hawthorn could stay pretty close to L&D because the charge nurse in the newborn nursery liked to teach students; but she still had to flit back and forth between L&D and the post-partum floor. Carol was glad she was around now.

Cecelia Claiborne was being rolled into L&D via wheelchair, by an orderly from Admitting. Cecelia sat calm, serene, attractive, and fully dressed. Her face was pale, her sleek dark hair was swept up off her neck into a loose, but neat, chignon on top of her head as if to show that she was prepared to get down to business, but might as well be as well-groomed as possible in the meantime.

"Okay, Welles," said Hawthorn hustling Carol over to meet her new patient. "Beth says she's to be admitted to room three. Do your stuff."

Carol stood wide-eyed before Claiborne's wheelchair as the orderly swiftly turned to leave L&D, obviously not wanting any part of the goings-on in the place, and the staff nurses moved away to get Claiborne's chart in order. This was *her* patient, a lady in labor with her first child. Carol had scanned L&D's procedures sheet, which Hawthorn had handed her and Minnie in preclinical, and was now expected to take over the care of this, her first OB patient. The whole experience would be new; she had never been in a labor or delivery room before, had never been in the presence of a woman in labor. All the knowledge she had to draw on was from her textbook; *Maternity Nursing,* chapters I, II, III, and IV—and the procedures sheet. She knew she should be scared, or at least nervous as she had been with her first fundamentals and pediatrics patients. That she wasn't, surprised her; and she attributed her lack of hesitancy to Cecelia's serene and friendly demeanor.

Carol said, "Hi, Cecelia; I'm Carol. I'll show you to your room."

Claiborne's mouth dimpled at the corners as she said, "Hi, Carol." Then wincing briefly she clutched her abdomen but never ceased smiling. "I'm really glad my time has come."

Carol wheeled Cecelia into room three. The room was small, but large enough for a bed, a sink, a private bath, one window, a clock on the wall facing the foot of the bed, and a shelf containing equipment

110

mounted on the wall over the sink. Under the clock a chart was tacked showing the actual size of the cervix when dilated to each centimeter from one to ten.

Cecelia got up a little awkwardly from the wheelchair.

Carol said, "While I take the wheelchair out, please remove your clothes, everything, and put on the gown there on the bed. The sack on your overbed table is for your underthings." It occurred to her once to wonder why the rooms had overbed tables when the patients weren't allowed to have meals.

When she wheeled the chair to the alcove near the nurses' station, she looked around for Hawthorn. The instructor had disappeared. Carol suspected what Hawthorn's thinking was; that she wanted her to draw on her own resources about the enema. She'd never given an enema before. Suddenly she resented Peavyhouse and Ross Street Presbyterian.

But the enema was down the list a bit yet. First, somebody had to check Cecelia to see how much she had dilated because there was always the risk of somebody having a baby in the toilet while they were expelling an enema. But Carol wasn't allowed to do a vaginal exam on a patient yet, and wouldn't have known what she was feeling anyway. "Checking for cervical dilation isn't something you get out of the textbook," Hawthorn had told them in preclinical. "It takes experience and skill; and then sometimes the doctors don't believe you."

She reentered Cecelia's room and began to help her out of her underthings. In one swift glance she was able to note Cecelia's distended abdomen and thought it was terribly grotesque. Its size was alarming and she wondered if Cecelia was going to have twins or triplets or something. It was a classical pregnant abdomen. There were the stretch marks the textbook had referred to, dozens of white streaks just beneath the skin, radiating out from the protruding umbilicus. The linea negra, the dark brown line reaching from the umbilicus to the pubic area, was there — just as the textbook described; and Cecelia's breasts were enlarged, their nipples dark, just like the picture in the textbook. Carol was just helping her into the bed when Liz entered the room briskly.

"Hi, Cecelia," she said. "Carol's going to take your vital signs while I listen for fetal heart tones. Just get comfy now and relax."

Carol took vital signs and watched as Liz took the stethoscope off the hook on the wall. The instrument was fixed with a brace which fitted over the nurse's head so that she would not have to hold the stethoscope; so that her hands could be free to feel for contractions. Liz pressed the diaphragm of the stethoscope into Cecelia's abdomen, making a small dent in her skin. Carol grimaced, but Cecelia only smiled up at the ceiling.

"Sounds good," Liz said. Carol wished she could listen, too. Maybe later.

"Had any bloody show yet?" Liz asked.

"No," Cecelia replied.

"Membranes haven't ruptured either, have they?"

"No."

"Soon as I'm through with the vaginal exam, Carol will give you a specimen cup for you to void in for a urine specimen. Okay?"

"Sure."

Carol was envying Liz's easy manner, her self-assuredness, how she never wasted a word or a moment of time. Busy as L&D was becoming, there was no time to waste.

Carol, standing beside the bed, listened as Liz chattered to Cecelia and positioned her for the vaginal exam—the lithotomy position. Cecelia lay flat on her back, her knees bent, her feet flat on the bed. Liz snapped on one sterile glove, lubricated the fingers with a water-soluble gel, and from a "peri bottle" she took from the shelf, squirted a Phisohex solution onto Cecelia's vagina.

Cecelia exclaimed, "Wow! That's cold!"

"Sorry. I forgot to warn you." Liz knew that Cecelia was embarrassed, so as she ran two fingers gently into the patient's vagina, as far as she could, she looked at Carol. "The unit's filling up. Dr. Reda and Dr. Costein have sent in two patients each to be pitted. Plus we've called O'Hara's doctor to come in and do the caudal if you want to watch. We always call the doctor when the patient is dilated six centimeters. In O'Hara's case, we called when she was dilated four. She has a history of rapid dilation."

"Will you explain to me what 'pitted' means?" Carol said.

Liz never changed her expression. "Sometimes when a patient has gone full term and the doctor thinks she's ready for delivery, for the patient's convenience and the doctor's too, he decides to induce labor, sends her to L&D. We start an IV on her and put Pitocin in the IV to induce the labor."

Carol nodded. Liz's fingers were turning slowly in Cecelia's vagina.

"Know what a caudal is?"

"Yes."

Cecelia had almost forgotten what Liz was doing as she listened to her talk, but Carol hadn't. Liz's fingers, which had disappeared into the vagina, searched for the cervical opening, and somehow the exam did not seem as bizarre as she had imagined.

"Three," said Liz as she slowly withdrew her fingers. "Three centimeters, Cecelia. You're well on your way."

Cecelia smiled hugely. "How long?"

Liz shrugged. "Oh—who knows? Everybody is different; but I guess six hours," she replied as she went out the door.

Cecelia and Carol scowled at the same time. Cecelia had waited nine months and now that the time had come for delivery, she was impatient for it to be over. Carol was sick with disappointment. In six hours she'd be driving back to the campus for lecture and wouldn't be here to observe Claiborne's delivery. Maybe Minnie got the better deal after all; for she would almost surely get to go to the delivery room with her patient.

Luckily, the enema kit was prepackaged. Carol had learned that any treatment kit that was prepackaged was simpler than a hospital-packaged one. It came with directions.

While Cecelia was in the bathroom voiding into the specimen cup which she had given her, Carol was able to figure out what to do with the enema kit; she thought that some things you learned in nursing school, you had to learn on your own. It was simple. All she had to do was to fill the plastic container with warm water, empty the contents of the packet of soap solution into the water, hang the container from the IV pole at the head of the bed, and give the enema.

It seemed cruel to give an enema to a patient in labor because an enema was a discomfort any time. But Carol explained every step of the enema as she gave it—according to *Fundamentals* in the chapter entitled, "Maintaining Bowel Integrity." She asked Cecelia to lie on her left side, knees drawn up a little. Take a deep breath . . . here comes the water now . . . try to hold as much of this as you can . . . Pant slowly if you begin to feel too full . . . if you get a pain tell me and I'll clamp off the water for a moment. . . .

Cecelia cramped and expelled water all the way to the bathroom.

Carol patiently cleaned water up off the floor with towels while Cecelia moaned with abdominal cramps and labor pains in the bathroom. It was cruel, all right, but Carol knew there was a reason for it. The patient must empty her bowels to allow more room for the passing of the fetus, and so that the pressure of delivery would not cause her to inadvertently evacuate her bowels and contaminate the delivery area.

The enema went well for Carol, if not for Cecelia, who emerged red-faced and weary from the bathroom. Carol helped her into her bed again. Now would come the perineal shave. She had never done a perineal shave.

Again, the prepackaged "prep" kit spoke for itself. There was a package of Betadine prep, disposable drapes, and a plastic razor.

It occurred to Carol only once that she actually had her head between Cecelia's knees; but after all, this was perfectly necessary. Shaving the pubic hair from the patient's perineum was just one more effort to protect the vagina from contamination—and the fetus, too, although lately some obstetricians were doing away with the perineal prep. Cecelia's was a half-prep—just the vulva and perineum were shaved, not the entire pubic mound as in the old days.

After Carol had finished the prep and had taken Cecelia's vital signs again, Cecelia seemed sufficiently exhausted and told Carol she wanted to rest. Now came the waiting; the Lamaze method must now come into play. Cecelia must psych herself into relaxing, and her husband was supposed to play the supporting role.

Carol got permission from Beth to let Mr. Claiborne into the room, and she went to the waiting room just outside L&D's pneumatic doors.

The father's waiting room was named the Stork Club and was full of people, mostly young men looking embarrassed, weary, nervous. Carol called for Mr. Claiborne. An anxious, burly young fellow jumped up and followed her into what he must have regarded as the mysterious inner sanctum of labor and delivery.

No sooner had she escorted Mr. Claiborne into Cecelia's room than Hawthorn swooped down upon Carol and ushered her into O'Hara's room to observe the installation of the caudal anesthesia.

Dr. Thomas was St. John's obstetric prima donna. He stood very tall, well over six feet, and was very thin, very blond, and very handsome. When Carol entered the room, he was sorting out the instruments he would need for the anesthesia; his blue eyes, arrogant but with overtones of melancholy, swept over the pack. St. John's went to a lot of expense to purchase prepackaged caudal trays, but, Hawthorn told Carol in a low voice, Thomas didn't like them. So the delivery nurses had to wash, rinse, wrap, and autoclave Thomas his own private tray.

"That's right," Thomas said flashing Carol a glance. For all his apparent aloofness and obliviousness to the nurses' presence, he must have overheard Hawthorn's comment. "The prepackaged caudal trays have too large a needle, too small a syringe, too small gloves for my hands, not enough sterile drapes, and the catheter is too large."

Suddenly O'Hara moaned low and softly. "Oh, oo-ooh." Her hands flew to the bedrails and clutched them.

"Turn her on her side, please. Flex her right knee, extend the left. In a modified Sims position," the doctor said.

Carol stared. Thomas was looking at *her*. She looked at Beth who was standing on the other side of the bed. Beth only jerked her head toward the patient. While Carol did as she was told, Dr. Thomas said, "Nobody stands around in here unless they make themselves useful. You've got to bend your knee up near your chin, Jackie, like the student is trying to get you to do."

"Easy for you to say. You haven't got a stomach like mine and you're not having labor pains. Ohhhhh Christ," O'Hara yelled.

It was then that a little insight flashed into Carol's student brain. *Nobody could get by with talking back to a doctor except a patient.*

"Hold her in that position," Thomas told Carol.

"Hold her *still!*"

Carol wondered why the doctor couldn't be a little polite about it as she held on to O'Hara, and Thomas told Minnie, "Now hand me the lidocaine. Hold it while I stick this needle into it. Tilt it, damn it, toward *me*. Okay, hold it still."

Minnie shakily held the vial of lidocaine while Thomas inserted the needle of the syringe into its rubber top and withdrew 10 ccs of medication.

"Oh God, you promised me I wouldn't hurt," O'Hara gasped.

"You won't in a minute, Jackie," the doctor said as he adjusted the equipment on the caudal tray.

Carol murmured consolations to Jackie she didn't understand herself. While everybody watched, Dr. Thomas swabbed the area at the base of Jackie's spine, then began to palpate for the caudal hiatus, located it, and inserted the needle into the caudal canal where a network of sacral nerves passes. O'Hara jumped, then remained still. The doctor threaded a small-lumened, but long, catheter through the needle and attached the syringe to the other end; then he injected a small amount of lidocaine—the anesthetic agent—into the catheter. "Feel that, O'Hara?"

"Feels like you're filling me full of air."

"Where?"

"My legs."

Dr. Thomas straightened. "Beth, goddamnit, where's the tape?"

"On the bedrail, Dr. Thomas, right under your left elbow," Beth told him.

The ends of six wide pieces of adhesive tape were fixed to the rail. Dr. Thomas secured the cathether to

Jackie's back with the tape.

"Ow!" O'Hara shouted. "Why isn't it working?"

"Shh. It will soon," Carol said patting her hands which gripped the rails.

"One more six-inch-long piece of tape," Dr. Thomas told Minnie.

Minnie grabbed the tape from the shelf, unrolled a piece, and reached for her scissors—which all students were supposed to keep in the pockets of their uniforms at all times. She couldn't find hers.

A good workman is never without his tools, Lena Black had said over and over again on her tapes in fundamentals. Students were supposed to carry bandage scissors, a pen, a pencil, a notebook, a paperclip or two, and rubberbands in their pockets. Horrified, Minnie looked over at Carol.

Carol whipped out her scissors and handed them across the bed to Minnie, feeling rather sanctimonious.

But Dr. Thomas said, "Forget the scissors," and told Minnie, "Tear the tape."

Minnie looked puzzled.

"You're not a real nurse until you can tear adhesive tape with your bare hands," he told her.

Minnie tried, got the tape tangled, twisted; and Dr. Thomas told Carol, "Get Jackie's legs up on a pillow and get her BP."

Carol kicked herself mentally for not remembering that a patient who has a caudal must have her blood pressure taken often, because sometimes a patient experiences hypotension after a caudal or epidural. Hypotension could threaten the fetus's life. Jackie's BP was normal.

119

To Carol's horror, Dr. Thomas then took a sterile needle, pulled back Jackie's buttocks and stroked the anal sphincter with the needle.

"If the sphincter doesn't react, then she's anesthetized from her umbilicus down," Beth told Minnie. "And her toes should be warm and red." She felt Jackie's toes. "She's getting there."

"You can turn on your back, now, Jackie," Dr. Thomas said.

Jackie tried, but her legs wouldn't move; she was truly paralyzed from her waist down and Beth had to position her legs for her.

"How do you feel, Jackie?" the doctor said laying one of his large hands on her abdomen.

"You made the contractions stop," she accused.

"You're wrong," he told her. "You're having a contraction now. You don't feel it?"

Jackie pondered that. "No."

Dr. Thomas almost smiled. "See you later," he told her and without another word, he left the room.

Carol regarded the patient; Jackie was dilated six centimeters, over halfway; and according to the textbook, she should be beginning to have a great deal of pain. Jackie looked at Minnie. "It's stopping. There's a pain coming, I think, but I can't really feel it."

Carol went out into the corridor. Evidently Liz had done another vaginal exam on Cecelia because the "scoreboard" showed that she was now dilated four centimeters. Moving right along. Probably because she did not require medication which would have slowed down the progress of her labor, and because she was determined to remain relaxed.

A patient in another room screamed, and Carol's hair stood on end. Already that morning she had learned that a patient in labor had a scream like no other, very high and shrill. Sometimes it started low, but it always ended up on that high, shrill note. Carol observed that the two nurses at the station did not even seem to notice the scream. She slipped into Cecelia's room.

Jim Claiborne was exceedingly pale as he sat beside the bed, and when Carol entered, he looked relieved. "Look, Miss Welles," he said, "I think I'll—er—leave if you're going to stay in here with her."

Carol regarded him, thinking, Can't take it, eh?

Cecelia let go of his hand. "Go ahead, Jim. Carol will stay. Won't you, Carol?"

Jim Claiborne escaped and Cecelia smiled. "Hospitals make him sick. Sickness scares him, and seeing me like this terrifies him. It's just as well. This is a one-person job anyhow, right?"

Not really. Throughout her pregnancy, Cecelia had come to classes for psychoprophylactic childbirth with her husband. The classes were designed to teach the patient all about childbirth and what to expect in order to help alleviate her fears. She learned exercises that strengthened her abdominal muscles, and exercises to teach her to relax the perineum. This was what Cecelia was concentrating on now, relaxing all the muscles, particularly the perineal muscles. Now that she was in labor, she was breathing slowly and deeply at the beginning of each contraction. The husband was supposed to stay with the patient to remind her to relax, to breathe slowly and deeply, and to give moral support, but it looked to Carol as if she'd have to fill in for Jim Claiborne.

Meanwhile, it was time to take vitals again—and fetal heart tones. She knew there was an instrument, which could be placed on the patient's abdomen, that would amplify the fetal heart tones enough for the patient to hear, but the nurses were all busy with other patients and Carol was hesitant to bother them.

As if she had done it hundreds of times, she pulled the stethoscope, called a fetoscope, on over her head and plugged the earpieces into her ears. She pressed the diaphragm to Cecelia's abdomen and listened. Nothing.

She wet her lips and moved the fetoscope to the side as she had watched Liz do. Nothing.

Perspiration beaded her forehead as she moved the instrument to the other side. *Swish, swish, swish* . . .

Fetal heart tones? No, placental circulation. The textbook had described the sound.

Carol moved the diaphragm down a little. *Swish-clop, swishclop, swishclop* . . . Fetal heart in there somewhere? She moved the diaphragm down a little more. *Clop-clop-clop gallop-gallop-gallop clop-clop* . . . The fetal heart! The fetal heart! Smiling she counted one hundred forty-four beats per minute.

She wrote down the FHTs on the vital-sign sheet with the other vitals.

Sighing, Carol took the hand that Jim Claiborne had dropped in his haste to leave the room and told Cecelia, "The baby's fine and so are you. I'll stay with you and give a little moral support."

Presently Hawthorn appeared in the room saying, "Let's time contractions!"

Hawthorn had a warm, motherly manner and her presence always made Cecelia smile. Hawthorn told Carol, "You keep your hand palm-down on Cecelia's distended abdomen. Don't be afraid of it."

Carol put her hand on the patient's abdomen and could *feel* the contractions as the abdomen rose slowly, and became hard. Sometimes Carol could even see the pulsebeat as it rose. During the next few moments, she learned to time the duration of contractions and the intervals in between. She was surprised at how regular they were—the distinguishing feature between true labor and false labor.

As the morning wore on, Carol kept watching the clock; Cecelia's labor was progressing, but time was running out. She prayed for Cecelia's labor to hurry, for Cecelia's sake and for her own. She did so want to observe the birth of Cecelia's baby—her first.

At 10:10 Carol saw O'Hara wheeled by Cecelia's room on a stretcher pushed by two L&D nurses; Minnie, following, was pulling up a surgical mask. *Minnie was about to observe Jackie's delivery.* Carol was suddenly miserably jealous and glanced at the clock on the wall opposite the foot of Cecelia's bed; then at her patient. Cecelia frowned, but that was all. Carol continued to time her contractions. They were five minutes apart. Cecelia moaned.

"Easy," Carol said softly. "Relax. Breathe slowly and deeply."

According to the Lamaze method, the patient was supposed to tell herself over and over to relax, to rest, to think pleasant thoughts. It didn't occur to Carol that her own young face was calming, that her soft voice and gentle manner were helping Cecelia remain relaxed.

Time passed. After a while it seemed as if Cecelia's contractions were becoming more painful; perspiration broke out on her face. Carol was beginning to think that she should be examined again when Hawthorn appeared.

"How's it going?" Hawthorn said.

Carol didn't have to reply. Cecelia frowned, bit her lip, and grasped the side rails of the bed.

Students were not exactly allowed to examine patients, Beth had said, but Carol read Hawthorn's thoughts now. *Fiddle dee dee. Everybody's busy. I'll examine, let Carol examine, and then we'll compare notes.* Cecelia was not scared, and she seemed to trust and like Carol so—

Hawthorn snapped on a glove and handed one to Carol. As Carol put on her glove, Hawthorn pulled back the sheet covering Cecelia's legs. Cecelia positioned her legs, spreading them and bending her knees while Hawthorn chatted about something else. Hawthorn's hand went inside, came out blood-tinged. She nodded for Carol to examine the patient.

Hawthorn had already squirted the Phisohex solution on the vulva so Carol had only to part the labia majora with the same hand she pushed into the vagina, slowly, gently, in, in, all the way. The tips of her fingers touched something spongy and she felt the rim—the cervical rim, sort of— She looked at the chart on the wall. Then she withdrew her hand.

"Well?"

"Well what?" Carol said timidly.

"How many centimeters?"

"Five?"

"Good guess. Six. It takes a lot of experience to get it exactly right and then you miss every now and then."

Carol pulled off her glove and washed her hands as Hawthorn went to the "scoreboard" and charted "6 cms" by Cecelia's name.

Today the other nurses were too busy to care that Hawthorn had done an exam. They were too busy watching pitted patients. The "pit group" had to be watched carefully in case the Pitocin caused a uterus to remain contracted, endangering the fetal circulation and the uterus itself, which could rupture if it remained contracted for long. Also, nurses could titrate the drops of Pitocin solution upward to cause the uterine contractions to increase in intensity and frequency, and therefore become more effective in thinning out and opening the cervix.

The morning wore on with Carol taking vitals every thirty minutes. It became apparent by eleven that Cecelia was not going to deliver within an hour. At eleven, she was dilated seven centimeters. Carol considered skipping lecture, then remembered they were going to have an exam in pharmacology. Disappointment overwhelmed her. To be able to follow a patient all the way through labor from beginning to end was ideal—and unlikely. She might be able to witness a couple of deliveries during the three weeks in L&D, but never see a patient all the way through.

"Oh God, Carol. I can't do it anymore," Cecelia gasped suddenly.

"Sure you can, Cecelia," Carol said as her thoughts came back to her patient. Realizing that the severe pain was a surprise to Cecelia and that it was beginning to frighten her, she put her cool hands on either side of Cecelia's face. "Your cheeks are flushed and it makes your face look so pretty. And did you know your lipstick is still on and there's not a hair out of place?"

Cecelia smiled for a moment. Then, "Oh, oh, oh—"

"Breathe slow and deep. Slow and deep."

"I liked the merry-go-round when I was little," Cecelia said speaking rapidly. "There was one at a carnival near our house. There was one pony I especially liked; he went up and down slowly, much slower than the other ponies. I liked *him*. I don't know why. So I'm going up and down on that pony. Oh Carol . . . Carol . . ."

"Up on the pony? Breathe slow and deep, slow and deep."

Cecelia obeyed, determined, urged on, and at the end of her pain said, "It helps to know somebody's rooting for me from the sidelines." Her blue eyes flickered open and she smiled.

It was then that a short man in a black-and-white hound's-tooth blazer plodded into the room. "Good morning, good morning," he said striding to Cecelia's bed. "They tell me you're seven centimeters along."

Cecelia nodded. "Hi. Where have you been?"

"No need for me, honey. You're the star of *this* show. All I'm going to do is bring down the curtain when the time comes." Dr. Cooper ignored Carol as he felt Cecelia's next contraction. The patient bore the pain patiently, a little restlessly.

"How'd ya like to hurry things along?" the doctor asked her.

Both Cecelia and Carol brightened. "Not by that IV stuff though," Cecelia said.

"No. By breaking your water," he said. Then he glanced at Carol. "Get the amniotome."

Carol stared a moment then looked over at the shelf where a packaged instrument lay. She didn't know what an amniotome looked like, but she took it off the shelf as the doctor snapped on an examining glove. "Open the package," he told her.

Open it? She pulled on the arrow end and the end of the instrument appeared miraculously. She held the wrapper open and the doctor took it. Then he examined Cecelia, said she was eight centimeters, stuck the amniotome inside her, and water from her vagina flooded the towels beneath her hips.

Carol knew from her reading that the next most important thing was to listen for the fetal heart tones. If the fetal heart had slowed to one hundred ten or below, it could mean that the cord had "prolapsed" during the rush of water, cutting off the fetal circulation. She listened as Dr. Cooper peeled off his gloves and watched her. She timed the *thump, thump* of the fetal heart tones and counted one hundred forty-two beats per minute. Normal. She raised her head and reported it to the doctor.

He was still watching her. "How long have you been in L&D as a student?"

"This is my first day."

"Are you married? Have you been around pregnant women before?"

"No."

"You're a natural Labor-and-Delivery nurse. Think about becoming one." And with that he strode out of the room.

She? An L&D nurse? She'd never considered it. She had always wanted to be a nurse in the surgical ward.

The doctor stuck his head back into the room. "By the way, catheterize her, will you? Her bladder's distending."

Catheterize? My God. Catheterize a patient in the latter phases of labor? With blood and fluid and —

After she had taken the wet towels away, Carol left the room desperately searching for Hawthorn. The instructor had vanished.

The doctor must have mentioned to Liz at the desk that Carol was going to catheterize Cecelia, for she looked up at Carol's pale face and motioned toward the glass-fronted shelves that stood beside the nurse's station. "Catheter kit's in there."

As Carol found the kit she was again resenting Peavyhouse and Ross Street Presby. But, thank God, the kit had been packaged by the same manufacturer as the one she had used at Presby. She stole quietly into Cecelia's room. Might as well act like I've done this a hundred times, she thought. Actually she *had* done it a hundred times, in her fantasies. She had failed to accomplish it with poor Mrs. Oglesby at Presby and since then had gone over the procedure in her mind again and again.

She opened the kit, explaining to Cecelia what she was going to do. At that point Cecelia, too busy to care, was concentrating on breathing correctly, relaxing, taking slow, deep breaths.

Carol did not perform the procedure. She floated up away and apart from the little blonde student and remote and cool, watched her—observed a mechanical robot named Carol, cleansing, picking up the catheter, inserting it into the urethra. Urine flowed amber into the plastic tubing and into the basin. She waited until the urine stopped flowing, then removed the catheter. She'd done it. She had catheterized somebody, and under a most difficult situation.

"Mmmmm," Cecelia groaned.

Liz appeared in the room as Carol was cleaning up after the procedure, and did an exam. "You're getting there, lady. Feel like pushing?" Liz asked cheerfully.

"Mmmm," Cecilia said nodding.

While Liz studied the patient's perineum, Cecelia gasped and moaned, "Oh God I can't stand it."

"Yes, you can," Carol said. "You've only got a little way to go now." She thought, Listen to me. How would *I* know?

"That's a long way," Cecelia panted. "Especially when you're on *this* angle to the bed."

Carol and Liz smiled and Cecelia said, "Oh, I gotta push!"

Carol glanced at the clock. The pains were only three minutes apart now.

"Bring your knees up and hold your knees with both hands," Liz said. "Like you learned to do. Now push!"

"Ungghhhh," strained Cecelia pushing down. "I can't stand this. Ya gotta gimme something, I'm going to die."

"Lady, you're getting there fast now. Anything I could give you now wouldn't have time to take effect. Besides, ready to give up?"

129

"Not really," she panted. Then, "Unhgggg . . ."

Carol went to the foot of the bed. From her new vantage point she could see that the labia majora of the vulva was gaping—it was a great, gaping slash, bleeding a little; something very white was leaking out.

"Ugghhh," Cecelia grunted loudly, panting and perspiring between pushes. When she pushed, something alarming appeared at the vaginal opening, then retracted when she ceased. And with each push, it progressed a little more and retracted less.

"What's that?" Carol said pointing to the dark, streaky thing.

"The baby's head," said Liz. "She's crowning." She looked up. "Go tell Dr. Cooper she's crowning. He's in the coffee room behind the nurses' station. And find Boston and tell her."

"Ugghhh," strained Cecelia loudly.

Carol flew to the coffee room, babbled something to the doctor, then ran into the nurse named Boston in the corridor. "She's crowning!"

Boston asked, "Who?"

Carol forgot her own patient's name for a moment. "My patient!"

"Honey, there's six patients in here and I—"

"Claiborne."

"That's better." Boston sauntered over to one of the stretchers that lined the corridor, humming some pop tune, and then pushed the stretcher into Cecelia's room.

"I'm gonna yell. I'm gonna yell," Cecelia was saying, as Carol hurried over to her bed.

"No you're not, kid. You're gonna pant and push

and then when the pain's over, you're gonna climb onto the stretcher for us. Okay?" Liz said as she stepped down on the wheel brakes of the stretcher.

"No. I've gotta have a shot. I give up. This is hell. To hell with Lamaze. Oh, here it comes . . . ungghhh . . ." In spite of her threats Cecelia remained as relaxed as possible between pains, panted exactly right, and pushed when she was supposed to. After her pain, she scooted sideways onto the stretcher with the nurses helping her.

Carol was alarmed at all the blood Cecelia left behind on her bedsheets, but she trotted in a sort of blur behind the two nurses and the stretcher. From somewhere Hawthorn materialized and told her to get on a mask.

Mask?

"Get your mask on, twinkle toes," Hawthorn told her, "and put on one of those fashionable paper caps. Then, see these booties? You put them over your shoes."

Suddenly Carol knew. Hawthorn had been in the delivery room with Minnie, and maybe she had gotten Bret to observe a delivery or two. She had been here all the time because she was wearing cap and booties, and her mask was dangling under her chin.

Carol put on the mask—for the first time ever. Then came the cap.

"Tuck all your hair in," Hawthorn told her.

And suddenly Dr. Cooper was there at the sink close by scrubbing.

I'm in the scrub room with the doctor. I'm in the scrub room with the doctor. I'm in—It was incredible.

He went into the delivery room holding his hands

up as she'd seen surgeons do on TV. And she and Hawthorn followed him into delivery.

Cecelia was lying on the delivery table, her legs already up in stirrups, her hands clutching a handle on both sides of the delivery table. "Unghhhh," she grunted.

The doctor, humming, snapped on the gloves as he looked between Cecelia's legs. "You want a boy or a girl, Cecelia? I forgot."

"I wanna shot. I want you to put me out. I want . . . unghhhh . . ."

Boston was fixing a mirror above the delivery table. "Can you see your bottom, Cecelia?"

"Ugh."

"What?"

"Yes. What's the matter with it? Oh . . . oh . . ."

Liz was uncovering the draped table of instruments, and Hawthorn maneuvered Carol over to stand behind the doctor as he sat down on a revolving stool, his head at a level with Cecelia's feet.

"Do you really want a shot?" said Boston standing now at Cecelia's head.

"No. Only when the pain comes. I'm a coward and I'm getting another one and—"

"It's a big one," Dr. Cooper said. "Cecelia, I'm going to insert a forceps to help turn the baby's head a little," he said taking the forceps from the table.

Carol thought it looked like a fat barbecue tong.

"It's going to feel a little cold," Dr. Cooper said.

"It'll feel good," panted Cecelia.

There was several moments in which the doctor slipped the forceps inside the vagina, applied a little pressure, made a quick deft incision between vagina and anus—the episiotomy to prevent tearing—and then waited.

"Unghhhh . . ."

And suddenly an awful thing happened. A wet blue head with a flattened orangutan's face and squinty eyes emerged.

"Big," Liz said as she drew up a medication in syringe. "You're not going to breast-feed, are you Cecelia?"

The doctor was suctioning out the infant's mouth. Cecelia answered, "No. What's happening?"

Before anyone could answer, the rest of it emerged, blue and wet and awful, coated in fluid. It stirred, gasped, screwed up its face, and as the doctor continued to suction out its mouth, it mewled moistly.

Carol must have expected thunderbolts to come out of the blue at the moment of birth, or maybe a voice out of heaven saying, "This is my beloved. . . ." Or at least a comment from the doctor or nurses.

"You ever see *Star Wars?*" the doctor asked glancing at Liz as he clamped the twisted, awful-looking umbilical cord in two separate places.

"You kidding? I've got twin boys remember?" Liz said. "The first day it hit the neighborhood theater I had to take them, otherwise I'd have had no peace."

"I went," Dr. Cooper said.

"You? You don't have small kids."

"I like science fiction."

"Hey, I can't see," Cecelia interrupted. "Is it a girl or a boy?"

"A boy. Probably . . . mmmm . . . about four thousand seven hundred grams," Dr. Cooper said.

"Oh, a boy. Oh, a boy. Jim will like that. How

many pounds is that?" Cecelia droned sleepily.

"Nearly ten and a half pounds," the doctor said cutting the cord. He handed the mewling infant to Liz and Liz took it to Cecelia to see. "Apgar score is nine," the doctor told Boston who was writing on a sheet of paper. "He didn't pink up as quick as he could have."

Hawthorn bent forward to whisper in Carol's ear, "Ten is perfect, you know, and few babies score a ten when they're born."

Carol saw her patient smile, and she began to coo, "Oh, look, look. Oh, he's beautiful. Isn't he beautiful? He's beautiful."

Carol was a sentimental idiot. Her eyes were full of tears and her chest felt like bursting with what she had just witnessed—birth. The birth of a human being. But blinded by tears and bursting with delight, she still could not empathize with Cecelia now; for the thing she had just produced, which everybody else seemed to regard as normal, looked to her like a pink, wet Neanderthal!

Hawthorn told her, "I've got to go on to post-clinical. You come as soon as you can, but watch him deliver the placenta and take a few stitches in the episiotomy first."

Carol nodded, unable to take her eyes away from Dr. Cooper's hands as he massaged Cecelia's abdomen and delivered the placenta, a purple mass of veins and flesh.

"What you'd enjoy is *Planet of the Apes,*" Liz told him as she gave Cecelia an injection in the side of her hip.

"I hate apes," Dr. Cooper said. "I hate their beady eyes. I hate monkeys," he said as he took a stitch in the episiotomy, tied the stitch, cut it.

Carol slipped out of the delivery room after that.

"Hey," the doctor called to her. "Remember. When you graduate, L&D. You're a natural."

"Thank you," she said and left. She had a vague memory of pulling off her cap, mask and booties; of attending postclinical, of the test in pharmacology later. But for days she drifted in a haze of pleasant ambience. She had witnessed the birth of a child, and she knew she would never quite forget that very first wonderful experience.

Hawthorn asked, "Cecelia Claiborne is now a what?"

"A primapara, or primip, as they say in L&D. She was not one of the pit group but Liz gave her an injection of Deladumone to keep her milk from coming down."

"Deladumone, Deladumone," chanted hazy faces beside her bed, reminding her of the ghosts in *Fiddler on the Roof*.

"On old Olympus' towering top a fat-assed German views his hops," Professor Murphy informed her as he gathered Phyllis Richards into his arms. "You must learn to be objective."

The telephone rang, and suddenly Carol was in her apartment. She knew it right away because the bedspread beneath her was the one she'd owned for three years.

The telephone rang again. She rolled over, her head still fuzzy from sleep. She thought, Every time I fall asleep studying I can hardly wake up. Was it only yesterday that Francis Gorham had told a group at the table in the cafeteria that she had opened up Murphy's office door to put her assignment on his desk and there he had stood with one of the students, Phyllis Richards, in his arms, and that he had had his hand inside her blouse? Oh, it was so awful. So disgusting—

The telephone rang again.

Murphy had told them just last semester that the way you could learn the cranial nerves was to memorize the little ditty, On old Olympus' towering top—olfactory, optic, oculomotor, trochlear—

The telephone rang again and Carol moaned and answered it. "Carol."

"Si-lent night. Ho-oly night. All is calm, all is bright," sang a male voice over the line. "You asked for it. Is that enough?"

It was *his* voice. Carol laughed.

"Hi, Carol. Duane Duren. Remember me?"

Of course she did. She sat up delightedly saying, "Let me see. Uh . . . it's the custodian at UTE."

"Nope. It's the sanitary engineer, the one who picks up your garbage every few weeks. How about going out for dinner some evening for smorgasbord. Anything your heart desires. A little stale maybe, but—"

She was laughing.

"Naw. I know a small Italian restaurant, lovely, not too expensive, and they specialize in lasagna. Do you like lasagna?"

"Love it. But I don't date engineers."

"How about a poor, broke, and exhausted med student who has studied until his eyes are burning out of his head and who finally took his test in bacteriology and has a day off and remembers a little strawberry-blonde student nurse he met on the elevator at Children's? Besides, calling it 'dating' is old-fashioned. Fifties stuff. Now you call it 'getting together' or something."

"You're nuts."

"I gotta tell you about this past few weeks. Fantastic. And about the surgery I assisted with this morning. Carol, I'll come by for you at seven."

"Now wait. Seven when?"

"Tonight."

Her eyes flicked to the mirror over her dresser. Her hair was a mess, and she had a test in OB to study for. "Okay."

"Tell me where you live."

She did and hung up; flew to the bathroom, took a shower, and washed her hair. He wanted to talk about the last few weeks; so did she. Though Cecelia Claiborne had been her first and most interesting patient, she had been able to follow three other patients through labor and delivery. Lynn and Jo Ann had yelped and hollered during the last phase of their first stage of labor. They had been given only Demerol when their pains were bad, and gas at the very end. *Not gas, stupid, cyclopropane! Stay professional even in your thinking.* Glenda had breezed through her labor and delivery with epidural anesthesia. Epidural was like a caudal except that the Xylocaine was injected into the caudal space higher up in the lumbar region. The thing had anesthetized only one side of her abdomen, though, and Glenda had been able to feel pain on her right side. Her doctor, Dr. Dixon, wouldn't admit he hadn't gotten it in the right place and she patiently bore the pain in one-half of her abdomen until delivery. Still, her labor and delivery were a breeze compared to Lynn's and Jo Ann's.

Dr. Dixon then gave her what he called a "whiff" of cyclopropane at the very end of delivery, and while she was under lightly, he inserted the forceps into her vagina around the baby's head singing, "Nothing could be fina than to be in your vagina in the mo-orning. . . ."

That was for Carol's benefit. "Some doctors are like that," Hawthorn had told her. "They've got to show off and it's usually something in that sort of vein." Carol did not like Dr. Dixon.

Now Carol dried her hair vigorously and looked at herself in the mirror over her sink. A freckled-nosed imp with amber-colored eyes; small, upturned nose, and hair naturally long, thick, and straight. She plugged in the hair dryer and bent over letting her wet hair fall as she turned on the dryer.

Suddenly she thought of Bret. He had sat through many films of childbirth and reproduction. Hawthorn had managed to slip him into delivery to observe four births; however, he had been swathed with mask, cap, booties, scrub suit—camouflaged, Hawthorn said. Poor Bret. Talk about discrimination! There was no limit to how many things a student nurse could see, if the student was a female. But the male nurse . . . It wasn't fair.

Carol slung her hair back over her head and began to comb it. It was full and shining with glittery gold highlights. Her face was still flushed from the heat of her shower. "Not bad," she said studying her face.

She dressed in the green velvet blazer she had gotten for Christmas, and a green and brown-tweed skirt and cream-colored blouse. She fluffed the high lacy collar of the blouse and told herself she didn't look bad.

Duane rang the doorbell at exactly seven. She answered and he gave her an obligatory whistle. "I'd invite you in," she said, "but—"

"But not on the first get-together. Right?" he said grinning.

She locked her door and walked with him to his neat maroon sports coupe. "Gosh," she said, "are you rich?"

"I'm poor. My father's sort of upper middle class, divorced from my mother. She is married to a bank president. This was my graduation-from-college-present—from Mom."

Duane slid into the seat beside her and stared at her, smiling. "It's startling to notice the little student nurse is also a girl. A lovely girl."

"Really?"

"I've been thinking a nurse is a nurse. She's one thing. A girl is a girl, that's another thing. It hasn't really occurred to me until now that they are one and the same." He started up the car and pulled out of the parking area.

Carol thought, Well, come to think of it, it never really occurred to me that a doctor is a man—somebody who grew up, went to college, went through four years of medical school, through several years of residency. She thought of Dr. Dixon singing, "Nothing could be fina—"

Duane was handsome in slacks, a sport shirt open at the neck, and a tweed blazer, but she noticed there were great, dark crescents under his eyes from lack of sleep; his face was thinner than when she had seen him last, his hair was longer—down on his neck and over his ears—probably because he hadn't had time to go the barber. But he exuded an electric excitability that communicated itself to her, electrifying her, too, causing her to live the thrills of the things he had experienced over the past few weeks. His tired eyes glowed with eagerness as he kept glancing at her as he drove.

"Lectures in pharmacology, physiology, obstetrics, pediatrics, pathology . . . most of that's behind me, now, Carol. Last semester, when I met you at Children's we were beginning to make rounds—you know—Baker was the resident who taught us stuff, how to listen for heart defects in infants, all about Down's syndrome. You know, Mongoloid kids."

"I know."

"We observed every kind of congenital defect there. Then we went to Bennet. God, I love Bennet! There we learned to do femoral sticks, to draw arterial and venous blood, to start IVs, to do blood and urine studies—"

"CBCs?"

"And sed rates."

"Urinalysis, bacterial studies, specific gravity?"

"All of it."

"We did some of that in—"

"*Then.* I spent three weeks on ER rotation. The pace was a little slower. Know why? I had night rotation. Nothing much happened, but I learned to suture wounds, Carol. Every night we had one or two stabbings. I did a suprapubic tap once too."

"Like a paracentesis—"

"Yeah, except that you aspirate only a little fluid

from the abdominal cavity just to see if there's blood or fecal material in it. Like when somebody's stabbed or comes in after an auto accident."

He was still rhapsodizing about his last few weeks making rounds and learning procedures when they entered the restaurant door, and his discourse continued while they ate. "Then today, my first surgery. I've got a test tomorrow as you do, but I had to see you. Carol? There's nobody I can talk to about all this except the guys and they all have girls somewhere tonight or they're on duty. No girl understands all this, but you do because you're a student nurse. At least you've seen some of it. Have you been to surgery yet?"

"As I said earlier, I've only had fundamentals, Pedi, and have just finished L&D, and am going to the newborn nursery Monday."

"L&D?"

She smiled smugly. "Labor and Delivery."

"Oh. I haven't had that rotation yet." He fell silent for a moment, as if disappointed that she had done something that he hadn't, but presently he brightened. "I didn't expect to assist in surgery even a little for a few weeks yet. I'm on surgery rotation, first day today. Okay I walk into this doctor's lounge where I'm supposed to meet my new group, the group I'm to make rounds with. My senior resident, Basil Novak, introduces us. I'm in a group with two other med students—third-year like me—one first-year intern and one junior resident. Okay Novak turns to me and says, 'Duren, today you scrub with me.' I almost wet—"

They laughed. "Who was the doctor doing the surgery? Residents don't do surgery without a doctor present, do they?"

He covered her hand with his own. "Carol. Once a person graduates from medical school, he *is* a doctor. He's an M.D. But he can't practice yet, right? He has to go through several years of internship first."

"What's the difference between an intern and a resident?"

"It varies only in terminology from one hospital to the other. At Bennet a new graduate who is practicing within the hospital under the supervision of senior residents and chiefs of staff and so on, is called an intern his first year. After that, he is called a resident. Depending on his specialty, he'll spend anywhere from four to seven years as a resident, before he goes into private practice. In my case, I want to become a surgeon, a general surgeon, so I'll rotate my first year through all the departments, but the second year I'll be on constant rotation in surgery and will spend probably four more years as a resident surgeon. You move up the ladder; you're a junior resident, then a senior resident, then you're an assistant chief resident, then, hopefully, you're chief resident. After that, you're turned loose on society in private practice." He smiled. "But to answer your original question, when a patient comes into the hospital and does not have a private physician, or his G.P. doesn't do surgery, if you're a senior surgical resident, you can operate, especially if it's something simple like an appendectomy. Besides, the one I assisted is Basil Novak. Anyway, I scrub, I go in, hands up like this—"

They giggled when Duane knocked over his empty wineglass, picked it up. "I go in, this nurse gowns and gloves me. Then I'm across the table from Novak. God, he's good! Just an assistant chief resident!"

"So what did you do?" Carol asked, her chin in her hand.

"I held the retractors."

"Gosh, that's terrific!"

"Well, it wasn't much, but it was a beginning," Duane said a little subdued.

"This Dr. Novak sounds familiar."

"Does he?"

"That name rings a bell—"

"Carol, that man we did the appendectomy on wasn't like the cadaver I learned anatomy from."

"I hope not."

"He bled more. And he was warm. And he had pulses. My God, he was beautiful."

She laughed.

Later they went to a small, expensive café where the lights were dimmed and a band was playing old-fashioned songs like Elvis' "Love Me Tender," and really old stuff like "Blue Moon." Carol would have liked to dance, but wasn't sure she could slow-dance, and anyway Duane was still talking.

"We'll be doing little stuff like appendectomies, prostatectomies, tonsillectomies on this rotation. Of course, I won't do anything but observe or maybe hold retractors and aspirate blood from the surgical field. You've no idea what it's like."

"No, but I've had some surgery patients and I have been through three weeks of L&D."

"L&D?"

Carol sighed. "Labor and Delivery."

"Oh yeah . . . There was this lady who came into

143

ER last week in labor. She didn't have a doctor. We had to send her to Brookline."

"I hope she made it."

"She did. It's a shame, but Bennet has a ten percent allowance in the budget for charity patients; that's ten percent of the average hospital census. When that ten percent is filled, they have to turn away the rest, send them to the county-run hospital. I felt bad having to do it. I called Brookline later to see if she made it."

"Did she?"

"Yes."

"I'm glad you called to check on her."

"Then we had this wino. Name's Felix Seifert. He's a regular. Comes into ER complaining of chest pain. Nobody believes he has chest pain, but how can we be sure, right? Okay, all we can do is send him up to CCU for observation. He spends three days in CCU in perfect luxury."

"If he's charity, why don't they send him to Brookline?"

"He's a fixture. Been around Bennet for years. Hey! And then this guy came in, his face all out of shape like this and twitching." Duane made a face while Carol laughed. "I think, my God a stroke? And I start trying to remember all the cranial nerves. Know how I remember the cranial nerves? We learned this thing; 'On old Olympus' towering top a fat-assed German views his hops.' It helps me remember the cranial nerves in their proper order; olfactory, optic, oculomotor, trochlear, trigeminal, abducens . . ."

Carol was bursting to tell him about old Mr. Wolfe, about Nancy andthe electric bed, about Willy Fry, about her experiences in L&D, but Duane never stopped talking. Finally, as they were driving late back to her apartment, she asked him, "Did you really take the Jell-O with the June bug to the administrator at Children's?"

Duane had to think a moment, to bring his mind down to less loftier times. "Oh, yeah. I did. I took it in, set it on his desk and said, 'Sir, I just thought you'd want to see this.' He leaned over, looked at it, and said, 'Don't tell me. I know. It came from our dietary department, didn't it?' I said, 'Right out of the kitchen.' He looked horrified. 'Please don't tell me you found this on a patient's tray.' I said, 'Nope, I bought it at the steam table in the cafeteria.' You know what he said? He looked at me and said, 'Where do you suppose a June bug came from in October?' "

They laughed. Carol said, "Then what did he do?"

"I don't know. He thanked me; I left. He didn't even ask my name, thank God. Not that I'd have minded telling who I was. It's just that—why rock the boat if you don't have to?" He pulled up to her apartment and turned toward her. "Carol, let's make this a regular thing whenever I can get a night off. You and me."

She smiled. His eyes were flashing in the light of a neighbor's porch light. "Okay I'd ask you in tonight, but—"

"Yeah, I know. Not on the first date. I don't agree with your old-fashioned philosophy, because what we could do in your apartment, we could do here in my car if I was a jerk and you were willing. But, I've got a test to study for and so have you; therefore, tonight I respect your philosophy." Grinning, he helped her out of the car, walked her to the porch, and said softly,

"What's your philosophy about a kiss on your first date?"

Very frankly she was *wanting* him to kiss her, to hold her. She wanted it more than anything in the world at the moment. She shrugged, and taking this as permission, he drew her to him and kissed her gently, briefly, on the lips. Then he let her go. He backed away, his eyes flashing. He went to his car, got in, and drove away without another word.

Why did her face tingle? Why did her lips burn? Why was her mind racing? Why were her eyes blurred?

Cranial nerves: olfactory, optic, oculomotor, trochlear, trigeminal . . . On old Olympus' towering top . . .

She turned, unlocked her door, went into her apartment. Study? She couldn't. She went to bed and dreamed and dreamed and dreamed. And this time the girl in Murphy's arms wasn't Phyllis Richards. She was Carol.

Chapter Nine

Neonatal Nursing

Seeing Bret bathe a tiny newborn infant was hilarious. But she didn't dare laugh. He looked embarrassed but interested and bathed the tiny infant gently, carefully, as if he were handling something made of such fragile stuff that he was afraid it might crumble and blow away.

They bathed "the kids" on a stainless-steel counter using wads of cotton balls. Then they rubbed lotion on their sleek fat bodies, diapered them, dressed them in T-shirts, wrapped them in receiving blankets, and tucked them back into their small, metal cribs.

Infants hated being bathed, but the nurses loved doing it. Bret was allowed to participate in the clinical experience in the newborn nursery in every aspect, except taking the infants to their mothers. The nursery nurses reasoned that new mothers wouldn't pop out a breast to feed a crying infant in the presence of a male nurse, not in these days and times, so carrying infants to their mothers was left to the female nurses and Minnie and Carol.

Bret was bathing baby boy Folsom when Carol noticed that he was staring down at the infant alarmed. She and Minnie were dressing infant girls at the moment and Carol had been wanting to laugh at Bret because his muscular, hairy arms looked ludicrous holding a small infant. She said, "Bret, what's the matter?"

He looked up at her, frowning a little. "This baby," he said and paused. "This baby's—uh—beeps are leaking."

"What?" Carol carried baby girl Forrester to where Bret was holding Folsom down on the counter with his hands on his chest.

"There," he said pointing to the infant's nipples. "His beeps are leaking milk."

Minnie peered at the infant. "Those aren't beeps; they're toot-toots." Minnie was the mother of three small children and *she* should know.

Carol laughed. "Bret, you didn't read last week's assignment in neonatal nursing. That's normal for a newborn's nipples to leak milk."

Bret regarded baby boy Folsom a moment longer and said, "Did it say anything about . . . about . . ." His face turned red. "Carol," he said desperately, "there's something terribly wrong with this kid."

Carol looked at baby boy Folsom. He was a chubby nine-pounder with a deep, loud cry, a thatch of straight black hair on a perfectly round head. He was regarding Bret with dark blue eyes, his arms waving jerkily in the air, his left leg pumping up and down, his right leg jerking a little—all perfectly normal. "I don't know what you mean," Carol said.

"Carol," Bret began apologetically, his expression pleading with her not to be offended. "Carol, my bathing this kid *turns him on.*"

Carol then noticed Folsom's tiny, erect penis and laughed. "Bret, silly. That's normal too." But she felt her face flush, nevertheless.

"Sometimes baby boys do that before they wee-wee," offered Minnie who had not yet mastered medical terminology.

At that moment baby boy Folsom let go a stream of urine that caught Bret on the chin and dribbled down his chin and dribbled down his neck onto his scrub smock. Bret never changed his expression and neither did baby boy Folsom.

While Carol and Minnie laughed and laughed; Bret regarded the infant solemnly. Then he looked at Carol. "Carol," he said, "they didn't warn us about this in the neonatal chapters."

When Carol caught her breath, she said, "Haven't you learned yet that there're some things we're going to have to learn on our own?"

Something else nobody ever mentioned in the textbooks happened within the next ten minutes. Dr. Beauregard, a tall, wide-shouldered pediatrician swept into the newborn nursery and began to throw verbal orders at the nursery nurses.

"Okay, Doctor."

"Sure, we'll do it."

"Certainly. We'll see to it."

"But write all of this in the kids' charts will you? We can only remember twelve orders at once," a nurse told him.

Then Beauregard blustered into the area where the students were bathing infants. "Who has Scott?"

"I do," Carol said.

"Bring him into the treatment room and put him into the infant seat for circumcision."

Carol picked up baby boy Scott and carried him to

what she guessed was the treatment room. She found an infant seat, and strapped him in.

After a few moments of tension on Carol's part, and puzzlement on Scott's, Dr. Beauregard came in. "Well, that's dandy. But how do I circumcise a kid with his diaper on?"

Embarrassed, Carol had only to loosen the tabs on Scott's disposable diaper while Dr. Beauregard washed his hands in the nearby sink.

Carol was nervous taking orders from doctors. Only twice had she taken orders, once in Cecelia Claiborne's room when Dr. Cooper had asked for the amniotome, and once when Dr. Thomas had asked her to position Jackie O'Hara for a caudal.

Now Minnie and Bret watched the circumcision procedure through the door of the small treatment room.

Dr. Beauregard used the Yellen clamp, an instrument resembling something Carol had seen on her father's worktable in the garage with his electric saws. Beauregard cleaned Scott's penis with Phisohex, stripped back the prepuce or foreskin, fitted the cone of the Yellen clamp over the glans or head of the penis, and stretched the foreskin over the cone with sutures. By then Scott was red-faced and screaming with rage. Circumcision hurts, Carol thought; no matter what people say, it hurts. Dr. Beauregard drew the foreskin through the hole in the clamp, screwed the clamp down crushing the foreskin which clamped off the bleeders, and while he waited the four or five minutes it took for the clamp to finish its job on the bleeders, he said over Scott's screaming, "Get a diaper. I'll diaper him myself when I'm through. I don't want to risk your breaking open the bleeders for the next hour or so."

Carol had only to reach over and lay a diaper beside the infant seat.

"I said get a diaper, not a disposable pad," the doctor said.

"This *is* a diaper—a disposable diaper," Carol said.

"It is not. That's a pad."

"The tabs on the sides of this diaper show it's a diaper."

Beauregard's eyes riveted to her face. "I see by your nametag that you are Carol Welles, S.N. Does S.N. mean snotty nurse?"

Carol was about to cry. "Student nurse," she said, her lips trembling.

"Well, student nurse, you'd better learn the difference between a diaper and a disposable pad." The doctor then turned and with three circular strokes of a scalpel, cut the foreskin away and removed the clamp from Scott's penis.

Scott howled in pain and fury and Beauregard stalked from the room.

Tearfully now, Carol lifted the baby from the infant seat and placed him on the counter where she diapered him with what she knew was a diaper. She glanced once out the door of the room and saw Bret pointing to a box of disposable diapers and talking to the doctor. She hoped he wouldn't get into trouble on her account.

Even through her anger something occurred to her as she diapered Scott and then held him to her, patting his back. Having been raised in a religious household, her family having rigidly attending the same Baptist church for more than twenty years, she had been taught Bible stories from as far back into her childhood as she could remember. God had commanded Abraham to circumcise his son and his male servants when they were eight days old. In yesterday's reading assignment in neonatal nursing, Carol had read that prothrombin time—the amount of time it takes for the blood to clot—is highest at birth, then declines until the eighth day when it returns to normal. Cutting on an infant before eight days meant he would bleed longer and more profusely than he would at eight days or older. In modern times, with sutures and clamps, bleeding wasn't a problem in the circumcision of infants, although nurses had to watch for bleeding after a circumcision, just in case. But back in Abraham's day, circumcision on the eighth day, when the prothrombin level was again normal, insured that bleeding would be at a minimum. Since studying anatomy, physiology, and disease processes, Carol had begun to notice that many of the laws Moses had given to the Hebrews had sound medical and hygienic principles.

Bret appeared in the door of the treatment room and grinned. "Beauregard offers his grunt to you."

When she smiled, he went on, "I showed him the difference between a diaper and a disposable pad and he grunted and left the nursery."

"Thanks, Bret, but you needn't have done that."

"Did it to prove a point. We nurses know more about our own jobs than the doctors do."

She left the treatment room and put Scott in his crib. At St. John's, infants were allowed to have pacifiers to suck on between feedings. They were makeshift pacifiers, a bottle nipple with clean cotton balls stuffed inside to prevent the infant from swallowing air. Carol fixed Scott a pacifier which he fell to nursing rigorously as if the sucking would stop the pain and rage he was feeling in his new world.

Happily, all nineteen infants in the nursery were normal in every way—except for Penny. Penny was a premie, born three months early. She weighed less than two pounds at birth. Penny was the star of the nursery, though she was isolated in the premie section by herself. Carol didn't understand the monitoring apparatus attached to Penny. It had been touch-and-go for this infant. Some days she lost an ounce, some days she gained. Penny was a month old now and weighed just over two pounds. She drew much of the attention away from the other infants during visiting hours because she was so tiny, like a small doll, and she was ugly. She resembled a little monkey, but the students knew the older she got, the prettier she would become.

Penny had not yet developed a sucking reflex and had to be fed through a feeding tube inserted through her mouth and into her stomach. She could not suck, but she could chew the tube, a mystery which delighted everybody who saw her.

During the three weeks that Carol, Bret, and Minnie spent in the newborn nursery, Penny gained slowly, chewed on her tube, and slept for long intervals. That she was alive, that she was gaining, was one of the miracles of modern medicine. Fifteen years previous, Penny would already have been dead.

Chapter Ten

Post-Partum

Carol's three-week tenure on the post-partum floor began in OB recovery. There she received all the experience she would ever need in catheterizing patients—and under difficult circumstances.

New mothers came from the delivery room exhausted, exhilarated, and very sore. Hawthorn showed Carol and Minnie how to get the perineal ice packs from the refrigerator in the supply room and to apply them on either side of each patient's sanitary pad, called a peripad in OB recovery. Patients appreciated the ice packs, they appreciated the sponge baths the nurses gave them, they appreciated everything. They were undecided as to whether to moan because of the discomfort of their episiotomies and after-birth pains, or to extol the virtues and beauty of their new babies. They had no idea how close to danger they were. That's why St. John's had created an OB recovery room.

OB recovery was on the post-partum floor, on the second level. It was not a large room, but it could accommodate as many as four stretcher patients at once, or five if there was a busy day in L&D. The room contained a sink, a cabinet for medications, a window, and one nurse per shift.

Mothers fresh from the delivery rooms were covered with warmed blankets and wheeled into an elevator that carried them to the second floor and into OB recovery where they were kept for one hour. After that, they were rolled down the corridor of the post-partum floor to their rooms.

New mothers were a mess. Their breasts were enlarged and streaked with swollen veins and stretch marks, their abdomens were more or less flat and flabby with a grapefruit-sized lump just below the umbilicus. They were sweaty, disheveled, and bleeding. Episiotomies were puckered, vaginas were swollen, and almost every patient had hemorrhoids. And yet they lay on their stretchers smiling as they dozed, or talking euphorically about their wonderful delivery or asking again and again, "Did you see my baby?" Or, "What did my husband say?" Or "When can I see my baby?" New mothers were all alike. And every one of them was different too.

Carol could tell that Hawthorn liked OB recovery and enjoyed instructing them about how to check the patients' peripads for excessive lochia—or bleeding—and how to place ice packs on the patients' perinea. The students, each having given only three or four injections while in fundamentals, were carefully supervised by Hawthorn in giving steroids to prevent lactogenesis in patients who were not going to nurse their babies. And if the doctor had ordered it, they often gave injections of Ergotrate or a similar medica-tion to induce uterine contractions. They took the patients' blood pressures and pulse beats every fifteen minutes and kept careful watch over each patient's uterus.

Divested of its fifteen or more pounds of fetus, water, and placental tissue, the fundus of the uterus during the immediate post-partum period could be seen and palpated as a lump about the size of a grape-fruit just below the umbilicus. Hawthorn taught the students how to palpate the fundus to judge whether it was firm or soft. They knew from their reading that the fundus of the uterus after birth should be round and firm, which meant that it was contracting and retracting, clamping down on the bleeding vessels. The uterus of most patients stayed firm naturally, but occasionally one needed massaging to cause it to contract. It was rare when a patient's fundus did not respond to massage.

Carol and Minnie stayed busy, taking vital signs, checking peripads, replacing ice packs, giving injections, catheterizing patients who couldn't urinate, and keeping the recovery-room records.

One day, after Carol and Minnie had been in OB recovery for six days, Hawthorn left to check on her students in L&D and the newborn nursery. Riley, the staff nurse in charge of OB recovery checked the three patients in the room before she told the students that she needed to go to the bathroom. She'd be back in just five minutes, she said.

Carol and Minnie were gleeful. They were now in charge of OB recovery.

For patients they had Opal Hollingsworth, a gravida four, who had delivered a ten-and-a-half-pound boy at eight A.M.; Carolyn Peace, a primip who had delivered a six-pound-six-ounce girl at 8:10; and Juanita Gomez, also a primip, who had delivered a seven-pound girl at 8:20.

Carol gave Carolyn a brief sponge bath, checked her peripad, checked her fundus, recorded her vital signs. Then she checked Juanita. Carol thought she could feel that Juanita's bladder was distended and she helped her lift her hips into the bedpan. But Juanita couldn't void in the bedpan. Carol wished she could consult Hawthorn or Riley, although she knew she had the prerogative to catheterize a patient if she judged it necessary. "When in doubt, catheterize," Hawthorn had said.

While Carol was catheterizing Juanita, Minnie was checking Opal's vital signs and chatting about her own three children. After a few moments, Carol heard Minnie say, "Opal? You need two pads instead of one. This will be uncomfortable but—uh . . . Carol?"

Carol was withdrawing the catheter from Juanita. *Seven hundred ccs urine,* she thought, noting the amount of urine in the calibrated bedpan into which the catheter drained. Good thing she had decided to catheterize. A full bladder along with the discomfort of everything else in the vicinity of the abdomen must surely be the pits.

"Carol?" Minnie said again.

"Yeah?"

"Would you come check Opal's pad, please?"

"Just a second." Carol emptied the contents of the bedpan, and wrapped and stuffed the used catheter kit into the wastebasket near Juanita's bed. She placed a new peripad on Juanita's perineum, replaced the ice packs, covered her, and went over to Opal's stretcher.

Minnie pointed first to Opal's peripad. There were a few blood clots—not always a sign of something wrong. You just had to watch to make sure there weren't too many and that they weren't too large. But what Minnie really wanted Carol to check was Opal's fundus. It was boggy.

"I can't get it firm," Minnie said softly.

Carol guarded and massaged the fundus, placing one hand below it and massaging it with the other. But the fundus wouldn't contract. Instead, blood gushed over the sheets between Opal's knees. Minnie jumped back. Carol massaged gently, but nothing happened. She raised her eyes to look at Minnie. "Find Ms. Riley."

"I don't know where she went."

"Go to the post-partum floor and get a nurse."

For a moment, Minnie hesitated; Carol was aware that she had suddenly become pretty damned bossy and that Minnie didn't like it.

Neither of them knew that the bossiness was a sure sign of a charge nurse in the making. Minnie turned and hurriedly left the room.

Carol smiled at Opal. "Your fourth child?"

Opal sensed something was wrong and was watching Carol carefully. She nodded. "I've never had no trouble before."

"That's good," Carol said as if nothing were wrong, and glanced at Opal's chart. She had not received an injection of Ergotrate or Pitocin or any of the other drugs that would make her uterus contract, but that wasn't unusual; most patients didn't. She noticed Opal's doctor's name. She didn't recognize it. "Your doctor is Dr. Timyrus?"

Opal nodded. "He's my family doctor. Delivered all my kids. He hasn't delivered babies in six years, though, but he agreed to deliver this one for me as a favor."

"An obstetrician?"

"No, just an M.D."

Carol smiled to herself. To some patients, "just an M.D." meant the doctor was a general practitioner. To them, anybody else was a "specialist."

Again she tried to massage the fundus to get it to contract. *You can understimulate and you can over-stimulate. You have to know what the happy medium is,* Hawthorn had said. Opal's fundus did not respond. Instead, more blood and clots issued from the vagina. Now Carol was more alarmed than ever.

A nurse in a white uniform and cap strode briskly into the room followed by Minnie. She took one look at the sheets under Opal, at the inadequate peripads. "Vital signs?" she snapped.

Carol was ready with the answer. "Pulse one hundred. BP one twenty over forty-two."

The nurse palpated Opal's abdomen. Then turned and walked briskly out of the room. The students could hear her shoes padding swiftly down the corridor, *tap-tap-tap-tap-tap*. Two minutes later they heard the switchboard operator page, "Dr. Timyrus, call 284 stat. Dr. Timyrus, call 284 stat."

Minnie knew not to remove the bloody sheets or pads so that the doctor could estimate the amount of blood loss. Carol took vital signs every two or three minutes.

Meanwhile Juanita and Carolyn, unaware that anything was amiss, were dozing blissfully.

Dr. Timyrus appeared within ten minutes. He was short, swarthy, bespectacled, and middle-aged. He looked at the sheets. "Glove," he said to Carol.

At that same moment, Riley returned to the room

looking horrified; her horror turning to anger and fear as she glared at the students. "What happened?" she demanded.

Minnie only answered by pointing to Opal. Carol was opening the pack of sterile gloves for Dr. Timyrus as he silently stared at Opal. After he put on the examining glove, he massaged Opal's uterus, keeping one hand inside her vagina, then he began to bring out handfuls of clots.

Oh my God! Carol thought. Shouldn't the doctor *do* something?

The nurse from the post-partum floor appeared at the door of the room again, watched for a moment, then hastened out of the room. Again Carol could hear her feet going *tap-tap-tap-tap-tap* down the corridor rapidly. Two minutes later, Carol heard the operator page, "Dr. Cooper call 284 stat. Dr. Cooper, call 284 stat."

Dr. Cooper had been Cecelia Claiborne's obstetrician and Carol knew that he was chief of the obstetrics department.

Timyrus kept bringing out clots and massaging Opal's uterus, while Riley took vital signs with a tight mouth and an occasional accusing glance at the student nurses.

Carol and Minnie knew they'd done their best, the best anyone could do, and they were determined not to let Riley's glances disturb them.

Hawthorn came into the room just behind Dr. Cooper.

Dr. Cooper hurried to Opal's stretcher and stood beside Dr. Timyrus. "Hello, Augusta," he said. "What's the problem?"

160

The more clots Dr. Timyrus had brought out of Opal's vagina, the more sober he became, and by the time Dr. Cooper entered the room, he was clearly worried. He did not answer. Dr. Cooper stood looking down at Opal, at Timyrus bringing out clots, and said, "Let's take her back to delivery for a D&C."

Not another word was said by anybody. The two doctors hurried from the room to prepare for the dilation and curettage, and Riley and a nurse from the post-partum floor wheeled the stretcher from the room.

Both student nurses felt guilty. Why, they did not know. They had done nothing wrong. They had been twice as vigilant of their patients as any staff nurse for several reasons: taking care of new mothers was new and interesting; they wanted to learn everything they could as fast as they could; they had not yet grown bored with their work.

Hawthorn said nothing; she couldn't in the presence of the other patients. But she set about helping her students do vital signs on Carolyn and Juanita and check them.

At last Riley returned and without looking at the students told Hawthorn that it was time to take both Juanita and Carolyn to their rooms.

Still feeling guilty, Carol and Minnie took first Juanita, and then Carolyn to their rooms on the post-partum floor. They raised the electric beds in the rooms and had the patients scoot off onto them. Then they lowered the beds, rolled the stretchers out of the rooms, and helped their patients into fresh gowns.

By the time they returned to OB recovery, Opal was there.

Hawthorn met the students in the hallway and crooked a finger at them. The girls approached quickly. Hawthorn put a motherly hand on each of their shoulders. She told them that Opal had had to have the D&C, which both students knew was a dilation and curettage, the dilation of the cervix and a scraping of the uterus to remove remaining placental tissue. "Do you know why?"

Carol said, "The uterus can't clamp down on the vessels when placental fragments are left."

"Exactly. And you girls did well. You did exactly right. The charge nurse on the post-partum floor didn't say so — you must never expect praise for doing a job well in this business — but she was pleased that you caught the problem before Opal bled too much."

"I think Riley blames us," Minnie said.

"Ms. Riley blames herself, but dares *you* to blame her. Don't worry about Riley."

"Why do we feel guilty?" asked Carol.

Hawthorn smiled. "Carol, as a nurse, every time you have a patient go bad, no matter why, no matter how long you've been a nurse, you'll always feel a little guilty. It's a kind of paranoia we all develop along the way. It keeps us on our toes."

Later, when Carol was walking down the corridor with Bret just after postclinical, they met Dr. Cooper hurrying down the corridor.

"Hey!" he said pointing a finger at Carol which frightened her. "You were in OB recovery this morning, weren't you?"

Carol nodded hesitantly.

"You are a natural. Remember, L&D after you graduate," and he strode on down the corridor.

Remember L&D? Indeed. How could she ever forget?

Chapter Eleven

Pharmacology

"Tablets."

"Tablets are preparations of powdered drugs molded into small disks."

"Toxicology."

"The study of poisonous effects of drugs."

"Name the doctor who discovered penicillin."

"Uh, Dr. Alexander Fleming."

"Give the name of the med student who finds you most attractive."

"Alexander Alpheus Poindexter," Carol replied. "The third."

"Poindexter gets a dose of formaldehyde in his next beer. Come here, student nurse. You've got sixty answers correct out of sixty-nine on your study sheet. That deserves a reward."

"Like what?"

"This."

On the thick-carpeted floor of her apartment, Duane overpowered her gently, easily, and pressed her back into the carpet with a long, lingering kiss. Then he raised his head to look at her. "I'm not sure who's getting the reward, me or you?"

"You promised you wouldn't do things like that if we came back to the apartment to study," she said smiling and tracing the vertical vein that always appeared in the middle of his forehead at times like this.

"I promised no such thing."

"You said you didn't want to get involved because we're both in school and it would interfere with our studies."

"Who's getting involved?"

"You just kissed me involved, and your hands are getting involved."

"Right now, lady, I don't give a damn."

Carol laughed. "That sounded like Rhett Butler in *Gone with the Wind.*"

"Ah, Carol." Duane rolled over on his back and stared up at the ceiling. While she propped her head on her hand and studied him, he said, "I'm depressed. You've learned as much about medicine in three semesters as I have in six—certainly not in as much depth or detail, but the same stuff. It's like the powdered drugs; it's all there pressed into a neat tablet. And you know more about patients and patient situations than I do. I've studied OB, but I have never observed labor and delivery. Besides that, we haven't studied nutrition and you've got an entire textbook on nutrition and diet therapy. I've never observed a circumcision, and you're even about to go into a state mental institution for your psychiatric training."

"I dread that. I'm terrified of it and it's only three weeks away. The summer semester begins in only three weeks and I'm already waking up in the middle of the night dreading it, drenched in a cold sweat. Oh, why do we have to go to Farley? Why a state mental institution? Why not a private clinic or—or a psychiatric wing of a hospital?"

"Because the private clinics and hospitals are determined to protect their paying patients from being discovered during their mild tenures of madness, by forbidding outsiders—like students—from doing their training there."

"But that's perpetuating the stigma of mental illness. The department of mental health and mental retardation keeps spending millions to dispel the stigma, to educate the public about mental illness; yet, the mental health clinics hide the patients away as though they had committed some awful crime. Oh, Duane, I'm scared. We are all a little scared. What if we get—assaulted or something?"

"My God, Carol, they're only people. Think of how lucky you are to be allowed—invited—to train in a state mental hospital with two thousand patients. Mc, I'll probably never get to set foot in a state mental hospital. God the things I *haven't* done."

"But you're getting into it now. You must be patient."

"I'm not getting into it fast enough. You're getting ahead of me."

"Are you jealous of my nursing?"

"It gripes my ass."

Carol sat up. "But why?"

"Your nursing school seems more structured than medical school, more neat, more organized. Compared to you I feel like a will-o'-the-wisp."

She laughed. "A what?"

"Will-o'-the-wisp. Skipping around from rotation to rotation, never settling in and doing anything for long. Just when things started getting exciting in surgery, I got shunted off to oncology rotation—going around seeing terminal patients with a resident who acts like a shrunken Frankenstein monster."

She scooted over and lifted his curly head and laid it in her lap. How long had they been seeing each other? Six weeks? Erratically. Taking breaks from their studies to study together or go out for dinner or a walk in Dove Creek Park. "One year from now," she began, "you'll be into your residency—"

"Internship."

"—Internship. Two years from now you'll be into your surgical residency. Then you'll be so busy that you'll think back on today and *wish* for it."

"Never."

"You're a brilliant student. I expect you to be a brilliant surgeon."

"I intend to be. I have to be. I have to be the best or die."

"I know a little bit of how you feel."

"And I can't fall in love, Carol. I can't get involved."

"I know."

"So don't try to make me."

"I don't intend to."

"Even though I may beg you, don't let me get involved."

"We've been through all this before, Duane. Besides, what does 'involved' involve?"

"Falling in love."

"It doesn't involve—sex?"

"I don't know. I haven't gotten around to that with you yet."

"What if you do and you get involved?"

"I'll have to leave you alone. Drop you like a hot potato."

"What if I become more important to you than your residency?"

"Don't let me."

Carol said softly, "What if I can't help it?"

Duane lay there, his head in her lap blinking up at the ceiling, and said nothing.

This was what her parents had been afraid of, her alone in an apartment with a man. But this was what she needed; someone to talk to, to comfort, to share both the exciting moments and the bad. And she needed love, too. She needed Duane more than he needed her. She needed love; he would only *react* to love if she allowed it or encouraged it. She knew she would allow it or even encourage it someday, but this wasn't the time. Not yet.

He lay staring at the ceiling in a bad mood because of his rotation through the cancer wards. Her exhilaration over the post-partum nursing only made him more glum. He seemed to admire her knowledge but he resented it too. He was reacting again, not living, not really feeling anything but his own desperate, driven, nameless desire to succeed and to do it in a damned hurry.

He liked to help her with her tests, for he knew the answers himself by heart, and he loved to laugh at her wrong answers, liked her more every wrong answer she gave. Yet, he admired her for her good grades.

Pharmacology wasn't an easy course, but the lecture instructor, an M.D. from North Central Medical School, taught the student nurses by taking each category of drugs and teaching them the way in which the drugs affected the human body, system by system. It was not only a course in pharmacology, but also a terrific review of anatomy and physiology. His method of teaching caused the students to categorize every drug, stuffing each type into a specific, labeled pigeonhole in their brains. When they would recall a drug, they would recall every system it affected and how it affected them.

Carol's aunts would often call her now and describe a new "pill" the doctor had given them, and expect her to tell them what the pill was. The average person had no idea of the hundreds of thousands of tablets, elixirs, powders, ointments, and capsules that were on the market. They had no idea that no one could possibly know every medication. *The Physicians' Desk Reference,* or PDR, listed every drug and its uses and actions and dosage. The PDR was over two thousand pages long, like a fat dictionary. If the aunt could give the name of her medication, Carol might or might not know what it was, but she could certainly "look it up" in the PDR. If the aunt only described the pill, it was impossible to know for sure.

One thing Carol had noticed about medications—doctors prescribed too many of them. For a post-partum mother aching from after-pains, an over-the-counter analgesic would stop the cramps most of the time; yet, the obstetricians consistently ordered an analgesic that contained narcotics. At Ross Street Presby, she had observed that the elderly, particularly, were overmedicated with tranquilizers; some were mummified from them. Doctors often used narcotics when a mild analgesic would have done just as well.

Nurses were guilty of overmedicating too. If a doctor had ordered a mild pain medication and a strong one, and left it to the nurses' discretion which the patient needed, most of the time the nurses would give the stronger one. The whole medication scene was like telling the patient, "Here, take your damned fix and leave me alone!" No wonder the world was full of narcs!

After three semesters as a student, Carol had it all figured out.

"Duane?"

"Huh?"

"Did you report that student for cheating on the toxicology exam?"

Duane sighed. "No. I wouldn't rat on a fellow student, at least not to the instructors. I discussed it with a few of the guys, though, and we cornered Bernard and told him next time we saw him cheating on an exam, we'd beat the hell out of him."

"Did it work?"

"As far as I know. At least nobody's seen him sneaking a cheat sheet out of his ballpoint anymore."

"I'm glad you didn't have to report him."

"Why?"

"Because he'd get kicked out of medical school."

"He *should* be kicked out of medical school if he can't pass the exams without cheating. If he can't learn the stuff in med school, he ought not to become a doctor."

"The final exams would weed out people like him eventually, wouldn't they?"

"Don't kid yourself. If he can cheat on semester exams, he can cheat on finals and that kind always manages to cheat his way through residency. How, I don't know."

"It makes me shudder."

Duane raised up and looked at her, grinned, took her in his arms. "Then come here. I'll keep you warm."

"No, I mean—"

"I know what you mean."

"Duane, you mustn't get involved."

"Who's getting involved?"

"We are."

"So?"

"You said . . . Duane. Leave me alone." She scrambled up and put her hands on her hips. "You made me promise not to let this happen."

He was on the floor still, on his hands and knees, his head down, not looking at her. "Carol, I was a fool when I asked that. This is impossible."

"Then don't come over here. Let's go for walks, to dinner, to the movies, but never here."

"No. I want you," he said to the carpet.

Oh, how she wanted to fall on her knees beside him, to take him in her arms, to love him and be loved. For a moment, a dreadful moment, she almost gave in. It was an intoxication. She wasn't really in control at all. Somebody else was, like the Carol who did that first mechanical catheterization while another Carol remained aloof, cool, and observing. The mechanical Carol said, "I think you'd better leave. I'm tired. It's 10:30, and I have to be up in the morning at 5:30."

"Carol, if I leave, I'm not coming back. This is hell."

"You made me promise and I don't go back on my promises."

He stood up and looked at her, his eyes tired, his

facial muscles slack with fatigue. "All right."

"I promised."

"Yes, you did."

"Then do please go, Duane. Please."

He went to the door, paused with his hand on the dead bolt, turned back. "We could—I would hurry. I wouldn't stay long."

"No."

He stared at her. "I'll go, but I'll never come back."

Somehow, she knew that he *would* come back.

"Good night," she said softly.

He left. As she locked the dead bolt of her door she heard the engine of his sports coupe roar, roar again, roar again. Gravel crunched under his wheels as he sped away.

Thirty minutes later her telephone rang while she was in the bathroom brushing her teeth. She answered, "Carol."

"Thank you," Duane's voice said. "The world looks a hell of a lot better after a cold shower."

"I'm glad. Call me?"

"Every night until I can see you again, which will be just as soon as I can. Good night, little nurse."

She shut her eyes, swallowed, said, "Good night."

PART FOUR

Chapter Twelve

Psychiatric nursing

"What really makes me mad is that we have to pay for the gas," Charlotte said.

"We're lucky we can carpool," said Carol, "—take turns driving our cars. And I'm glad it's with somebody I know."

Bret was riding in the back seat leafing through the nine handouts they had received Friday in their first lecture in psychiatric nursing. "Did you look at these handouts?" he asked.

Charlotte glanced over her shoulder. "If we're going to have to drive our cars forty miles to Farley to a state mental institution to subject ourselves to no-telling-what, you can bet your sweet . . . life . . . that I studied the handouts."

"Self-defense," Carol offered. She had drawn the short toothpick and had to drive her car on this their first week of clinical.

"I haven't had a chance until now. I worked all weekend," Bret said.

"Bartending."

"Best money there is," Bret said, "unless you have a college education. Listen to this, 'Rules for Students and Instructors; Number one. Never give a patient a ride in your personal car. Two. Always park in designated parking areas, never in out-of-the-way places. Three. Always take your keys out of your car and lock your car doors. Four. No firearms allowed on the premises under any circumstances.' "

"Sounds like a prison," Charlotte said.

"My mom would die if she knew we were having our psychiatric training at Farley," Carol breathed.

"You didn't tell her?"

"No."

"I don't blame you. Ted was furious. He doesn't think it's necessary if we're not going to go into psychiatric nursing. Actually, we're sort of in danger, aren't we? And on locked wards—"

"Duane says they're only people," Carol said.

Charlotte replied, "Yeah, so was Jack the Ripper."

"Duane says psychiatric nursing should be fascinating, not frightening."

"Has he ever been in a state mental institution before?"

"Well—"

Bret spoke up. "Who's Duane?"

Carol smiled; it was Charlotte who answered. "It's her boyfriend. A medical student from Bennet."

"Suppose we get assigned to the back wards," Carol said. "Suppose we have to—"

"There're no back wards anymore. Remember what Dr. Coker said? The unit system has mixed the chronics with the acutes."

"Whatever that means. What *does* it mean?"

"The long-time sickies with the short-time sickies, I'm sure."

"Bret, do you know?"

"Ask your medical school friend," Bret grumbled.

"Well, why don't you read us the interpersonal techniques we're supposed to use when we talk to those people," Carol said. "That's another thing, you can't even talk naturally to those people. You have to use therapeutic techniques. What was it Dr. Coker said?"

"He said the interpersonal techniques you use while talking with mental patients is designed to draw them out, to verbalize their feelings," Charlotte answered.

"Verbalize, Bret."

"Okay Number one: *using silence*. No example, it speaks for itself."

"Pun, pun," said Charlotte.

"Number two: *accepting;* example, 'yes,' 'uh-huh,' nodding."

"God."

"*Giving recognition,*" Bret went on, "example, 'Good morning. I notice you combed your hair.' "

They laughed.

"*Offering self*. Example, 'I'll sit with you awhile.' *Offering general leads*. Example, 'Go on,' 'and then?' *Restating:* Patient—'I can't sleep.' Nurse—'You have trouble sleeping.' "

"That's enough. Now I'm really scared," Carol said.

"Why are we scared?" Charlotte said.

"Because we don't know anything about mental illness or mental patients. It's an unknown. Something you don't talk about in polite society."

They drove in silence for a long while. Then Bret said, "It seems to me that as bungling students, we could do more harm than good to these people."

"That's one reason they don't let us practice on the paying customers in the private hospitals. Just the

177

wards of the state who are too poor to pay for private care."

"Why make us do it at all?" Carol said. "Why can't we just have lectures?"

"It's like everything else in nursing. You learn by doing," Bret said.

"Yeah, well, who wants to learn *this?*" Charlotte asked.

"Like it or not, ladies, we're gonna learn," Bret said glancing at his watch. "And if you don't speed up a little, Carol, we're going to be late to our first preclinical."

"Anybody want to back out of this and forget nursing?" Carol asked. They were silent. "Because if you do, you'd better do it quick. There's Farley's water tower up ahead."

They met for preclinical in a small barrackslike dormitory said to have been the student nurses' dorm at one time when student nurses were required to live on the premises. Their clinical group consisted of Carol, Charlotte, Bret, Myra, a quiet beautiful girl; and three others. Their teacher was Selma Cauthron, a white-haired widow of fifty-five with a B.S. in nursing and a master's in psychology.

Cauthron leveled with her clinical group immediately. "This is a whole new world here at Farley State Hospital. After a year of clinical training, you students are probably just getting accustomed to the clinical scene. And now it has changed."

They liked Cauthron immediately because she was aware of their apprehension and did not scoff at them. They sat in the tiled, sterile parlor of the dorm in comfortable vinyl chairs, gathered in a cozy circle in an unair-conditioned room fanning themselves with their notebooks and handouts.

Cauthron went on. "You'll be here three days a week, six hours a day, for nine weeks, as you know. In that length of time you'll be free to roam about as you please on the grounds and in the unit to which we are assigned. Our unit is number sixteen and contains two locked wards and two unlocked wards. You'll each be given keys to the locked wards. Guard those keys and never let them out of your sight. If you unlock a door, always, always lock it when you go in or out. Okay, you have freedom to spend your time talking with patients or going to occupational therapy or to physical therapy. But, you're expected to select a patient or patients and to establish a one-to-one nurse-patient relationship."

Carol and Charlotte looked at each other and Charlotte dug into the pocket of her slacks and brought out a roll of Life Savers.

"The one-to-one is to be a therapeutic relationship and you'll be expected to observe and remember everything you and the patient said in your interview and to write down both your own and your patient's verbal and nonverbal communications. Nonverbal communication means things like the wringing of hands, fidgeting, and so on. I'm particularly interested in your observations of your own feelings as well as the communication with your patients. You'll be expected to hand in a daily account of your one-to-one. These are due on the Monday after the week just past."

"There go the weekends," Carol said. Then,

realizing that she had spoken aloud, she covered her mouth with her hand.

Cauthron looked at her. "I'd advise you to go home after clinical and write down everything that happens the day it happens, otherwise you might forget some important details. Don't wait till the weekend. Meantime, I'll give you one week to find a patient or patients for your one-to-one. I've handed you this week's assignments: to describe your reactions to Farley State Hospital, and to describe some of its concepts. Any question?"

Of course there were a few.

Then Cauthron said, "Okay, group. We'll go over to unit sixteen and I'll show you through; then you're on your own. Postclinical is at 12:30."

Carol looked down at her first week's assignment.

Week one, day one: Utilizing the mental health concepts . . . describe the physical aspects of Farley State Mental Hospital and your personal feelings in regard to it.

She looked up, through a nearby window where dozens of brick buildings were scattered about on rolling grounds. This was going to be even more difficult than she had at first imagined.

*Psychiatric Nursing
Week I Day 1*

Assignment: Utilizing the mental health concept that self-awareness influences one's understanding of other persons, describe the physical

180

aspects of Farley State Mental Hospital and your personal feelings in regard to it.

Never having seen Farley State Mental Hospital before, I was unprepared for how many facilities it has, some old, some new. To me, the red brick administration building has a forbidding appearance, probably because it is ninety-three years old. I understand that it was the original building when the hospital was named Farley State Insane Asylum.

The grounds around the thirty-two buildings of the hospital are well kept. There are lawns and many old trees about the grounds. Around the buildings there are flower and shrub beds. There is always something blooming on the grounds, the nurses say.

Besides the administration building, there are newer one-story buildings of a more contemporary architecture, most of them built in the shape of an H. Each building is a separate unit with two locked wards and two unlocked wards. To my surprise, there are greenhouses scattered about the grounds filled with growing things with which the grounds are maintained, and there is a chapel, a general hospital, a rehabilitation center, an occupational therapy building, and a gymnasium.

Patients are strolling or standing about on the premises, either talking with friends or going to the canteen, a small, flat building which contains a snack bar and tables.

I love the grounds. The newer units are not as forbidding as I had expected because inside they're painted in bright colors — yellow, lime green, sky blue — with coordinating floor tiles and plastic furniture.

181

Unit sixteen is fairly representative of most of the other units at Farley. It is built in the shape of an H. Two long rectangular buildings, standing parallel to each other, are connected in the middle by a long corridor lined with vending machines. A door on the north side of the corridor opens out onto an enclosed patio; corridor and patio form the crossbar of the H. The east rectangular building houses two wards—one locked, one unlocked—also the cafeteria. The west building is like it, but without the cafeteria.

Physically there is no difference between the locked wards and the unlocked wards. In each there is a large dayroom, where male and female patients mix and mingle, and a small reading room lined with shelves of books and magazines. The female and male bedchambers are at opposite ends of the dayroom, but are identical, with rows and rows of beds, each with its own night stand. On one side of each room are rows of windows screened in steel mesh, and on the other the bathroom and showers.

In each bedchamber area, there is a nurses' station, enclosed in a glassed-in booth. There, the patient charts are kept, as are the medications dispensed to the patients. Physically, the units are arranged in an orderly fashion.

Recreation within the dayroom consists of watching television, playing table tennis and table games like Monopoly and cards. Mostly, though, the patients are just sitting or they are wandering aimlessly about.

I'm very uneasy around the patients. Most of them act strange in some way. Most of their faces betray their illnesses even if their manners don't. They're restless or statue-still, or they laugh too much or too little. They grimace inappropriately and their motor movements are either exaggerated or they are almost absent. They seem weary, befuddled, and suffering somehow. I feel very sympathetic toward these people, but I tend to want to avoid them rather than to befriend them. I expected to feel a certain amount of revulsion toward the hopelessly ill ones, those who have been at Farley for a long time, but I did not expect to feel this pity. I *must* feel pity because these patients are human beings to whom a horrible misfortune has befallen.

Carol Welles, S.N.

Psychiatric Nursing
Week I Day 2

Assignment: Utilizing the mental health concept that culture influences behavior, describe the unit system as you understand it.

Farley State Mental Hospital operates under the unit system which means it is divided into several semiautonomous units, each serving a specific geographic area. All patients, chronic and acute, mix together in each unit in a "therapeutic milieu." By working closely with other health-care agencies in the specific areas they serve, the units can help patients by placing them in jobs and by providing aftercare. The only exceptions to this system are the alcoholic and the adolescent units. Together these two units house fifty-six percent of the patients at Farley. Out of the two thousand five hundred and seventy patients at Farley, over seventy percent are from the city. This seems to be a statement that the cultural atmosphere of our cities (i.e. the noise, the faster pace, and the crowding), as compared to that of rural areas and small towns, is more conducive to mental breakdowns.

Three units at Farley are devoted to the care of patients from the city and the student nurses of UTE have been assigned exclusively to these three units.

Carol Welles, S.N.

Psychiatric Nursing
Week I Day 3
Assignment: Keeping in mind the mental health concepts that all behavior has a reason; that every individual is unique; and that behavior is ever-changing; describe the open-door policy and the therapeutic milieu.

The open-door policy can mean anything from open units with unlocked doors where patients may come and go at will, to patients governing themselves and being responsible for their actions whether within or without the hospital setting. The adolescent unit is an excellent example of the open-door policy in that the patients can come and go at will to and from the units, and they elect officers to serve as president, vice president, and so on as if they were an exclusive club. They govern themselves and hold hearings to discuss discipline problems. The doctor in charge of their unit is referred to as a counselor.

The therapeutic milieu: In a therapeutic milieu, every aspect of a patient's daily life is directed toward his eventual recovery and return to the community. Nurses, doctors, aides, social workers, psychologists, therapists, and volunteers all work together to this end. Although in the past chronic patients deteriorated mentally in back wards, they are now mixed together with short-term patients, are grouped into families of ten or fifteen, and encouraged to develop interpersonal relationships. All patients, chronic and acute, participate in social, recreational, and cultural activities as well as in group therapy. Patients are encouraged to take part in the planning of programs and improvements for their own units.

Psychiatric Nursing Clinical Record
(A detailed report of the one-to-one nurse-patient interview)
Nurse: <u>Carol Welles</u>   *Patient's initials:* <u>T.R.</u>
Week II Day 1   *Diagnosis:* <u>Manic depressive</u>

Communication of nurse: I was walking across Ward Five feeling sorry for myself because I had not yet found a patient for one-to-one. Seeing a black girl watching me as I passed, I said, "Hi" very automatically.

Communication of patient: "Have we met? Can you take me to get a Coke?" Her eyes were large with what I interpreted as hope. I obtained permission from the nurses to take her outside the locked ward.

Nurse: Slightly disgruntled because the patient did not have her own money for the Coke, and perturbed because her body odor was so strong, I handed her the Coke I bought her. "Are you ready to go back to the ward?"

Patient: She took the Coke, but I noticed that she had grown solemn. "I got slugged in the face last night by the attendant," she said to a nurse who was passing by in the hallway.

Nurse: As I unlocked the door of Ward Five, I rephrased her statement. "You were hit by the attendant?"

Patient: "Yeah," she said watching my expression. "I tried to kill myself with a fork."

Nurse: "You tried to kill yourself?"

Patient: Her shoulders were beginning to slump and her eyes had dulled as she watched my face intently. "Yeah, because I felt like it," she said.

Nurse: There were two or three minutes of silence as we walked toward the patient's bed. "You must have felt badly."

Patient: "My granddaddy died two months ago and I feel so bad." She set her Coke down on the bedside table and sat down heavily on her bed. Her shoulders were slumped, her face sad; her eyes were dull.

Nurse: "You must have been close to your granddaddy," I said sitting down on the bed with her.

Patient: Whining, said, "I felt so bad. My mother say, 'T., don't think about it no more.' But I can't help it. I been locked up in a state school an' now I'm locked up here. Why did my mother put me in this place?" She clenched her fists and beat on her knees. She was becoming agitated.

Nurse: Concentrating on eye-to-eye contact, I asked, "Why do you think your mother put you here?"

Patient: " 'Cause I was trying to kill myself." She watched my expression, her eyes grew brighter.

"I took all the pills I had. I felt so bad—because of my granddaddy. My mother said, 'T., you don't want to go where your granddaddy is do you?' An' I said, 'No.' That was two months ago." The patient began to rock back and forth with hands folded in her lap. "I had a baby," she whined. "My mother put her in a adoption home."

Nurse: "You had this baby at the time your granddaddy died?"

Patient: Beginning to cry and lie over the bed on her stomach, putting her head in my lap, she said, "I don' want to talk about my granddaddy no more."

Nurse: There was silence for several long minutes. I laid my hand on the patient's back. "You wanted to keep your baby?"

Patient: She sat up and nodded. Her eyes were red and damp, but there were no tears on her lids or cheeks. "They put me here and there was no place for her. I tried to kill myself and the baby."

Nurse: "You must have felt pretty bad to do that."

Patient: Her expression brightened and she watched my face. "I used to break car windows out and I was on dope, even L.S.D. Was locked up six times in jail. My brother in college got on speed once. I took pills, got drunk, that's why I killed my brother. I feel bad about breaking car windows an' taking dope. That's why I got sick— that and I missed my granddaddy." She picked up a picture and showed it to me. "This is my home. I went home Thanksgiving and Christmas. We have a shag carpet."

Nurse: "You have a nice home. Such pretty furniture. Do you live with your parents?"

Patient: She nodded and became silent as she rolled and unrolled the fringe on her shoe. Still rolling the fringe, she said after a few moments, "But I tried to kill myself. Swallowed all my pills and they took me to the hospital and pumped out my stomach."

Nurse: "You see why you are here now, don't you? Don't you think your mother put you here so you'd be safe? And this feeling bad will go away someday too."

Patient: She was looking past me now. "I'll feel better at home." She was sitting up straight. Her eyes were not dull. "Well, I'll let you go and talk to someone else now."

Nurse: "Do you have something else to do?" I asked standing up, noticing the untouched Coke on the bedside table.

Patient: "Well I have to take a bath." She stood up and began to walk away.

Nurse: "I'll see you tomorrow if you would like for me to."

Patient: She nodded as she began to turn away again. Her face was placid and her eyes were bright.

Psychiatric Nursing Clinical Record
Nurse: <u>Carol Welles</u>   *Patient's initials:* <u>T.R.</u>
Week II Day 2   *Diagnosis:* <u>Manic depressive</u>

Communication of nurse: I smiled and approached T. with the intent to look as happy as possible to see her, though I was dreading the interview.

Communication of patient: T. was watching me even before I saw her. She appeared pleased and not depressed as she sat with a group of other patients. She rose and came to me. "Hello, I forgot your name."

Nurse: "Carol. I came to see you as I promised I would. Are you feeling better today, T.?" I said as we began to walk in the hallway of the ward.

Patient: "Yes ma'am. Let's go for a walk." Her manner was somewhat detached.

Nurse: "I'm glad to hear you're feeling better."

Patient: "I had another bad dream."

Nurse: "You had another bad dream? What about?"

Patient: "My mother. I always dream she's dead an' I wake up screaming." T. had turned around and was walking toward her bed. When she reached it, she sat down.

Nurse: "How long have you been having this dream?"

Patient: "Since my granddaddy died." She laid her head on my hand and held my arm. She began to cry.

Nurse: "You're afraid of losing your mother?"

Patient: "Uh-huh."

Nurse: I remained silent.

Patient: She sat up and looked at me. No tears were in her eyes. Her shoulders were not slumped

189

as they had been the day before. "I screamed an' the nurse came an' talked to me. I guess I'm having these nightmares because I tried to kill my mother. I cain't sleep some nights and others I have nightmares."

Nurse: "When you tried to kill your mother, were you on dope after your granddaddy died?"

Patient: "Yes."

Nurse: "What do you think caused you to try to kill your mother; you or the dope?"

Patient: "The dope."

Nurse: "You weren't in full control of your thoughts?"

Patient: She nodded. Then sweetly she said, "I'm through talking now. Will you come tomorrow?"

Nurse: "No, but I'll be back Wednesday."

Patient: "I'm going to take a nap." She lay down on the bed.

Nurse: I covered her with the bedspread. " 'Bye. I'll see you Wednesday," I said as I walked away aware that today she had not once mentioned suicide.

Patient: She lay watching me as I left the ward.

Week II Day 3

Ms. Cauthron,

T.R. was transferred yesterday afternoon to unit seven by Dr. Diaz. I was able to secure a carbon copy of the doctors' progress report and it reads as follow:

June 6. Pt. suffering from acute manic depressive psychosis with the usual bouts of retarded depression and excitability. Because of recent attempts at suicide within the ward, though on large doses of Thorazine, I felt that the patient would benefit from a short tenure under the more custodial care of unit seven. Recommend EST three to four times a week to control excitability and depression.

Manuel Diaz, M.D.

Psychiatric Nursing Clinical Record
Nurse: <u>Carol Welles</u>   *Patient's Initials:* <u>L.N.</u>
Week III Day 1 Diagnosis: <u>Residual Schizoptrenic</u>

Communication of nurse: Intending to find a patient for a one-to-one interview, I entered ward eight, and noted a patient sitting on her bed taking off her shoes. Her face was sad. I approached her and said, "Hello, are you getting ready for a nap?"
Communication of patient: The patient looked at me and smiled. "I was going to lie down, but doubt that I can sleep." She appeared fatigued. She seemed to have a head cold.
Nurse: "It's quiet here today."
Patient: "Yes. But I seldom sleep during the day, and having this cold doesn't help." The patient seemed well-oriented, free from anxiety, but her face reflected sadness. Her posture was erect, shoulders back.
Nurse: "My name is Carol Welles. I'm a student nurse. May we talk for a few minutes?"
Patient: "Oh, yes. Let's do," she said pulling the

blanket aside for me to sit down. "What do you do here?"

Nurse: "We talk with the patients, and interview the same one each day," I replied. "What is your name?" I sat on the bed.

Patient: "My name's L.N. What you do must be interesting. Most people are afraid of mental illness. They think everyone here is crazy. I've never thought that. I brought my husband here several years ago. I brought the children to see him and everyone said, 'L.N.'s the one that's crazy for exposing those children to that.'" She leaned back against the head of her bed.

Nurse: "Then this experience is not very new to you."

Patient: "No. I understand these people. When all your problems hit you one after another, something has to give." Her face became even more sad.

Nurse: "Your problems hit you one after another?"

Patient: "For twenty years, one after another. I marvel because some people's husbands pay the rent, pay for the car, pay the bills. Why, I don't even know what that would be like. I've always worked."

Nurse: "Your problems consisted of working for a living?"

Patient: "Mostly. That and illness—other people's illnesses. Me, I've always been pretty healthy." Her foot began to move rhythmically.

Nurse: "Do you feel that you are well now?"

Patient: "Except for this cold. Obviously, I'm not

too well or I wouldn't be here, would I?" She smiled and patted her hair. "I guess I *look* sick. I just had a permanent and they didn't have time to comb it out. Yours sure looks nice."

Nurse: "Thank you. Was it very long ago that your husband was here?"

Patient: "Two years ago. I think there is still such a stigma about mental illness. Maybe you nurses can help to change that. My children have grown up unafraid of it."

Nurse: "So they are able to accept your stay here better."

Patient: "Yes. My son had me committed, but was afraid I was mad at him. But I figured this was a blessing. I had pneumonia three weeks ago when I was in unit six. The nurses were marvelous, treated me like a baby, petted me. At one point they thought I was dead, couldn't get a pulse. I could hear them talking. They would have taken me to the general hospital, but I was too sick to be moved. I got strength from somewhere to stay alive. I would have died outside of here." The patient was fingering her collar nervously.

Nurse: I was remembering that unit six was the alcoholic unit. I said, "You did feel sicker with pneumonia than with the illness that you are being treated for?"

Patient: "Oh, much more so. See, I'm here because I injured my back and took too much medication for pain. It was for this reason they referred me to a psychiatrist. This is his idea." She looked around her indicating her presence in the hospital. "But my son said I needed the rest, that I was on the verge of a breakdown — *but I didn't have a breakdown,* you understand."

Nurse: "And you are just resting here. Will you go back to the same job when you get home?"

Patient: Her face dropped. "No, no. I am learning to be a PBX operator over in the rehab building."

Nurse: Feeling that I had stumbled on to something by asking her about returning to her old job, I attempted to pursue the idea. "You did not like your job?"

Patient: She nodded once. "Do you have a patient to talk to every day?" She sat upright.

Nurse: "Not yet. What days do you go to rehab building?"

Patient: "Mondays, Tuesdays, and Wednesdays, from eight till twelve. I have group therapy on Thursday and Fridays from two in the afternoon till three."

Nurse: "Oh, that's too bad. I'm here on Mondays and Wednesdays when you're at the rehab building."

Patient: "Oh, I'm sorry. Maybe I could skip rehab for a few weeks."

Nurse: "No. Rehab is very important. I can see you on Fridays, just to say hi." I must have shown my disappointment.

Patient: "Oh, I'm sorry. I would have enjoyed talking." She did show her disappointment.

Nurse: "I have to go now. We have group activity at ten. Guess I'll see you on Friday."

Patient: All right. I'm glad you came to talk to me. Good luck to you."

Communication of nurse: After having learned that L.N., my only patient, had mysteriously disappeared from the hospital last evening, I was again strolling through ward eight in search of a patient for one-to-one when I approached a patient as she was spreading and smoothing the top sheet on her bed. "I see you're getting ready for inspection like everyone else." I was smiling but not "bubbly" as one patient had accused a student of being.

Patient: She turned and smiled. "Yes. I was straightening the sheet. It was a little messed up." She talked slowly, seemed friendly.

Nurse: "You haven't been on this ward long, have you?"

Patient: "No. Only three or four weeks. I'm new." She stopped working on her sheets. Her posture was erect; her arms hung limply at her sides.

Nurse: "I'm Carol Welles, a student nurse from UTE."

Patient: She squinted at my nametag. "Oh yes. I see."

Nurse: "What is your name?"

Patient: "W.A.," she replied. "My daughter is a student nurse in New York, one of those big hospitals there. She really likes it."

Nurse: "Really? That's a fine place to learn. I

think everybody likes nursing who gets into it. Do you have more family?"

Patient: "My son in Beeville." She was smiling. When mentioning her children she had a very pleasant look on her face.

Nurse: "That's nice and close. Does he come to see you often?"

Patient: "Oh—well, yes. But I haven't been here long." She changed the course of the conversation. "What do you do here?"

Nurse: "We talk to the patients. We try to find someone to talk to for thirty minutes to an hour each day we are here—the same person, hopefully. I would enjoy talking with you if you feel comfortable about it."

Patient: "Well—" She pulled at her fingers. "I don't have much to offer. My problem is religious more than anything." She looked away from me, beyond me; her face lost its pleasant look and became sad.

Nurse: "Your problem is religious?"

Patient: "God just picked me up and shook me and sat me back down again. I haven't been living right and He's telling me about it." She looked at me, smiling, but it was an ambiguous smile, for the rest of her face was still sad.

Nurse: Feeling a special liking for the patient to begin with, I did not have to try hard to begin to develop empathy with her. "You seem tired; let's sit down." We sat on chairs at the end of her bed. "Do I have your permission to talk with you three times a week?"

Patient: She nodded. Her face held no expression, but her mouth smiled politely most of the time. She seemed tired. Her posture showed it; her shoulders were slightly stooped. "I'd like that. I feel comfortable talking to you, but I have no more to say than what I've already said. The Lord just shook me and made me realize I had been going my own way too long."

Nurse: "How did he shake you, W.?"

Patient: "I became unconscious, all of a sudden."

Nurse: "You felt God did that?"

Patient: "Yes." She nodded emphatically. "I could almost hear Him say, 'These are my children; you aren't one of them.'"

Nurse: "Did you mention hearing Him to your doctor?"

Patient: "No. These Cuban doctors don't believe in God. They would never understand."

Nurse: "You feel God is punishing you?"

Patient: "Yes, I know He is." She nodded again emphatically. "He's done it before; three other times I passed out. This is my third time here."

Nurse: "Were you from a religious family?"

Patient: "My parents were, but we went our separate ways."

Nurse: "Are your parents living near your home?"

Patient: "My mother lives in _____ right across the street. We wave from our apartment windows and I have a sister who lives down the street."

Nurse: "Then you didn't go your separate ways physically." I cringed inside myself after this. I had already learned that mental patients don't like jokes about themselves.

Patient: She smiled pleasantly as she had when mentioning her mother and sister. "No, we didn't."

Nurse: "But you feel you went away from your parents' religious teaching?"

Patient: "Yes." She nodded vigorously. "Absolutely!" She sniffed. "I only know I love Him. I feel a love for Him I couldn't have felt on my own. It must c-come from—" She stopped in the middle of her sentence.

Nurse: "Him?"

Patient: She nodded. Tears were in her eyes.

Nurse: Silence.

Patient: She had been looking beyond me seemingly ashamed of her tears.

Nurse: I felt a little anxiety at seeing her tears. *Empathize,* I told myself. *Feel* with her, dumdum.

Patient: She broke the silence. "My mouth says I love Him, but I'm afraid my heart is black and it's saying something else—like two people arguing."

Nurse: I was resisting injecting some of my own religious teaching, but that was forbidden. In fact Bibles are forbidden in the wards here. "You feel something inside you saying you don't love Him?"

Patient: She nodded. "I'm so afraid, my heart's so black." She put her hand to her chest. "I feel so peculiar."

Nurse: I was alarmed, wondering if I had really goofed. "I hope I didn't say anything—"

Patient: "No," she interrupted. "I just feel so— In fact since I've been talking to you, I felt God near."

Nurse: "Maybe He was. Was it a pleasant feeling?"

Patient: She hesitated. "Yes."

Nurse: "Do you think He would be near if He were mad at you?"

Patient: She shook her head, but did not appear convinced. She was slightly agitated now.

Nurse: The personnel were making unbelievable noise; shouting, rushing up and down aisles. I was distracted.

Patient: W.A. was distracted also. She chuckled. "Inspection day."

Nurse: "Do I have your permission to talk to you on Monday, Wednesday, and Friday mornings for thirty minutes or more?"

Patient: She was smiling. "Yes, I guess. I've just told all there is, though. But I enjoyed talking to you. I don't have much to offer."

Nurse: "I enjoyed talking to you, too. We don't expect people to just pour out everything unless they want to."

Patient: She laughed slightly. "Well, I don't have much to pour out."

Nurse: "I'll see you next Monday, W. I surely enjoyed talking to you."

Patient: "I enjoyed talking to you, too. Good-by. And thank you."

Psychiatric Nursing Clinical Record

Nurse: Carol Welles   *Patient's initials:* W.A.

Week IV Day 1   *Diagnosis:* Catatonic schizophrenic

Communication of nurse: Before I was due to meet with W.A., I studied her chart and discovered that she had been brought to Farley in an acute catatonic state. She had been given seven electroshock treatments before she was able to respond to verbal stimuli or to function on her own. She has been in a mild agitated state since the last treatment. After searching the dayroom, lobby, and occupational therapy, I finally found W.A. napping on her bed. She had changed beds.

Communication of patient: She saw me as I approached, got up, and smiled. "Guess I overslept." She folded her bedspread carefully.

Nurse: "It's a beautiful day outside, not so hot. Would you like to go sit outside on the patio?"

Patient: "Yes. I'd like that."

Nurse: While we found folding chairs to sit on, I said, "I'm sorry you couldn't talk last Friday."

Patient: "I was sick. My son didn't come for me on Thursday like he promised. I think he must have forgotten. But I feel better today."

Nurse: "I'm glad to hear you're feeling better."

Patient: "But I had a bout with the Lord this weekend."

Nurse: "Tell me about it."

Patient: "There's not a whole lot to tell."

Nurse: Silence.

Patient: "I was just feeling so bad. I suddenly . . . Well . . . something carried me into the bathroom, then into one of those . . ." She chuckled. "One of those little closed places. I cried and cried. I felt so guilty. But pretty soon I

thought I heard Him say, 'Go in peace.' Ever
since then I felt so much better."

Nurse: "You feel all the guilt lifted?"

Patient: "Well, no. I still feel guilty a little."

Nurse: "When you feel bad, have you ever asked
for medication?"

Patient: "No. Medication won't help this."

Nurse: "How do you know that?"

Patient: "Because you can't get rid of guilt with
pills. And I *won't* feel better either until I find
out what's the matter." She folded her hands in
her lap.

Nurse: "What's the matter?"

Patient: "Whether I'm being chastised or
punished."

Nurse: "You still feel that God is punishing you?"

Patient: "I certainly do. If I thought he was chastising me I'd lay down and tell Him to chastise
away. But I'm afraid it's worse than that." She
shifted about in her chair, pulled her skirt down
over her knees.

Nurse: I was very disappointed, angry at mental
illness, angry at my patient for her persistent
guilt feelings, so maybe I launched out on forbidden grounds. "You feel guilty. You feel God is
punishing you."

Patient: "Or chastising me."

Nurse: "I'm sorry if I sound dumb, but what is
the difference in chastisement and punishment?"

Patient: "Chastisement is correcting His children. Punishment is brought on those who are
not His children."

Nurse: "W., have you ever thought that maybe

you are punishing yourself and that it's not God at all?"

Patient: She locked her hands behind her head. "No. Because I don't have that much sense. He had to do it. I was set in my ways."

Nurse: "Then you feel He is making you feel guilty."

Patient: "Yes."

Nurse: "Maybe you're trying to handle your guilt all by yourself."

Patient: "I don't understand." She glanced at me quickly.

Nurse: "You feel those blackouts were his chastisement?"

Patient: "Yes." She locked her hands behind her head. "Or worse." She shifted in her chair, pulled her skirt down over her knees again. "And I could understand Him to say that I had blasphemed."

Nurse: "*Did* you blaspheme?"

Patient: "No. Not unless my heart is saying something *I'm* not."

Nurse: "Do you think God punishes us for an unconscious thought?"

Patient: "The Bible says He looks on the heart, not on outward appearances."

Nurse: "I see. He's looking for sins to punish us for."

Patient: "No, no. He takes our sins away if we let Him."

Nurse: "You believe that He takes away sin, but leaves the guilt?"

Patient: "No," she said almost irritably. "He took the guilt on Himself."

Nurse: "Everybody's guilt but yours."

Patient: She was silent. She was not moving her foot back and forth. She stared into space. The usual fixed smile was not on her face. Finally she looked at me. "I feel better."

Nurse: I was surprised. It was too easy and too quick. "Oh?"

Patient: "I'd never thought of it like that."

Nurse: "You've told me before how you believe. I wonder why you never thought of it like that?"

Patient: "I guess I wasn't thinking, or maybe my eyes were closed and it took you to open them for me."

Nurse: I felt flattered, I felt great, I felt that I'd done something of value for her. But I was still slightly apprehensive. "But what if you get rid of your guilt and turn it over to God completely and it doesn't work? I mean, what if you feel no better after that?"

Patient: "Then it would be something else."

Nurse: "What would it be?"

Patient: "I guess the guilt is myself punishing myself, like you said."

Nurse: Bingo!

Ms. Cauthron,

Since the beginning of this study, Mrs. W.A. was discharged from Farley State Hospital on July 9, 1978. As stated in the nurse's prognosis, it seems that long-range therapy should have been employed. Mrs. A. would have, in my opinion, benefited from group therapy, vocational rehabilitation, and job placement.

Whether or not "getting rid of her guilt" helps Mrs. A. on a long-range basis remains to be seen.

Carol Welles, S.N.

Psychiatric Nursing Clinical Record
Nurse: Carol Welles   *Patient's initials:* F.T.
Week VI Day 2   *Diagnosis:* Undifferentiated
schizophrenia

Ms. Cauthron,

I apologize for day two of this report which follows. I admit it isn't usual, but this really is the way it happened, only condensed. F.T. is an eighteen-year-old girl diagnosed as an undifferentiated schizophrenic. All of us students have tried to be polite to her but we don't choose to select her for one-to-one because of her demands on our time and because of the fact that she is switched back and forth between our unit and the adolescent unit.

Communication of nurse: I was at the nurses' station reading the discharge notes for W.A. when F. came into the room.

Patient: "Hi. Are you reading my chart?" she asked smiling and swinging her arms back and forth.

Nurse: "What makes you think I'm reading your chart?"

Patient: "I don't know," she said, still smiling and swinging her arms. Then she asked the nurse in charge, "Can I have some Thorazine? I'm so nervous today."

Nurse: "C'mon, F. Let's go walking. That should help."

Patient: "Okay," she agreed very readily.

Nurse: We walked outside the unit to a bench under a tree.

Patient: "Let's talk here." She sat down on the bench.

Nurse: Silence. I sat down beside her.

Patient: "You've talked to me before, haven't you?"

Nurse: "Several times."

Patient: "What do you think about me?"

Nurse: "What do you mean?"

Patient: "I mean how sick do I seem to you?"

Nurse: I thought a moment. "Well, today you seem fine. You act pretty normal."

Patient: She appeared irritated. "I mean most of the time."

Nurse: "Well, you usually seem pretty well."

Patient: She shifted on the bench. "You don't understand me at all!"

Nurse: "Why do you say that?"

Patient: "You disappoint me. You put me in a corner like I'm some freak."

Nurse: I swallowed and was silent.

Patient: Silence. Her hands were between her knees.

Nurse: "F., how have I made you feel this way?"

Patient: "By not knowing how sick I am."

Nurse: Silence.

Patient: "Some people say I put on a good show. Outwardly I seem well. Inwardly I'm feeling like hell. I'm disappointed in you for not knowing me. You don't know me at all. Nobody does but the doctor and a social worker."

Nurse: Fighting an urge to defend myself, I said, "I'm sorry I've disappointed you, but you do put on a good front."

Patient: "Don't you see anything about me that's abnormal?"

Nurse: "Sometimes you're depressed. Sometimes you don't want to talk."

Patient: "That's abnormal?"

Nurse: "Well—most people feel that way at times."

Patient: "See? You don't understand me at all."

Nurse: "I understand that you're much more depressed at times than is normal."

Patient: She looked at me almost cheerfully. "I don't mean to be critical of you. It's just that everyone acts like I'm well and I'm not. The doctor says I'm a very sick girl, but nobody else thinks that. I just want them to know *I'm sick!*"

Nurse: "They know that."

Patient: "Then why don't they pay attention!"

Nurse: "To what?"

Patient: "They act like I'm normal. Have you read my chart?"

Nurse: "Yes."

Patient: "What's my diagnosis?"

Nurse: I thought about that. I decided to stick my neck out. "You're schizophrenic."

Patient: "That's me."

Nurse: "Does it help to know?"

Patient: "It helps to know they know I'm sick. I've thought they thought I was neurotic. All my life I've tried to tell people I was sick and no one believed me. I get so jealous of other patients."

Nurse: "How do you mean?"

Patient: "When they get shots. I get jealous."

Nurse: "Why do you get jealous when they get shots?"

Patient: "I'm attracted to pain and I get so jealous."

Nurse: "You're attracted to pain?"

Patient: "That's the only time my parents ever showed me attention—it was associated with pain. I guess that's why."

Nurse: "You seem to have some insight about your jealousy."

Patient: "I've been told that before, but I don't have enough to get rid of it and get me well, do I?"

Nurse: "Do you want to get well?"

Patient: "I don't want this hell I'm going through, but I don't quite want to get well either."

Nurse: "You don't feel ready to function outside of here?"

Patient: "No, people would be mean to me."

Nurse: "What makes you think that?"

Patient: "Because they always were." She started to cry and covered her face. "I want somebody who really cares for me. I just want somebody to care."

Nurse: Silence. I was thinking that F. was putting on an act to keep my attention.

Patient: She recovered and said, "Have I told you about talking to the plugs?"

Nurse: "No."

Patient: "Light plugs. I say, 'How are you today?' Stuff like that and I pretend the plugs care about me."

Nurse: "How would they care if they could?"

Patient: "They'd understand how I feel. Have I told you about Taxpayer?" She lowered her voice.

Nurse: "No."

Patient: "I pretend I'm this plastic doll. I'm attracted to plastic because that's what they use to cover the table with when you go in for shock treatments. I use pieces of plastic to masturbate with. Taxpayer is my owner and I pretend it's him doing it. He says, 'How does that feel, baby doll?' He also likes for me to be hurt. If I get mad at somebody or get my feelings hurt he says, 'Ah ha! You're going to get a nice shock treatment, baby doll.' "

Nurse: This was no act. I was mortified.

Patient: She seemed exhausted. "I've talked to students all morning."

Nurse: "Has it helped?"

Patient: "I feel like you know me better now and understand. Will you be here tomorrow?"

Nurse: "I won't be here again until Friday."

Patient: "That's what the other students said. How can I go till Friday without talking to someone?"

Nurse: "Can you talk to a nurse?"

Patient: "The only ones who understand are the doctor and the social worker."

Nurse: "F., we'll all be back next Friday."

Patient. "Okay. Well, I'll go get my cigarette. I'll see you. I won't tell anybody that you told me my diagnosis."

Nurse: "Tell whatever you need to, F."

Patient: "Okay. Good-by."

Psychiatric Nursing Clinical Record

Nurse: <u>Carol Welles</u>   *Patient's initials:* <u>F.T.</u>

Week VII Day 3   *Diagnosis:* Undifferentiated
                                          <u>schizophrenia</u>

Communication of nurse: Walking with Charlotte across the parking lot, we saw F. striding across the lot. I did not want to call to her because once she sees me it's hard to get away from her. But Charlotte called, "Hi, F."

Communication of patient: She turned, saw us, came to us. Obviously she thought it was I who spoke. "Hi! Where you going?" She appeared cheerful.

Nurse: "To ward eight. How are you today?"

Patient "Okay. Can you go for a walk with me?"

Nurse: "Sure. Where do you want to go?"

Patient: "Oh, anywhere, I guess."

Nurse: I was silent as I fell into the fast pace F. had already set as we left Charlotte at the outside door of unit sixteen.

Patient: "I'm so nervous since I've been off shock. I've been worried about something," she said as we walked along.

Nurse: "Oh?"

Patient: "Some of the girls on ward six told me

209

some things about shock that bothers me. One girl said they forgot to give her the shot in the arm before the shock and she felt this awful pain from the shock."

Nurse: "But—"

Patient: "And this other girl said they didn't give her enough of the medicine in her arm and she felt the shock. She said it was awful. Painful."

Nurse: "F., would you slow down a bit? Let me tell you what I know about it. From what I've read and from hearing a lecture by Dr. Diaz here, there is no pain with EST (shock). The minute the doctor pushes the button the patient is unconscious, feels no pain. That's in standard EST. In the modified, like you had, you are given the shot of Pentothal and are asleep before he pushes the button."

Patient: "Gee that makes me feel better."

Nurse: F. was walking very fast and was headed in the direction of the administration building. I was quickly getting out of breath. Her energy was incredible. Never had she vocalized with such rushes of energy as she did then. "F., a little slower. Okay?"

Patient: "You know I told you I get jealous of other people when they get shots?"

Nurse: "Mm-hm."

Patient: "Well, I almost want to kill myself when I get so jealous. Do you know what I really want?"

Nurse: "No."

Patient: "To kill myself. That's what I really want."

Nurse: "You really want to kill yourself."

Patient: "My biggest problem is my jealousy. If I could only get rid of it. I told you how jealous I am. What makes people get jealous? It's hell."

Nurse: "Why do you think you get jealous?"

Patient: "I told you. The only attention I ever got from my parents was when I was hurt."

Nurse: "That's good insight."

Patient: She nodded. "I would kill myself, but some girl told me I'd go to hell if I did. I have enough misery now; I don't need misery in hell forever too."

Nurse: Silence.

Patient: "You understand. You didn't used to, but you do now."

Nurse: "I'm glad you feel that way. F., tell me. Is it the pain you're jealous of?"

Patient: She thought a moment. "I guess."

Nurse: "Then it looks as though you'd like pain. Why did you ask me if EST treatments hurt? Was it because you wanted them to hurt?"

Patient: "Gosh, no!" She thought a minute. "I guess it's the attention."

Nurse: "Do you feel jealous when the nurses give someone a tablet?"

Patient: "No."

Nurse: "Did your parents give you attention when you were sick?"

Patient: "No. But once my sister got sick and they gave her a lot of attention. But when I got sick I got yelled at."

Nurse: "How did they give your sister attention?"

Patient: "They gave her presents and when I

asked if any were for me, my daddy yelled at me and said I was selfish."

Nurse: "What else?"

Patient: "They seemed worried about her and they took her to the doctor."

Nurse: "Did they take you to the doctor?"

Patient: "No, they ignored me."

Nurse: "How?"

Patient: "They acted like I wasn't very sick. They didn't show me much attention and they didn't take me to the doctor."

Nurse: "Did you want to go to the doctor?"

Patient: "No. I was afraid I'd get a shot."

Nurse: "What made you afraid you'd get a shot?"

Patient: "The doctor gave my sister one."

Nurse: "And you've been jealous of people who've gotten shots ever since?"

Patient: "I don't remember. Ever since I've been here, I've been jealous."

Nurse: "F., I have to go back to the unit now."

Patient: "Can I walk with you?"

Nurse: "Sure."

Patient: "I wish I could understand my jealousy."

Nurse: "Don't you understand at all?"

Patient: "I don't know."

Nurse: "Are you going to be jealous from now on of people who get shots?"

Patient: "I don't know."

Nurse: "You do realize that people are getting shots all the time in this hospital."

Patient: Nodded only.

Nurse: "I just saw a patient get a shot on ward eight; patients get them all the time. Are you just jealous at certain times?"

Patient: "Who got the shot?"

Nurse: "I don't know her name, but—"

Patient: "*Why* did she get the shot?"

Nurse: "I don't know."

Patient: "If I had seen that, I would have . . ." She began to cry. "I *knew* something bad would happen today."

Nurse: "You mean because somebody had a shot?"

Patient: Nodded only.

Nurse: "F., I'm sorry I told you."

Patient: "It's not your fault. It's this misery. I wish I were dead."

Nurse: "F., I have to report to ward eight now. Will you start working on your jealousy problem?"

Patient: "I'll try. When will you be back?"

Nurse: "Next Monday."

Patient: "That's a long time."

Nurse: "I'll see you then. Okay?"

Patient: She nodded, waved, and walked away still crying.

"This is funny," Carol said as they drove out of the hospital grounds through the opened iron gates. "I think I drove on our first day of clinical. Nine weeks, three people, how did I end up driving on our last day?

"Charlotte was sick for two days and threw us off schedule," Bret said from the back seat.

They fell silent for a while. Then Charlotte said, "Carol, do you think I ought to write Janice and let her have my address? I feel terrible leaving her like this."

Charlotte had established her one-to-one the first week. Her patient had been a girl of twenty-five who did not speak, but wrote hundreds of letters to non-existent persons, and during their nine weeks of clinical at Farley, Charlotte had been able to communicate with Janice enough to talk with her about her problems. Like all the patients who were chosen by—or had chosen—a student, Janice had come to look forward to Charlotte's visits. Janice had cried when Charlotte had said good-by for the last time.

Carol said, "All I know is that Dr. Diaz said for us not to give our addresses to our patients. They've been known to leave the hospital and show up on students' front porches. That's kind of callous of him to say that, though. Some people have no feelings."

"I'm going to consider it. I'll really miss her."

Carol stared at the road ahead. "Somebody should visit Margaret. I took her a gift. She wasn't my one-to-one, but we were able to talk."

"You mean she was able to talk to *you*, and she had never talked to anyone else the entire seventeen years she was at the hospital."

"What are we? We're users, that's what. We used those people to gain knowledge for ourselves, taught them to trust us, and then we left," Carol said.

"You get attached to them, your Wilma, your Margaret, my Janice, Lanny. I even got attached to Fran."

Carol laughed. "No, Fran attached to us, poor kid. Now she'll start talking to light plugs again."

"Yeah, probably."

They were silent awhile.

Then Carol said, "Bret, you're quiet. What's wrong?"

"I feel lousy."

"Why?"

"Tom cried. I don't think he's far enough along to trust anybody but me."

"Being a bartender, Bret, you were a natural sounding board."

"Bartenders keep more people out of mental institutions than doctors do."

Charlotte said, "The sickest people we saw were the alcoholics. Remember that next time you serve a drink."

"And the narcs," Carol said.

"I won't remember anything but the look on Tom's face when I first began to prepare him to accept that I was leaving Farley and wouldn't be back."

"Maybe you ought to be a psychiatric nurse," Charlotte said.

"I've got to keep my original goal in mind."

They were silent again; then Charlotte said, "Do you think the doctors should have let Myra take Lanny out on the picnic?"

Carol shook her head. "I don't know. She shouldn't have let herself get that attached to a patient."

"Attached nothing. She fell in love with him; everybody knows that. And everybody knows that you can't take a patient out on pass unless you're family."

"But Lanny's not even psychotic. He's just brain-damaged and his parents don't want responsibility for him."

"It's a shame. Even if Myra were to do what I think she wanted to do—take him home with her and keep him—it's better than Farley."

"Anything is better than Farley."

"For charity patients it's the best we have."

"It will haunt me forever." Carol hit her fist on the steering wheel. "What's so bad is, we're leaving. We established a relationship with those lonely people and now we're leaving them."

"Well, I guess what we should remember when we feel guilty about leaving our patients is that there'll be other students along soon to take our places."

"Let's hope so. UTE *could* change the curriculum, you know."

"Yeah. That'd be a lousy deal for the patients," Bret said as he gazed out the window at the country-side, crisp and dry in the August heat. "And for the students, too," he added morosely.

PART FIVE

Chapter Thirteen

Medical-Surgical Nursing I
Patients and Problems

Carol had become more acquainted with Bret while car-pooling with him and Charlotte to Farley and back. She had learned that he had been in a skirmish in Vietnam where he had been hospitalized with fragments of shrapnel in his right thigh. He'd spent two weeks in the army hospital in Vietnam and several weeks in a nearby veterans hospital for complications from the wounds. He had seen some "pretty lousy" medical treatment in both hospitals, though he never specified what, and was determined to work his way into the hospital where he was last hospitalized, and up the ladder to correct the mismanagement there in whatever ways he could.

As a student nurse, Bret had discovered he "had a way" with patients, especially the elderly, and Carol was glad he did after her first day of clinical at Bennet.

Carol, Mae, Joe, Shelly, and Bret had been assigned to Bennet at last—their choice of hospitals, their heaven on earth, their medical Utopia. Bennet was a twenty-eight-hundred-bed teaching hospital, the training grounds for two medical schools and five nursing schools, including Bennet's own R.N. school, which was a four-year program and their own LVN school, which was a one-year program. The local Cedar Crest Community College's two-year R.N. school took part of its training at Bennet, as did a four-year R.N. school from nearby Davenport. The Baptist four-year school also sent their students there for part of their training.

Medical interns and residents from North Central and from Bennet University medical schools abounded, and Bennet's own staff was enormous; its corridors teemed with white-clad professionals, pink-smocked volunteers, red-and-white candy stripers, and housekeeping personnel in gray. The nurses' stations clamored with activity. Elevators, which carried patients and visitors and personnel, were always full.

Bennet medical complex was a cluster of twelve large buildings, old and new of various heights, connected by underground tunnels and twisted corridors. Its main cafeteria was enormous and the culinary fare was excellent; the steam tables would have made the city's largest cafeteria look like a neighborhood delicatessen. Bennet was the ultimate goal of every student nurse who wanted to learn a lot quickly.

Ellen Child's clinical group, consisting of eleven students, was required to arrive for preclinical at 6:00 A.M., in time to have thirty minutes of preclinical from which they would disperse to their designated stations where they would sit in on report along with the regular nursing staff. This was the first time the students had been allowed to sit in on report.

Carol, Jo, and Bret were assigned to the fourth floor of Dowell. Dowell was one of the older buildings and housed mostly the medical patients—those with medical rather than surgical problems. Eagerly they hurried to the nurses' station where a ward clerk dressed in blue motioned for them to go into the small lounge behind the nurses' station to join the nurses for report.

Report was a thirty-minute overlap in shifts during which time the charge nurse of the off-going shift gave a report on each patient on the floor to the nurses of the on-coming shift. As a guide, the charge nurse referred to the Kardex which was a tablet of capsuled information on each patient on the floor. Report insured a smooth transition of nursing care from one shift to the next, and during this time any special information concerning a patient was conveyed to, and any unusual problems were discussed with, all the nurses coming on duty.

The students were amazed at the diversity of patients in Dowell, and when the charge nurse gave report on the patients to which they had been assigned, they eagerly took notes. They were expected to read charts, write nurses' notes, graph vital signs, give medications, see that their patients had their baths, and that their beds were changed; total patient care. The only thing they could not do yet was to regulate, start, or inject medication into IVs.

"Mr. Fred Pride," said the charge nurse, a tall, thin red-headed nurse with freckles. She glanced up from the Kardex at Carol. "Mr. Pride is an eighty-two-year-old patient of Dr. Moore's, admitted seven days ago, August 25th, with a diagnosis of bacterial pneumonia. Mr. Pride was put on a regimen of strict bedrest, IPPB treatments, and gentamicin and kanamycin. His progress has been excellent—up until two days ago."

"Tell me about it," said a plump LVN.

"We've had to fill out two incident reports on our shift because Mr. Pride has gotten up out of bed twice and fallen both times in his room," continued the eleven-to-seven nurse.

The nurses all looked at Carol, who was assigned to Pride.

"Day shift reports that he has quit eating his meals," she went on.

"He also cries," said the platinum blonde charge nurse on day shift.

"Didn't you talk with him, Louise?"

"Yesterday," said the day-shift charge nurse. "I sat down on his bed and took his hand and asked him what was wrong. Somehow, he's got it into his head that he's not in his own room. We took him to x-ray two days ago and ever since then, he's been thinking that we brought him back to the wrong room."

"Nothing was changed in his room," offered the LVN.

"I showed him all his things in the drawer of his bedside table—his toothbrush, his electric shaver—but he wasn't convinced," said the platinum blonde.

The LVN spoke up again. "I've been assigned to Mr. Pride for a week, and yesterday he told me we'd taken him to a different room by mistake. And he's been worried and depressed ever since."

The platinum blonde nurse on day shift leaned over and squinted at Carol's nametag. "Welles?" she asked.

Carol nodded.

"Welles, Mr. Pride can sit in his bedside chair now and Dr. Moore suggested yesterday that we take him for strolls in a wheelchair for a change of scenery. He's a sweet old fellow. See if you can persuade him to eat today, will you, since he's your patient today?"

"Sure," Carol said feeling like a "full-fledged" nurse for the first time.

The charge nurse on night shift turned the page of the Kardex and began report on another patient.

The head of Mr. Pride's bed was rolled up all the way when Carol went in carrying her pink stethoscope—a present from Duane—and rolling the mercury sphygmomanometer. He looked at her. His teeth were out and his nose almost touched his chin, his cheekbones were prominent over the hollows in his face which his teeth would have filled out.

"Hi, Mr. Pride. I'm Carol. I'm going to be your nurse this morning."

"Oh yeah?" he said pleasantly, observing her with watery blue eyes.

"How do you feel this morning?"

Mr. Pride looked at the painting of a farmhouse on the wall opposite the foot of his bed and said, "Oh . . . all right, I guesh."

"Hungry?"

"No-oo, can't shay ash I am."

"Well, I'm going to take your vital signs now and then it'll be time for your breakfast tray."

"I'd feel a whole lot better if they'd put me back in my old room."

Therapeutic techniques were still fresh in Carol's mind from psychiatric nursing, and though Mr. Pride wasn't psychotic, Carol had decided the therapeutic techniques could work just as well with other patients. "You feel you aren't in your room?"

"That'sh right. They tell me I am, but they're mishtaken. It'sh all turned around."

"Oh. I see. You're turned around."

"No ma'am. *I'm* not. The *room* ish."

Carol bit her lip to keep from laughing as she wrapped the blood-pressure cuff around his arm.

"Do *you* know where my room ish?"

She took one of the earpieces of the stethoscope back out of her ears. "Sir?"

"Do you know where my old room ish?"

"Uh—this *is* your room," Carol said hesitantly.

"No," said Pride looking at the painting again, "itsh not. And I can't get anybody to believe me."

Step number one: before a student nurse or any nurse takes vital signs or gives meds to a patient she must always check the armband of the patient, no matter how well she knows the patient. Checking the armband is a double insurance against giving a med to the wrong patient, or recording the vital signs on the wrong patient. Carol had checked Pride's armband. "Fred Pride. Room 406," his armband read. This was room 406.

Carol took all Mr. Pride's vital signs except his temperature. She discovered that you can't take an oral temperature on patients unless they have their teeth in.

"Let's put your teeth in, Mr. Pride," she said. He nodded. She went to the sink in his room where a cottage cheese-sized box sat, and stared down at the set of teeth. She had never seen a set of false teeth before. However, fundamentals had instructed that the nurse rinse the teeth in tepid water before offering them to the patient. She washed her hands carefully, glancing at the teeth.

They were not very white and the gums glistened pink. Bits of . . . matter floated in the water in which the teeth were soaking. She hesitantly picked up the teeth. Her stomach lurched. C'mon, she thought, you've touched urine, feces, blood, amniotic fluid, and emesis. What's a set of false teeth? She rinsed them off, swallowed back a lump of something acrid that came up in her throat, and handed the teeth to Mr. Pride. He opened his mouth.

Which was the bottom plate and which was the top? She examined them, turning them around and around trying to decide. What looked like the bottom teeth, did not look as though they would fit there. "Er . . . Mr. Pride, put in your teeth for me, sir."

He put in his top plate, *chomp*. Then the bottom plate, *chomp*. His cheeks had filled out and the nose and chin separated miraculously. "Gee, you're almost handsome with your teeth in," Carol said.

Mr. Pride looked at her. "Well, I'd be a whole lot handsomer in my own room, young lady."

When Pride's breakfast tray came, Carol took the tray from the cafeteria helper, placed it on Pride's overbed table, pushed the table up in front of him, and tucked the napkin under his chin. She removed the cover over his plate of bacon and scrambled eggs, buttered his toast, opened his carton of milk, stuck a straw into it, and asked, "Do you take cream and sugar in your coffee?"

"Cream."

She poured cream into his coffee, stirred it, then stood aside.

Mr. Pride carefully pushed the overbed table away.

"Mr. Pride, you're not hungry?"

"Nope."

"Why not?"

"Because they're not bringing this food to me, they're bringing it to whoever belongs in this room. I don't eat other people's food."

Carol thought maybe if she left the room he'd eat. So she went to the nurses' station and charted Mr. Pride's vitals. She located the linen room, got towels, washcloth, soap, sheets, and a clean hospital gown, and carried them to his room.

Mr. Pride was still sitting up in bed staring at the painting on the wall, and hadn't touched his food.

While Carol helped Mr. Pride with his bedbath, and then changed the bed linen while he sat up in a bedside chair, she tried to persuade him that this was his room. She knew that the doctor and the nurses were concerned about Pride not eating and she was determined to be the heroine of the day by persuading him to eat; she figured the way to get him to eat was to persuade him that this was his room. But he didn't eat and he didn't believe the room was his.

At mid-morning Bret came by while Carol was watering the cut flowers and plants which Mr. Pride's friends had sent him.

"Hi, Fred," Bret said coming into the room. "Your nurse here tells me you haven't eaten your breakfast."

Carol had put Pride's tray on the cart in the corridor at the same time Bret had put his patient's tray there to be carried back to the kitchen, and she had told him about Mr. Pride not eating.

Mr. Pride said, "It wasn't my food. Who are you, a doctor?"

"No, I'm a student nurse."

Mr. Pride thought about that. "Well, I never heard of no man being a nurse."

"Well," Bret said coming to stand beside Pride's chair, "there're men studying to be nurses now."

Pride eyed Bret steadily. "Well, seems to me you could find something better than that. I don't believe in people mixing things up. Women are supposed to be nurses. Men are supposed to be truck drivers and such, and I don't believe they ought to mix things up."

"Like your room."

Pride looked at Bret. "Yeah. How did you know?"

Bret smiled at Carol. "Everybody's heard about it."

"Yeah?"

"Sure. You know, everybody makes mistakes."

Pride stared. So did Carol. "Bret, what are you doing?" she said through her teeth.

Bret ignored her. "Fred, I've come to take you to your room," he said.

Carol looked quickly at Pride. His face had brightened as he watched Bret go out of the room and return instantly with a wheelchair which he must have parked just outside the door. Bret got Pride up from his bedside chair and into the wheelchair, hung his IV and the IV pole attached to the wheelchair and said, "Like to come with us, Carol?"

She was still staring. "Me? Oh, I suppose so. I *am* his nurse, aren't I?"

Bret tucked Mr. Pride's robe around his knees and got behind the wheelchair and wheeled him out of the room. He pushed as they strolled down the corridor going east, Carol padding softly beside him.

"You're nuts, you know," she said. "We learned in psych not to go along with a patient's delusions."

"Pride's not that kind of patient. And there's a difference between delusion and confusion."

"Still, I don't know what you're doing."

"Mr. Pride hasn't been out of that room since they brought him back from x-ray. Right, Fred?" he said leaning down near Pride's head.

"That's right," Pride snapped.

They turned right and started down another corridor. "You're a super little nurse, Carol, but you've got a lot to learn about human nature."

"Oh, yeah?" she said folding her arms as they strolled.

"As a bartender, I learn a lot about human nature."

"And so you have all the answers."

"All but one."

"What's that?"

"How to compete with a good-looking medical student for a certain girl's attention."

Carol laughed. "I see you more than Duane. I see him only once or twice a week."

Bret grinned at her. "Now what makes you think the girl is you?"

Carol blushed.

"You see? I know human nature. To make a girl blush these days takes skill and a knowledge of human nature." He bent down to Pride. "Ain't that right, Fred?"

"You betcha," Mr. Pride replied.

Bret turned right into another corridor.

"Chalk one up for you then, Bret."

"The girl *is* you, of course. Do I have a chance at asking you to go out?"

"Sure."

"I do?"

"You have the *chance* to ask, but that doesn't mean I'll go."

"Oooof. Chalk one up for you, Carol."

"Duane and I are . . . pretty friendly."

"I gathered that." Bret turned right into another corridor and they walked silently for a while. Nurses in white uniforms and white caps bustled by them. The paging system almost constantly summoned doctors and other hospital personnel. The corridors were busy with carts full of breakfast trays, housekeeping personnel in gray uniforms, candy stripers passing by carrying vases of flowers.

Bret turned right into another corridor again and they passed by the nurses' station where Mr. Pride's chart was kept. The charge nurse looked up from her work.

"Hi there, Mr. Pride," she called to him.

"How do you do?" Mr. Pride said, nodding.

"Hi, Fred," called the LVN who had been Mr. Pride's nurse during the past week.

Mr. Pride smiled and waved.

"We're taking him to his room," Bret told them.

"Oh? Well . . . " they heard the charge nurse say.

Then they came to room 406. Bret briskly rolled Mr. Pride into his room. "Here we are, Fred."

Mr. Pride looked around the room. "Yessir," he said hesitantly, his near-bald head swiveling around as he studied his room.

"Look," Bret said flinging open Pride's closet. "There's your luggage and your clothes," he told him.

"Yessir. That's my luggage, all right," Pride said.

Bret rolled him to his bed while Pride gazed across the room wonderingly. As Carol stood, hands on her hips at the door, she saw the bright look on the old man's face.

"Okay, Fred?" Bret said bending down so that he could see Pride's expression.

"It's my own room," Mr. Pride said wondrously. "Yessir, it's my old room. Sure as the world."

While Carol helped Bret get Fred Pride back into bed, she said, "Chalk two up for you, Bret."

At noon Mr. Pride ate all of his lunch, and for the rest of the week until his discharge from the hospital on Friday, he was happy, cooperative, ate all his meals, and told every nurse on every shift how glad he was to be back in his old room again.

Medical-surgical nursing. The students had taken their cocktails, their hors d'oeuvres, their appetizers, but med-surg was the main dish, the entrée of nurse's training. They were practiced in taking vital signs, giving bedbaths, doing simple treatments. They had given oral and rectal medications and several injections each. They had gained experience in taking care of medical patients, surgical patients, and in dealing with psychiatric patients. They had experienced much, but they hadn't yet experienced death. Shelly was the first.

Nobody knew much about Shelly. They knew she was working her way through nursing school as a flight attendant for TWA. They knew she had an ileostomy. They knew she was either the top student in the class or next to the top. And that was all they knew about Shelly.

Jo had gotten better acquainted with her in psychiatric nursing when they had been assigned to the same unit at Farley, and Carol heard the story about Shelly from Jo.

Just prior to her enrollment in the prenursing courses at UTE, Shelly had been brought into ER at Bennet with severe abdominal pain and vomiting. X-ray had revealed that she was suffering from complete lower bowel obstruction. Conservative measures to relieve the obstruction had proved unsuccessful and Shelly had been rapidly going into shock.

Emergency surgery had been performed by the chief of the surgery department, Dr. Whitehall, who was assisted by a young surgical resident, Basil Novak, who had been on call at the time Shelly was admitted. Most of Shelly's large intestine had been necrosed so the surgeons had been forced to remove most of her lower intestine, and to bring the severed end of the small intestine to the surface of her abdomen to form an abdominal anus called an ileostomy.

During Shelly's recovery, young Dr. Novak had visited Shelly's room often. Jo had no romantic illusions about that, any more than she had romantic illusions about anything else. "When resident surgeons are just starting out, they're always fascinated by their first surgery patients. It's nothing personal. They are so proud that the patient is still alive because of something with which they helped, that they keep going back to check the patient."

Jo was probably right.

Shelly wasn't attractive, but she wasn't unattractive either. She had black eyes, very short black hair, a pale complexion. She was petite from her waist up, but from her waist down, she was slightly plump. Shelly had a quick, bright wit that kept students laughing in pre- and postclinical, but there was something desperate in her wit—her eyes were too bright. Her wit never quite extended to her eyes. And she did not form close friendships. Jo was her only friend, and Jo was the most skeptical about Shelly's love affair.

According to Shelly, after she was discharged from Bennet, Novak had come to her apartment a few times and even given her a bracelet, which she never removed. She claimed they had had sex once. Now, he was avoiding her, she said, because he didn't want to get involved. He was a brilliant surgical resident, ambitious to become chief resident; according to Shelly he had promised her when he had given her the bracelet that if she'd be patient and understand why he couldn't see her, once he had finished his residency and established his practice, he would come to her and they would be married.

Everybody in clinical with Shelly knew that she often sent Basil Novak gifts, every Christmas, every birthday. She had telephoned him repeatedly until one day she called and he had obtained an unlisted number. In pre- and postclinical, Carol and the other students caught only brief snatches of insight into Shelly's affair. She would mention buying him an engraved pewter cup for Christmas, a hand-tooled belt. She mentioned a surgery she had heard that he had assisted with and she had pored over that surgery patient's chart looking for Dr. Novak's progress notes, operative report—anything that was *his*.

The only firsthand observation that Jo and Carol had of Shelly's affair was a unique one. On one rare occasion at the beginning of the fall semester, Shelly joined Jo and Carol as they walked to their cars in

Bennet's huge parking lot after postclinical. Shelly did not usually join anyone in anything; she simply vanished after postclinical. That day she laughed brightly. "Can I join you? What did you guys think of that respiratory test yesterday?"

"I didn't think," Jo said as they passed between the cars. "I just reacted."

Carol gave the test a thumbs-down.

"I think I did badly on it, too." Shelly laughed. "I don't do as well on the medical questions as I do on the surgical ones. The surgical ones I know before they ask—for obvious reasons."

Jo glanced at Carol.

"My God!"

Jo and Carol stared at Shelly as she suddenly stopped and stood as though frozen to the spot. Her face turned pale as she again whispered, "My God."

They looked in the direction of Shelly's stare. A young man, in an adjoining parking lot, *the doctors' parking lot*, was sticking his keys into the lock on his car door.

"It's Basil. Oh my God, it's Basil."

Carol had never heard words wrung from the depths of a human soul before: agonized, tortured, desperately hopeful; every human emotion was condensed into that one whispered word, "Basil."

And while Carol and Jo stood still and gaped, Shelly went flying across the parking lot shrilling, "Basil! Basil! Basil?" Her books were scattered on the ground at their feet; a piece of notebook paper flew out of a book and went sailing across the parking lot in the wind.

The young doctor paused, looked up. They were

not close enough to see what he looked like, or to see his expression; only that he was tall, only that he froze when he heard her calling his name.

While they stood watching, Shelly stopped before the young man. They stood like statues. Then Shelly's body shook with what they guessed was her usual forced laughter. She gestured. The doctor did not move.

"If you ask me," said Jo, "any man who tells a girl he doesn't want to get involved until after a certain period of time, ain't aimin' to get involved at all—ever."

Carol shuddered involuntarily. For the only difference between Shelly's love affair and her own was that she at least got to see Duane occasionally; and that was a big difference.

While Carol and Jo pretended to talk near Carol's car, Shelly spoke with Basil. The girls did not see Basil do anything but stand there motionless beside his roadster, and watch as Shelly gestured and talked. Neither Carol nor Jo wanted to leave. "Who gets up and leaves the room in the middle of a good dramatic scene on TV?" Jo said.

After several tense moments, Shelly came back to them. Her face had changed from its deadly pallor to a scarlet red. Her eyes were bright. "I peed my pants. I did," she said. "I stood there and peed my pants."

Jo said in her flat monotone, "Why?"

Everything Shelly had to say rushed out before she could check herself, just like her urine had done, and it made about as much sense. "I told him that I never hear from him anymore and asked if it was all over with us. He told me no. I asked if he wanted his bracelet back. He told me no."

234

The girls waited for more. There was no more.

"That all?" asked Jo.

"That's it," Shelly said picking up her books off the hood of Carol's car where Carol had stacked them. "You see, he can't be seen talking to me because other residents might question him and then the story about us will be out."

"What story?" Jo asked. Jo had a way of getting around all the fluff.

Later, as she drove homeward, Carol recalled Shelly's flushed, perspiring face; her too-bright eyes, her panicky expression.

Don't go spreading it around that we're seeing each other. I don't want anybody to get the idea that I'm getting serious about a girl. See, it could hinder my prospects of being accepted at Bennet for my residency. Residents who are in love or married don't perform at their best. Everybody knows that. Ask anybody. No, don't ask. Just—just trust me.

It wasn't Basil who had said that. It was Duane.

He called that evening. "Do you know a Dr. Basil Novak?" Carol asked him.

"I sure do. He's the senior resident I assisted during my first surgery, remember? Why?"

Carol was not about to betray Shelly's secret, so she said, "I just heard the name mentioned in preclinical."

"Basil Novak is Whitehall's fair-haired boy. He's grooming him to be chief resident at Bennet next year. He'll be *my* chief resident if I get accepted at Bennet, and by the time I'm chief resident, he could be the chief of surgery, for all I know. He's assisting

Whitehall with experimental gynecological surgery at the moment. He's brilliant, Carol. What did you hear about him?"

"He was just mentioned. I don't remember," Carol said.

It was Shelly's patient who died their second week at Bennet.

Shelly had asked for a terminal patient. Ellen Child assigned her to Mr. Likes who had cancer of the liver. Shelly took care of Likes on Monday. Tuesday as she was taking his vital signs, he died.

Because of Bennet's size, patients who died were not left in their rooms for the funeral homes to pick up as was the case in some smaller hospitals. At Bennet, the body had to be readied for transfer and moved from the room by stretcher to the morgue in the basement of Dowell.

Carol was sitting at the nurses' desk when Ellen Child, the instructor, came to her. "Your patient has gone to surgery?"

Carol nodded. "I gave her the preop injection and checked off her preop list. First time. But I wish I could have gone to surgery with her."

"You will later. But right now, Shelly needs help."

"Oh?"

"Her patient just died. The nurses are letting her get the body ready to move, but she could use help."

Carol stood up. She was curious; yet she was hesitant too. The only time she had ever seen a dead person was at a funeral. Ms. Child told her what room Shelly's patient was in and Carol hurried down the corridor and into Mr. Likes's room.

Shelly was unfolding a plastic sheet beside the still, gaunt form of Mr. Likes. The room was semidark.

"I came to help," she said softly as she approached the bed.

Shelly was her usual cheerful self, her voice only a little more subdued than usual. She could have been preparing to wrap a gift.

First they stripped Mr. Likes of the hospital gown. His chest, arms, and legs were cool; his back was still warm. Carol reasoned that without the heart pumping the blood through the veins, the blood pooled at the lowest center of gravity. They tied his hands together at the wrists with the twine that was provided in the shroud packet. Shelly had already written his name and room number on the tag and they tied the tag to his wrists. Then they tied his ankles together and attached an identical tag to them. Then they rolled him over, tucked a plastic sheet under him, rolled him back, wrapped him cocoonlike in the plastic, and tied the bundle in four places—neck, waist, thighs, ankles. Shelly then hurried out of the room to get a stretcher. Carol was left alone in the dimly lit room with the dead man.

Fear?

Fear did not come. Carol, having become introspective from the moment she entered the room, felt the same for Mr. Likes in death as she would have felt for him in life. They had taken care of him. They had prepared him as they would have prepared any patient, for whatever was in his future. He was not scary and he was not repulsive. He was no less a man in death than he had been in life. She regarded the lifeless bundle on the bed with no emotion other than absolute respect. As she waited for Shelly to return, she began to gather his things and put them into his luggage; his after shave, his razor, his toothbrush, his shoes, his robe, his pajamas, his eyeglasses, trousers, shirt, coat—the items a man accumulates in life to meet his needs, which now having served their purposes, would be packed away in his luggage and given to his relatives.

Shelly arrived with two orderlies and a stretcher. Likes's body was "dead weight" as the two students, and the two orderlies lifted him onto the stretcher. They covered him with a sheet and strapped him securely. Then the orderlies wheeled him out of the room. They said they would take him to the hospital morgue, to be placed in a refrigerated vault until the mortician came for the body. Carol wondered about the morgue, the place where they performed autopsies on human bodies.

The body. For the first time in her life Carol understood what "the body" meant. They had taken care of the body. Mr. Likes had gone away, whatever and wherever away was.

"Ants!"

"Shhh. Keep your voice down, Carol," Ellen Child said. "I'll come and see."

Carol's patient was Mrs. Betty Lumas, a diabetic with cellulitis, a new disease process for her to learn. As seniors, the students had taken on more responsibility. Once they were assigned to a patient and were given information about the patient's diagnosis, treatments, and medications, they were expected to study the diagnosis, understand the treatments, and to know the different methods for administering medications, their usual dosages, and the side effects.

Carol had been especially interested in studying about diabetes mellitus because Charlotte had diabetes mellitus and Carol did not understand Charlotte's behavior at times; nor did she understand why, if she had high blood sugar—or hyperglycemia—she would take candy during a period of stress. When Charlotte became worried, she sucked on Life Savers or some other hard candy. Right before or after a test, Charlotte would eat an entire candy bar. Why?

When she was assigned to Mrs. Lumas, she found out.

Diabetes mellitus is a condition in which the islets of Langerhans located in the pancreas, fail to produce insulin. Carol learned that insulin promotes the storage of glucose in the cells of the body. Without insulin, the glucose remains in the bloodstream to be eventually excreted in the urine. In the body's attempts to make up for the lack of glucose in the tissues, the liver converts amino acids and fatty acids to glucose. When the fats are incompletely metabolized, ketone bodies appear in the blood causing acidosis. Acidosis causes hyperventilation and a loss of important electrolytes. Ketoacidosis could cause coma and death. Diet control and injections of insulin are the keys to controlling diabetes mellitus.

Insulin injections provide insulin which the body needs in order to store glucose in the cells of the body. However, if the patient omits a meal or vomits a meal, or exerts himself physically or comes under any other unusual stress, which uses extra glucose for energy, the additional insulin can cause hypoglycemia, low blood sugar.

At this point Carol knew why Charlotte took Life Savers when she became upset in lecture and why she became pale and perspired when she was upset — low blood sugar.

Diabetes causes many complications, but the one that concerned Carol and her patient, Betty Lumas, was the increased susceptibility to infection. Mrs. Lumas had three skin lesions, one on the left leg, two on the right, which became infected due to arteriosclerotic vascular disease, another complication of diabetes. The ulcers, once infected, had not healed because of the poor circulation in her lower extremities, and when she was admitted to ER September tenth, the resident in charge of ER diagnosed cellulitis.

Cellulitis in itself is as dangerous as gas gangrene. Mrs. Lumas had been admitted to Bennet two days before Carol was assigned to her care. Upon admission, Mrs. Lumas was suffering severe lethargy, disorientation, and tachycardia. In addition, the cellulitis ulcers were angry, swollen, and bluish-red.

Carol noted that Mrs. Lumas' treatments included dressing changes on her skin lesions once a shift. The doctors' orders concerning the dressing were specific:

Skin lesions dressed t.i.d. Irrigate with hydrogen peroxide, apply sterile gauze to lesions using aseptic technique, taping two ends only, leaving dressing loose enough to permit some exposure to air.

Simple enough. Carol had never done a dressing change before, but all one had to do was to follow directions. In this case the doctor's orders were clear.

On the first day that Carol was assigned to Mrs. Lumas, Mae's patient went to x-ray and Mae came into the room to help Carol bathe and change her patient's bed linen. Students often helped each other when they were through with their own work. That is, everybody helped but Jo, who always disappeared when somebody needed help getting a patient up out of bed or with some other task. Mae was always around. Today she was interested in observing Carol do the dressing change, something she had not yet done. Besides, Mae had discovered that if she stuck as close to Carol as possible, something unusual was bound to happen. That day she wasn't disappointed.

Carol had already taken Lumas' vital signs when Mae entered the room. The patient was quiet, lethargic, and answered Carol's questions slowly and drowsily. Carol filled her wash basin and laid all the dressing packets on the overbed table along with the towels and washcloth because she planned to do the dressing changes after the bath.

Mae and Carol chatted softly as they removed Mrs. Lumas' gown and began to bathe her gently, Carol on one side, Mae on the other. This bath would go quickly and not tire the patient much. Carol was glad because Mrs. Lumas was short of breath and had a temperature of 104°. The bath water was tepid and must have been cooling, for Mrs. Lumas smiled faintly as they bathed her hot face, neck, and arms.

When Carol pulled back the top sheet to expose Mrs. Lumas' right leg, it was then they saw the ants.

241

Carol's mouth flew open. Mae staggered backward, her hands going to her mouth. Both students stared as tiny sugar ants trailed along Mrs. Lumas' leg and disappeared under the dressings. Others were trailing out from under the dressings carrying—*oh God, what?*

Carol and Mae went berserk. They frantically began brushing ants off the bed, madly, mindlessly until they were gone. Carol peeled off the dressings on Mrs. Lumas' leg. More ants going in and out of her wounds. Holding her breath and still mindless with fury, Carol doused the wounds with peroxide. Neither girl had spoken yet. Their minds were only on one thing—getting rid of the ants.

Meanwhile Mrs. Lumas was dozing, unaware of the battle going on over her infected wounds.

Carol told Mae, "Stay with her. I'm going to find Child."

At the nurses' station Carol had Child paged. The instructor came off the elevator smiling and approached the nurses' station. Carol blurted, "My patient. We took off her top sheet and there were ants in her bed."

"What?" Child said, screwing up her face.

"Ants!"

"Sshhh." Child went with Carol back to Mrs. Lumas' room.

The ants were returning, marching resolutely up Mrs. Lumas' leg toward her infected leg ulcers, and Mae, pale and gasping, was brushing them off the leg, off the bed. But still they came, trailing up the leg of the bed from the floor, from a crack in the tile against the wall. Mae was brushing, stamping, gasping, fighting—and she was losing the battle.

It was like a nightmare, something out of a horror movie.

Child paled, then stepped back. Then she rushed forward. "Let's get that bed changed," she hissed.

It was the quickest bed linen change in nursing history.

That night Carol couldn't sleep and at 12:30 A.M. she telephoned Duane, something she had never done before.

"Duren," he mumbled into the telephone.

"Duane? Duane, are you awake?"

"Who ziss?"

"It's Carol. Duane, can you talk? I think I'm going to be sick."

"What? Carol? What's the matter?"

She told him about the ants.

"What?"

"Ants. There were ants going in and out of her wounds."

"Oh my *God*. Did you report it? Carol, those ants are carrying infection."

"Ms. Child said she reported it to the nurse in charge of the floor and the nurse said she'd report it to maintenance." Carol was sitting up in her own clean bed dressed in her favorite nightshirt with Snoopy printed on the front. She kept itching everywhere, slapping her legs and arms, and feeling stings of ants that did not exist.

Duane was silent a moment, then, "Carol, it's your duty to report the ants directly to maintenance. Somebody's letting down on the job. My God! Ants going in and out—and people are afraid of roaches and flies. My God! Carol?"

"Yes."

"Tomorrow, you find maintenance. It's down on the lower level of Baskin, that's the building next to Dowell. Go down there and ask for the head of the maintenance department. Tell him what you saw. And I'm going to write an anonymous note to the administrator. What floor did you say?"

"Seven."

"My God. If they're up on seven, they must be on all the lower floors. Carol?"

She felt weary. "What?"

"I'm sorry you experienced this. Bennet's really a terrific hospital. It's just that—"

"I know. Somebody didn't do his job right."

Carol did not report the ants to maintenance the next day, but ants were still in Mrs. Lumas' room, trailing along the wall. They were no longer parading to her bed, however. Carol reported the ants directly to the charge nurse who informed her coolly that she had done all she could do about the matter.

Mrs. Lumas died on the second evening after Carol had been assigned to her care. Cause of death: another complication of diabetes, a heart attack. The next morning Carol was assigned to Annie Rice, an elderly patient with a diagnosis of cholelithiasis, or gallstones.

When Carol went to Mrs. Rice's sink to get her false teeth from the little cottage cheese-sized carton, there were the ants, crawling all over the teeth. Carol went berserk again, took the teeth to the charge nurse. "These were in Mrs. Lumas' leg ulcers day before yesterday," she told the charge nurse.

Irritably the nurse looked into the carton. She was a

hardened old veteran nurse of twenty-five years, but she clamped her hand over her mouth, jumped up from the desk, and barely made it to the nurses' rest room before she lost her breakfast.

The next day Carol was sick and missed her first day of clinical and lecture in four semesters of nursing.

Chapter Fourteen

Surgery

"If you have an itis or a lithiasis and are lucky, you'll have an internist for a doctor. If you're smart, you'll have an ectomy," Duane told her.

The students had taken medical terminology to heart from the beginning, but there were still many terms to learn. Even though some of the things he said didn't make sense, Duane made it easy for her. "Learn your prefixes and your suffixes and you can understand anything the doctors throw at you."

She had learned her prefixes and suffixes before, but now that the students would be studying more about surgical procedures she wanted the use of medical terminology to become second nature with her as it seemed to be with Duane.

"Okay, Carol. I'll give the prefix, you tell me its meaning," he said.

They were lounging under a giant live oak in Dove Creek Park. The park was a long rectangular, green stretch of St. Augustine lawns, with flowering crape myrtle in fading shades of pink and red, privet hedges and oak trees, and a creek trickling down its center like a blue-and-silver spine.

She had spread Aunt Daisy's gift of two Christmases

ago upon the lawn. It was a lovely quilt with a scalloped edge done in a pattern called "around the world." Carol used the quilt for picnics and every time she used it, somebody came by to make her an offer for it, anything from fifteen dollars to a hundred.

Duane was leaning against the tree, twists of his curly hair blowing across his forehead. They had had a picnic lunch and were enjoying the lovely Indian summer day, but neither of them could really waste a day picnicking. She was studying for a test in med-surg; he had been poring over Gray's *Anatomy*, following some train of thought that had to do with surgery until he had decided then to help her with her medical terminology.

"Gastri," he said.

"Stomach," she replied.

"Hepato."

"Liver."

"Cholecyst."

"Gall bladder."

"Appendi."

"Appendix."

"Thora."

"Lung."

He said, "You've got your prefixes down, I think. Let's try the suffixes. Itis."

"Inflammation."

"Otomy."

"Incision."

"Ectomy."

"Removal of."

"Let's put the prefixes and suffixes together. What's a cholecystectomy?"

"Removal of the gall bladder."

"Appendectomy."

"Removal of the appendix."

"Gastritis."

"Inflammation of the stomach."

"You don't ever miss, do you, kid?"

"Easy," she said and leaned over and planted a kiss on his nose. She couldn't do that in the apartment. Duane kept trying. Because of her own reticence and the promise she kept making over and over, she kept fending him off. It wasn't easy. She wanted him, but she thought that if she was going to keep him, she'd have to keep him away from her now. Sure, it wasn't easy. It was hell, in fact. They were both young and eager and she loved him and thought that he loved her, but school came first. Getting involved, as he called it, clearly had its disadvántages. Basil Novak had said the same thing to Shelly, if she wasn't fantasizing the whole thing.

Surely Duane's willingness to befriend her and yet not have sex with her was a statement of his high regard for her, although it didn't make much sense. One could have sex and not get involved. Or one could get involved without sex. How many other med students deprived themselves of sex during school? Fat chance. Yet, how many med students were dead set on making perfect scores, set on climbing to the top, the very top? Duane was intent on it. He worked hard, he studied hard; his goal was never out of his mind—his primary and ultimate goal always, to be the best.

He caught her hand now before she could sit back on her heels, pulled her to him, brought her down upon the quilt. "Carol," he whispered. Then his mouth came down upon hers, so warm, firm, and *assertive*. "Carol." His hand stroked her head, moved down to hold her face.

"No," she whispered.

"Let's go."

She saw it in his eyes. His desire for her, intense, strangled, struggling. The vertical vein in the center of his forehead swelled, throbbed.

"Let's go or I'll take you here."

"No. Not here. Not anywhere." She was so weary of this. So tired of being the strong one when it came to this battle of wills. She'd have given in long ago if she could have won the ultimate prize—Duane forever, not just Duane for a night. She caught his hand as it went to her breast. Caught the other as it moved across her thigh. "No. Let me up. Please, please."

She held both of his hands as he tried to break free; he broke free, grabbed her wrists, lowered his face down to her throat. She struggled, fought a hand at her abdomen, a hand at her breast. She rolled away breaking free.

"Carol," he said and lunged for her.

Something tore.

He was as shocked as she. For a moment neither of them moved, neither of them knew whose clothes had torn.

His face displayed a look of profound surprise as his hand went to the seat of his pants. "I'll be damned," he said incredulously. "I've ripped my jeans."

What a wonderful release from tension it was to laugh. And to laugh loud and high and breathlessly. Duane, in a fit of passion, ripping the seat out of his jeans. The look on his face was a mixture of befuddlement, irritability, and frustration as he stared at her.

The people in the park stared, too, at the girl sitting in the grass, her head thrown back, screaming with laughter, and at the young man on his knees on the quilt, his hand covering the seat of his pants.

She did not let him come into the apartment that evening. The tear in the seat of his jeans had saved them from a terrible spat and she was not going to risk getting into one, not tonight, not while the thrill of his kiss still lingered hot and sweet on her lips.

She told him good-by outside the apartment door just at dusk.

"Go home. Go study. I have to study, too."

"I can't help but wonder what would have happened if my pants—"

"Nothing. And certainly not in a park in front of dozens of people."

He smiled. "What a rip-off!"

They left each other laughing.

She was assigned to Mrs. Reba Flowers during her fourth week in Med-Surg I. She was assigned to check Reba Flowers through the usual preop check, to give her the preop meds, and to go with her to surgery. This was the entrée to be sure! She was determined to remember every detail of it to tell Duane.

Mrs. Flowers was a forty-year-old mother of three girls—eighteen, sixteen, and thirteen—Carol noted on her chart at the nurses' station before she went in to see her for the first time. For the past three months Flowers' menstrual periods had been spotty and almost negligible. She had experienced abdominal cramping almost continually. Her doctor, Dr. Wendal

250

Moss, had examined her and diagnosed a tumor of the uterus. "Probably a benign fibroid," he had stated in her history and physical. But still, the thing was causing discomfort and needed to be biopsied at least. Flowers opted for a hysterectomy, removal of the uterus. The night before she was to go to surgery with Flowers, Carol read up on hysterectomies. She learned that a subtotal hysterectomy is the removal of the fundus of the uterus only; a total hysterectomy involves the removal of the entire uterus including the cervix; panhysterectomy is the removal of the entire uterus, tubes, and ovaries. Flowers was scheduled to have a total hysterectomy unless the ovaries and tubes were involved in some way. She would not have a vaginal hyst either, it would be an abdominal; the gynecologist would go for the uterus through the abdominal wall, and Carol would see it.

She pushed the mercury sphygmomanometer, which was attached to a little stand on wheels into Flowers' room. Flowers had the head of her bed rolled up almost ninety degrees; her hands were in her lap. She smiled when Carol came in.

"Hello, I'm Carol Welles. I'm going to get your preop vital signs. How are you, Mrs. Flowers?"

"Hi. I'm fine. I'm scared, though, because I've never had surgery before," Reba Flowers said, smiling.

"I'm sure surgery is scary. Is there anything particular that scares you about it?" Carol asked as she took the patient's thermometer from the little holder attached to the wall over her bed.

As Carol shook the mercury down in the thermometer, Mrs. Flowers said, "I'm afraid of the anesthesia, for one thing."

"Oh? Have you talked with the anesthesiologist who is going to attend you in surgery?"

"Last night. His visit helped a great deal. He's an Indian, name of Pashi. Very intelligent-speaking man."

Carol smiled. "I'm glad you like your anesthesiologist. He's a very important person when it comes to surgery. Let me put this under your tongue now."

Carol took Flowers' vitals and wrote them down on the preop sheet. Then she scanned the preop list.

"You need to empty your bladder now," she told the patient.

"I just did, the minute before you came in."

"Good. You don't have any prosthesis, do you? Like contact lenses or bridgework?"

"No. Nothing."

"Hairpins?"

"No."

Carol checked that off her list. "Have you had your Phisohex shower?"

"At five this morning." Reba Flowers laughed.

"Your prep?"

"Do you mean the shave? Yes."

"And you had your cleansing douche?"

"Last night."

"And you were NPO since midnight?"

"Not a sip."

"Except for your preop medication, you're ready to go. You're scheduled for seven."

"I know." Reba clamped her hand suddenly on Carol's wrist. "The other thing that scares me is the tumor."

Suddenly Carol realized how lightly she had taken

Reba's fear of surgery. God, she was as clinically sterile in her attitude as a seasoned nurse, forgetting the patient while attending to the routine. Bret's personable treatment of old Mr. Pride, who thought he was in the wrong room, had shown her that she tended to focus more on learning nursing routine and her personal achievements in it than she did on the patient. In that momentary flash of insight, she vowed never again to be that unfeeling.

"You're disturbed about the tumor?"

"Yes." Reba's attractive brown eyes studied her face. "What if it's malignant?"

Yes, what if? Carol's knowledge of uterine malignancy was scanty, but she used what she did know. "Reba, the majority of uterine tumors aren't malignant. Dr. Moss thinks yours is a fibroid tumor and those are seldom malignant."

"But he doesn't know?"

"No."

Just then a tall, distinguished-looking man with graying hair entered the room. He was dressed in a business suit and Carol remembered reading in Reba's chart that her husband was an oil company executive. Reba reached toward him as he approached her bed, took her hand. He nodded to Carol.

Reba said, "George, this is Carol. She's a student nurse. Isn't she precious?"

George Flowers smiled at Carol. "Indeed she is. This your senior year, Carol?"

"Yes."

"Our youngest daughter thinks she may want to go into nursing. Do you recommend it?"

"Oh, I certainly do."

Reba said, "Our oldest two daughters aren't married yet. They're both in college. One's studying to become a secondary-school teacher, the other wants to do something in music. I'm not sure what." Reba laughed. "We wanted a boy, of course—I guess everybody does—but our girls have been such wonderful children."

"They aren't children anymore," said Mr. Flowers. "The last one is thirteen, quite a young lady. Cheerleader in high school."

Carol chatted a moment longer with the Flowerses then left the room so that she could place the preop sheet on Reba Flowers' chart—it would be the first page in the chart until after surgery.

Ellen Child was at the desk to supervise Carol's mixing of the two preop medications. Carol withdrew the Demerol from the narcotics cabinet and recorded the withdrawal; then she placed the tubex of premeasured Demerol into the tubex cartridge as Child watched.

"So far so good, Carol. What's the Demerol for?"

Carol felt at ease with Ellen Child. She was a softspoken woman who had been an R.N. in ICU for five years. She was recently divorced and was built like a model, only she wasn't pretty. Carol liked her as an instructor because she knew nursing and did not intimidate or push or press or scare her students as Charlotte's clinical instructor had done.

"Demerol is for sedation, to lessen anxiety; and it also reduces the metabolic rate so that the quantity of general anesthetic needed will be less."

"Right out of the book. You have a good memory. What's the atropine for?"

"To reduce the amount of secretions in the mouth and respiratory tract," Carol replied.

"Good. I'll go with you when you give the injection."

Carol was at ease giving injections now. If her memory was correct, this injection of Demerol and atropine was her fifth injection.

She gave it in the upper outer portion of Reba's left gluteus medius, or hip. Flowers did not flinch.

Carol had just recorded the injection on her chart at the nurses' station when an orderly came with the stretcher, took Reba's chart, tucked it under the mattress, and rolled the stretcher toward her room.

Child and Carol hurried down the corridor into the Jenson building and took the elevator to the fourth floor. When the elevator door opened, they were facing a screen with a sign that read:

SURGERY SUITE
NO UNAUTHORIZED PERSONS PERMITTED

Today, Carol was authorized.

Surgery. The outer desk was U-shaped and manned by two nurses in surgical greens. The corridor to the right was long and lined with stretchers and OR rooms. Five of the stretchers waiting in the corridor were occupied. To the left of the elevator Carol could see a huge room with stretcherlike beds, IV poles, monitoring equipment. The sign near the door of the room read: SURGICAL RECOVERY.

Child and Carol moved to the nurses' lounge where they changed into surgical scrub dresses. Then they went down the corridor just behind the nurses' station where they donned the surgical masks, caps, and booties, identical to the ones she had worn in L&D. At last they entered OR number three.

It looked exactly as she had pictured it. Large, sterile-looking walls tiled in light green, asbestos tiles on the ceiling, floor tiles of an antiseptic green, op table in the center of the room, anesthesia tanks lined up against the wall at the head of the table like colorful torpedos. The instrument table was long and gleaming; stainless-steel instruments were lined up neatly on sterile drapes on its top, alongside with basins, snowy gauze sponges, green drapes, towels, sutures, and needles. There were cabinets displaying IV solutions and tubing, arm boards, gloves, gowns, more sterile green packs of instruments, and extra sterile drapes. There was an enormous light over the table, and there were a dozen smaller ones on goose-necked swivels. A cardiac and arterial blood-pressure monitor was attached to the wall over the head of the operating table, and on the wall facing the foot of the table was a huge clock. There were x-ray screens with lights. The predominant smell in the room was Betadine with overlays of Merthiolate and pine-scented disinfectant, and a dash of ether. No wonder Duane loved surgery. It was like the stage of a theater. In medicine the showmanship was in surgery.

Reba Flowers was already on the operating table. Dr. Pashi nodded briefly to Carol and Child as they entered. He was taping Reba's arm onto an arm board. Gowned and masked nurses were busily uncovering the supply of sterile surgical instruments on the nearby table and on the Mayo stand near the operating table. Pashi stuck monitor electrodes on

Reba's chest and glanced at the monitor on the wall over her head. Carol saw the electronic blip bobbing fast. The readout under the oscilloscope indicated that her heart rate was one hundred sixty-six. Reba was still scared even after fifty milligrams of Demerol.

A nurse draped Reba's body in sterile drapes, leaving her abdomen uncovered. Another nurse began to swab her abdomen with Betadine prep from her breasts to her pubic mound and upper thighs; she swabbed from side to side to the level of the table on both sides.

"So what did Broughman say, that she did or didn't approve of the football pot?" the nurse swabbing Reba's abdomen asked the other.

"You know Broughman. But who cares? She's only in charge back here. She can't have complete rule over our lives. So we got up the football pot. A dollar a throw. And every doctor back here has put in his. Likely it'll be one of them that wins."

"Well, it's only the preseason games. Wait till the regular season starts. There'll be football pots all over the hospital."

Carol and Child were standing off to the side of the room and some of the rules of surgery were running through Carol's mind: *Below the waist is unsterile. Never turn your back to a sterile field. Don't touch anything*. . . .

Pashi crooked his finger at Carol. "Come here, student nurse."

Carol moved hesitantly. If you pass between the operating table and the sterile table of instruments, which do you turn your back to, for Pete sake? Neither. Go sideways. She came to stand beside the anesthesiologist.

"Start the IV," he said.

"Sir?"

"Start the IV."

"I've never—"

"Nothing to it, dear. I'll hold your hand and guide you in. We'll go into the antecubital space. You can't miss there."

Carol glanced at Reba; she seemed too scared to have noticed this exchange.

Pashi handed Carol the intracath. "A little stick," he told Reba as he took Carol's hand. "We'll go in beside that vein right there. See? Then when we've gone through the skin, we'll angle over and go into the vein. You'll feel it pop when we go in. You'll feel it with your fingers." He guided her hand, sliding the needle into the skin, then angled over. She did not feel the vein pop, but blood backed up into the catheter. "We're in. Thread the catheter into the vein, sweetheart, and we'll remove the needle. Easy does it. That's it. Good girl!"

Carol was perspiring and trembling, but the catheter was in. Pashi taped it to Reba's arm.

"Now, Mrs. Flowers. I'm going to give you Pentothal. Remember? I told you last night that I'd inject it into the IV tubing." Pashi stuck the needle of a syringe into the rubber valve of the IV tubing and slowly pushed the plunger. "Count to ten for me, will you Reba?"

Reba began, "One, two, three . . ." She never made it to four. Anesthesia from IV Pentothal is almost instantaneous.

A bustling in the operating room caused Carol to look up as two doctors entered. One was tall and young, the other short and middle aged. The nurses became brisk. "Dr. Moss, we've a student nurse here today," said a "sterile" nurse as she held a gown for him.

Dr. Moss looked over at Carol. "Oh?" he said disinterestedly as he thrust his arms into the gown.

The scrub nurse asked the tall one, "Dr. Novak, may the student help me gown you?"

He looked at Carol. "Sure, why not?" he said.

Rats! Ellen Child had said that the students would only have to observe in surgery, not participate. Carol had studied the gowning and gloving procedure once, but not lately. And Basil Novak was Shelly's lover — or was he? — and if he was, he was a brilliant, ambitious horse's ass.

"C'mon," the scrub nurse urged Carol.

Carol looked at Child who winked.

Carol took her place behind Novak as the scrub nurse held the gown at the neck and Novak thrust his arms inside, but not before Carol had seen his eyes crinkling at the outer corners as he looked at her, his blue eyes laughing at her over the surgical mask.

Jeez, he's got to be incredibly handsome, Carol thought.

Now she grasped the gown by the inside shoulder seams as the circulating nurse watched closely. Carol was not "sterile" and could not touch the outside of the gown which was considered sterile. The inside of the gown was considered unsterile because it would go against the doctor's scrub suit.

Senior resident Dr. Basil Novak slid his arms further into the gown. "Ooops, hold tight, baby, till I get in. Okay Great," he said, and waited as she drew the red-tagged tie out of the gown at the side and pulled it around to the back.

"On around," said the circulating nurse. "Don't touch the gown anywhere but on the tag. Okay, grasp the other tag and pull it out. That's it. No need to be careful now as you tie them, his back is considered unsterile."

Carol tied the gown as Novak shrugged his shoulders to get comfortable.

"First year?" he asked glancing over his shoulder at her.

"S-senior. But this is my first surgery."

"Oh, it is? Well, so far you're doing better than med students. Most of them contaminate everything in sight on their first day."

She wanted to say, But not Duane Duren, I'll bet.

He reached out his hands toward the scrub nurse, who lifted a sterile glove from the instrument table. In the old days, nurses had to pour talcum inside the gloves to facilitate the surgeon's slipping his hands and fingers into them. Today, most sterile gloves are pretalcumed or lubricated.

"Come on around and see how the gloving's done," Novak told Carol.

The glove had a wide cuff so that the scrub nurse was able to slip her fingers under it, thumbs out, and Novak slipped his big hand into it. *Snap*. One fluid motion and he was gloved, the glove extending over the sleeve of the gown. *Snap*. Another fluid motion and he was now entirely gloved.

"That looks easy, but I know it's not," Carol said.

"Just takes practice," Novak offered. "What's your name?"

"Carol."

"Well, Carol, next time I see you in surgery I'll expect you to be scrubbed and know how to gown and glove me."

"Listen to him, Dr. Moss," the scrub nurse said. "He thinks he's a full-fledged surgeon."

"He *is* a full-fledged surgeon," Moss said. "The damned best resident surgeon I ever saw. Come on over here, Basil; you've done enough socializing now. I want you to do this one. This is just a simple fibroid. I'll assist."

Novak went over to stand at the operating table as Carol positioned herself near the anesthesiologist and Ellen Child.

"Shouldn't we do a D&C first?" Novak asked. "Because if it's cancer, we could spread it by operating before we have a biopsy—"

"I know my business, Basil, you young whippersnapper. Remember, you *are* still just a resident. It's a fibroid."

Novak didn't seem to like it, but he shrugged and folded his hands almost reverently above his waist. The scrub nurse came to stand beside him as Dr. Moss moved to the left-hand side of the table.

"The patient ready?" Novak asked the anesthesiologist.

Pashi gave an Okay sign with thumb and forefinger.

The curtain rises, Carol thought.

"Scalpel."

The circulating nurse placed a stool at Carol's feet. "Here, stand on this so you can see."

The lights glared bright and hot, especially the huge one over the table. Carol perspired profusely as the scalpel slit neatly into the skin. Dr. Moss sponged

261

as Novak incised fascia, adipose, muscle. Moss sponged the blood, tying off bleeders and applying clamps. Through her mouth, Pashi had installed an endotracheal tube in Reba's trachea and had attached a tank of anesthesia to the tube. It was probably ether.

"How's the patient, Pashi? She's a little blue," Dr. Moss said.

"Her pulse is still too rapid. I've got a die-limma. Take her down further to slow down the heart, or leave her up. If I slow her heart, she might perfuse better. On the other hand, she might need more O_2"

"She's tight, Dr. Pashi. Can you take her down some more?" Novak asked.

Watching the monitor, watching the patient, Pashi turned some gauges on the sophisticated machine attached to the tank. Carol was impressed by how very carefully he watched the patient and her vital signs, making a mark every few seconds on the anesthesia record.

After a moment Novak said, "She's red now. Just needed to slow her down."

"She wanted to wake up here before we took her to recovery. I think she wants to know she's still alive as soon as possible," Dr. Pashi said.

"We'll wake her up," said Dr. Moss.

Carol could barely see inside Reba Flowers' abdomen now through the small incision. The doctors' hands were in the way, busy, constantly busy, cutting, tying off bleeders, clamping, applying retractors. Dr. Moss asked for the suction tubing. The circulating nurse handed him the tubing and turned a valve on the wall. Moss aspirated blood from the abdominal cavity. *Sssssssst. Sssssssst.*

Carol was feeling faint. It wasn't the blood and the glimpse of the organs inside. It was the lights, the heat. The room itself was cool, but under the lights . . . and she had taken something for cramps that morning . . . and it was the first day of her period.

Damn it! She stepped down off the stool. Pashi glanced at her. "Are you leaving me, student nurse?"

She shook her head.

"Hot under the lights, isn't it? Well, I'll tell you when they get there—"

She headed for the door fast.

Outside of the operating room she sat down on the floor, put her head between her knees, and felt the grayness slowly lifting. The ringing in her ears slowly subsided and when Child found her, she was crying.

"Aw c'mon, Carol. It's your first surgery," Child said. "Don't take it so hard."

"It wasn't the surgery. It was the hot lights. They beamed right down on the back of my head. Besides, I started my period this morning and I took an analgesic."

"How are you now?"

Carol wiped her tears away with the back of her hand. "I feel Okay now, but I've made a fool of myself."

"No, you haven't. The surgeons aren't even aware you left and Dr. Pashi is completely understanding. If you can, let's go back in. It's like falling off a horse. If you don't get right back on immediately, you'll be afraid to ride forever more. Come on."

Hesitantly Carol followed her instructor back into the operating room, and Pashi motioned her to him.

"They're there, sweetheart," he said.

Carol climbed back onto the stool just in time to hear Novak say, "Endometriosis."

"Involves one ovary."

"Does it go?"

"It had better; otherwise she'll end up with a chocolate cyst."

"Even without the uterus?"

"As long as there're ovaries, the adhesions of endometriosis will bleed into the abdominal cavity and you've still got problems."

"Most women have a little of it."

"About half, I'd say, and—That tumor . . . see . . ."

"Uh-oh," Novak said.

"Oh, Holy Mother," Dr. Moss breathed.

Carol's heart beat faster. Was it cancer? Was there more wrong than Dr. Moss had suspected? She couldn't see. She couldn't see what they were talking about.

"What do we do now?" Novak asked looking up at Dr. Moss.

"We sew her back up, Goddamn it all to hell."

Novak's incredible blue eyes watched Moss. "Can't speak to the husband first?"

"Hell, no. She's got to have a say in this, too."

"It's a fetus, isn't it?" asked the scrub nurse.

"You're damned right," Dr. Moss said. "This is the shits. This is embarrassing. God, I'm an obstetrician and I didn't . . . Christ!"

"It's viable too," Novak observed.

"We've got to consult with the patient. She's got a fibroid and a fetus both in there. Look."

"Can't she carry the fetus to term?" the scrub nurse asked.

"No reason why she can't. If she wants it."

"Would you say ten, eleven weeks?" Novak asked.

"More like twelve or thirteen. Shit. Basil, let's close."

A fetus. A viable fetus! Thirteen weeks and the doctor didn't know? Dr. Moss was considered an excellent obstetrician according to the nurses. Carol noticed his beet-red face, his silence as he assisted Novak in closing. Carol watched them suture layer by layer.

Finally Basil Novak said, "Dr. Moss? Anybody can make a mistake."

"Sure," was all Dr. Moss could say.

Carol did not see Reba again that day, but the next morning she learned from report that Dr. Moss had presented his embarrassing revelation to Reba and her husband once she was awake. Reba was horrified that she was pregnant, being forty years old and her last child thirteen. Dr. Moss had given them a choice, he could go back in, remove the uterus as planned—fetus and all—or Reba could carry the fetus to term. He could do a Caesarean and hysterectomy—or save the hysterectomy for later and let her have a vaginal delivery. She had three choices, and he had left her and her husband to talk it over. Their conclusion was shocking. Reba wanted a hysterectomy. Now.

Rumor in the surgical suite was that Dr. Moss had had trouble finding a nurse to assist him, to scrub in, to circulate. The head nurse of surgery, Broughman, was Roman Catholic. She had refused to have any part in such an abortion. The other two nurses approached refused also. Finally Dr. Moss had persuaded two: one scrub nurse, one circulating nurse.

Reba went to surgery earlier than she had the day before, so Carol barely had time to gown and mask and rush into OR number two. Child was going into surgery that day with Mae for her first day so Carol was alone in surgery without her instructor.

This time Dr. Moss performed the surgery himself. A different, less experienced resident was assisting him. Carol noticed the difference between this resident and Basil Novak. This one was hesitant. This one had to be told to do almost everything.

Carol was feeling disappointed in Reba, and sick at the idea of what was happening as she saw the uterus, a gray-blue-pink glob the size of the baseball, come into Dr. Moss's hands. He dropped it into a jar. The circulating nurse tapped the plastic lid onto the jar and left the room with it.

Suddenly, Carol was consumed with curiosity. Was the baby malformed? Was it a girl or a boy? The nurse would be taking the jar to pathology. Duane had said that every organ, every vessel, and every tissue that was removed from every surgery patient in every hospital was always sent to pathology where it was dissected, inspected, and studied under a microscope for abnormal cells or microbes, or other abnormalities.

She left surgery immediately and went to the lounge to get back into her uniform. Mae was already there getting into hers.

"Hey, I observed cryosurgery on my patient before they did her D&C. Child left before the cryosurgery. Nothing to either procedure much. But boy did I get my eyes opened about some things," Mae exclaimed.

While they changed from their scrub dresses to their uniforms, Mae told about the cryosurgery. Cryosurgery was the destruction of tissue by the application of extreme cold. In Mae's patient's case, the woman had had recurring bouts of yeast infection within her vagina, which medication had not cured. She was scheduled for cryosurgery to destroy the infection. The machine used looked to Mae like a little box on wheels. The attachment the gynecologist used looked to her like a fat hair curler, about a foot and a half long and made of smooth chrome.

The patient was young, attractive, and clearly infatuated with her young gynecologist. As the anesthesiologist, also a young man—probably a resident anesthesiologist—was intubating her, she had begun to gag even though she had been given a light "whiff" of gas by mask.

The gynecologist she worshipped said, "Don't like that, sweetheart?" He knew she would never remember what he said. "Too bad. Take her down, Roger, we'll make her like it. You stuff up there, I'll stuff down here."

The anesthesiologist carefully inserted an endotracheal tube into her trachea.

"There, like that better, sweetheart?" the gynecologist went on. "Well, I know you'll like this," he said inserting the vaginal speculum. "Wait till you have this cold cryo in you." He laughed. "She'll be cold-cocked from both ends."

The anesthesiologist glanced at the gynecologist. "Cool it, Bob. We've got a student nurse in here today."

The young gynecologist glanced at Mae, the only female in the room besides his patient, for an attending nurse was not necessary in this case. "Yeah, well, she might as well find out how it really is," said the gynecologist.

"It isn't like that," Carol told Mae. "They don't make fun of patients. Not all of them."

"Just some of them," Mae said shuddering. "And all I could do was stand by and watch. I wanted to tell him what I thought. But who am I? How did your surgery go?"

Carol told her, then asked, "You don't suppose Child will give us permission to go to pathology do you? We've got two hours before postclinical."

Mae's eyes were wide. Carol never ceased to amaze her with her curiosity, her far-out ideas, her boldness. "Gosh. I don't know."

"Mae, will you go with me if we can?"

"You bet I will!"

"Let's go!"

Ellen Child was just going into surgery to accompany Shelly with her patient, and readily gave the girls permission to go to pathology.

Where was pathology? Downstairs in the basement, next to the morgue. In the basement of Dowell somewhere.

The students hurried down the corridor toward the elevator. They would have to cross over to the Dowell building and go down to the basement from there. They hadn't any idea how long it would take the pathologist to get to Reba Flowers' uterus, but they were determined to find out.

The elevator stopped on the first floor and Carol

and Mae hurried through the connecting corridor to Dowell. Dowell's elevators were slow and always full of passengers. However, they discovered that no passengers were boarding for Dowell's basement. Only Carol and Mae stepped in and Carol pushed "B."

The elevator hesitated. Its doors slid shut. It descended. The doors opened again. They faced a concrete-block wall.

The corridor was narrow here. Personnel were few: only lab techs, x-ray techs, and orderlies. Carol and Mae passed the laboratory, the laundry, medical photography, and radiology, and came at last to pathology. Inside was the pathology lab, next door would be the morgue. They pushed open the pathology lab door and went in. Sitting at an old metal desk was a secretary typing from a dictaphone. She looked irritated when Carol and Mae approached her desk.

But Carol had her spiel well planned. "We're student nurses from UTE and we're on surgery rotation. My patient has just had a hysterectomy and our instructor gave us permission to observe the—the pathologist when he studies the tissue. We were wondering when he would get to it. My patient's name is Reba Flowers. Dr. Moss."

The secretary leaned back in her chair, and called, "Dr. Robbins?"

"Yeah," came a voice from another room.

"Two student nurses want to know when you'll do Mrs. Reba Flowers."

"About two minutes."

"Can the students watch?"

"Why not?"

Mae nudged Carol as the secretary said, "Go on in,"

and pointed to the other room.

The room into which they entered was brightly lit. Counters lined three of the walls; the labeled cupboards over the counters displayed test tubes, beakers, slides, microscopes, solutions, and sample tissue floating in jars of liquid.

Dr. Robbins, a young pathologist, was sitting on a stool at a stainless-steel table dissecting something the girls couldn't identify. He was examining pieces of tissue under a microscope and speaking into a tape recorder located on a wall next to the table.

They watched, not understanding much of what the pathologist was saying, and were totally ignored by him. Then he reached for the jar with its uterus. He removed it, examined it, spoke in a monotone into the tape recorder. "Mrs. Reba Flowers, hospital number 3309083 dash six. Dr. Moss. Gravid uterus approximately . . ."

A moment later he took a scalpel and made an incision into the organ. Water shot out and sprinkled the front of his lab coat even though he jumped back to avoid it. He recovered his dignity instantly and, opening the uterus, took out its contents, cut the tiny cord from the tiny placenta, and laid the fetus out on the table.

The students gaped as the tiny porcelain doll's arms unfolded, and its legs straightened from their folded position. The pathologist intoned his observation into the recorder, "Apparently normal fetus approximately five and three-quarters inches in length . . ."

Approximately thirteen weeks old. It was a child. Every finger and every toe was there, and was well defined. Its nose, its mouth, its closed eyes were there.

Its genitals were there and were well defined. It even had some hair on its tiny head. The students did not wait to see if Dr. Robbins was going to dissect the fetus. They fled.

In postclinical Carol told the story of Reba Flowers, and of the trip with Mae to pathology. Clearly it was a case of abortion; not abortion because of illness or a threat to the life of a mother, but one of convenience. At forty neither of the Flowerses wanted another child. After all, their youngest was thirteen years old!

On her way home that day, Carol wondered what the Flowerses, with their three daughters, would have thought had they known the fetus they had just rejected was a boy.

Chapter Fifteen

Autopsy

Bret, Carol, Mae, and Shelly were among those who wanted to observe the autopsy. The three students out of the eleven in Child's clinical group who chose not to watch were all LVNs. Jo said she'd seen one autopsy years ago and that was enough. Shelly had told Child that she wanted to observe an autopsy and Child had notified the secretary in pathology to page her when an autopsy was scheduled. The secretary called right before postclinical and Child secured permission for the students to observe; then she had rounded up all eleven students and gave them the option to observe the autopsy or to be dismissed from postclinical early.

The students who had chosen to observe the autopsy trooped down the corridor from Jenson to Dowell, laughing and talking. As if they're going to a movie, Carol thought. The semester was nearly over, and after today, they had only one more week of clinical before final exams. Everybody was beginning to feel that the end of student days was close at hand.

The other course they had taken this semester was Community Health Nursing, a dull course that nobody liked because they had been given only one assignment for clinical in CHN. Carol's assignment had been to drive to the home of a Negro family and to teach a young, unmarried mother how to sterilize baby bottles. Maybe somebody got something out of Community Health Nursing, Carol thought, but she didn't. She had not felt welcome in the home. The old folks had sat around and watched her tell their daughter how to sterilize her child's bottles. But it was over now. The course had lasted only six weeks and had demanded very little of the students' time for studying.

Now, as they faced finals in Med-Surg I, they were tense, but happy that the end was in sight. One more semester left to go, Med-Surg II, before graduation.

Bret fell into step beside her. "You know we have to write a term paper next semester, don't you? It's supposed to be a thesis-type thing."

"So I've heard," Carol said.

"Why don't you write yours on that abortion?"

"It's a thought. Only can we really call it an abortion? Mrs. Flowers had a tumor." Carol pondered that a moment. "You know," she said as they paused in front of the elevators, "I used to think abortions were Okay, that a woman should have a right to decide whether to have a baby or not. I thought a baby wasn't human until it was born. Bret, remember Penny in the newborn nursery at St. John's? She was born three months early and she was human then. And the thirteen-week fetus that Mae and I saw, he was human too. He was alive before Dr. Moss removed Mrs. Flowers' uterus. Bret, is that right?"

"You're asking me to give you an answer that the scholars and physicians and philosophers and theologians can't answer?" He looked at her, kept looking at her, saw her stare down the corridor; his eyes followed her stare.

She was watching Duane as he came toward them with four other young men in white lab coats. He approached, looked right at her. She smiled, raised a hand; he deliberately looked away, not acknowledging her greeting as he passed on down the corridor. Her smile faded, her face reddened, her eyes moistened. Bret saw it all.

As the elevator door opened, he saw that she wasn't going to move. He took her arm and brought her into the elevator with the other students. They didn't speak as the elevator descended. The other students chattered and laughed.

"Better watch Shelly, she'll steal the colon," Gwen said.

"Not from a cancer patient, I won't," Shelly answered laughing.

Bret held Carol's arm until the elevator stopped. The door opened, the students stepped out. Gazing around them at the windowless corridor, they wandered past radiology, past the lab, and found pathology. Bret and Carol lagged behind.

Never, never, never had she been so hurt. Never had she felt such pain, such humiliation, such embarrassment. Couldn't he have just smiled? What harm could it have done if he had just spoken? Would speaking to her have hindered his career? If he felt no more for her than that, why did he come to see her? Why did he call every evening? Why did he take her out? Why did he seem proud of how she looked when they went to dinner? Why did he have the look in his eyes that conveyed to her that he loved her? He couldn't be leading her on to use her for sex—it hadn't happened. It was *he* who kept setting the rules about that.

Suddenly she felt her body slam into the concrete-block wall of the corridor. She felt its cold, rough surface against her arms as Bret pinned her shoulders to the wall. His face was close to hers; his blue eyes riveted her gaze to his.

"Was that your boyfriend?" he demanded. "The one who's the med student?"

She nodded and then the tears came.

Bret studied her face. Then he wiped the tears off both of her cheeks with the back of his hand. "What's with him, Carol?"

"I . . . don't know."

"Yes, you do. Tell me."

"He's afraid somebody will find out he's seeing me and it will hinder his chances of being accepted for his residency at Bennet. He says that students who are married or in love don't do their best work."

Bret kept staring at her. "Are you kidding me?"

She shook her head and started to cry.

Bret let her put her head on his shoulder and his arm went around her. "I don't understand," he said. "I'm trying but I don't understand."

She stepped away from him feeling ashamed and, incredulously, untrue to Duane. "He's really a nice guy, Bret."

Bret wasn't looking at her now; he was looking past her at the wall. "Yeah, *real* nice. If I'd known *how* nice, I'd have . . ." he began angrily. Then as she stood speechless, he backed away from her, leaned against the other wall of the corridor opposite her, folded his arms, and kept looking at her.

She laughed and dashed away her tears with both hands. "I thought you understood human nature."

He shook his head, still looking at her, and said, "That's not human nature, Carol. Maybe I was prejudiced against that guy before I ever saw him, but . . . Talk about blind ambition! I never knew what that cliché meant until now."

What could she say? Nothing. Anything she could say in Duane's defense would seem to be untrue to him, to their relationship.

"I don't think I'd better say any more," Bret said. "I have no right to. Maybe I should have *made* it my right. But you seemed happy, in love with the guy. It never occurred to me that the feeling wasn't mutual." He shut his eyes and shook his head. "See?" he said. "I've already put my foot in my mouth and I've got no right to. Who am I? To you, I'm nobody."

"You're a friend."

Bret smiled slowly, raised his brows. "Well, that's *some*thing."

It had never occurred to her to think of Bret as more than a friend. Of course, as her mother had always said, single friends of the opposite sex don't stay friends for long if they keep seeing each other. They either go one way or the other.

Well, she wasn't seeing Bret, only in clinical and occasionally in lecture. They had been eager to talk about their patients or to hash over exam questions together, but never alone.

She sniffed and wiped her eyes. A lab tech grinned at them as he strode by. "Let's go in now," she said.

Bret looked at her again. "If you say so."

"I wouldn't miss this autopsy for the world."

He didn't say anything else, just followed her into pathology.

As they filed into the pathology lab, the secretary at the desk pointed to a set of swinging doors. They knew that beyond the doors must surely be the autopsy room, for some irreverent soul had made a sign which read: MEAT LOCKER, and taped it to the door.

The room was large, tiled from ceiling to floor with gray tiles. The floor was concrete, and in the middle of it was a drain. On one side of the room were six refrigerated vaults. There were two stainless-steel tables in the middle of the room and on each one lay a body. The body nearest the door was that of an elderly man. On the other table lay a young woman. They were both naked. The students were huddled in a cold cluster just inside the door.

"Come on in, gather 'round," said a man dressed in a scrub suit. "Look all you want. We only ask that you not touch anything unless you have on gloves. Come on. They won't bite."

A big, burly Negro man dressed in surgical greens giggled through enormous white teeth.

There were three men besides the black man, probably resident doctors, dressed in greens. Each wore gloves; only one wore a surgical mask.

Mae clutched Carol's arm. Carol was feeling depressed anyway and her first reaction to the scene before her was one of revulsion. The huge Negro was plugging in something that looked like an electric saw. She hated this. Hated it because both bodies were naked and the female body was the one surrounded by the residents.

"This patient died of cancer," said the friendly pathologist. "The other one died of a heart attack, both just about an hour ago. Gather 'round. Look all you want."

"Question," said Shelly.

"Yes, ma'am," said the resident amusedly.

"If you know what the patients died of, what're the autopsies for?"

"We do as many autopsies as we can. Some autopsies are required by law. For instance, if someone dies in the hospital within forty-eight hours of admission. Another time it's required is when foul play, such as a poisoning or whatever, is suspected. In other cases, we just secure permission to do an autopsy because the physician is curious about what-all was wrong with the patient, especially if he's insecure about his diagnosis. Many times, the family is curious also and grants permission for an autopsy so that they can find out. Remember, we have learned anatomy and physiology mostly from dead bodies."

Carol thought of the little mouse in A&P. She backed against the wall while Mae froze on the spot. The other students moved slowly forward as the pathologist, with three bold strokes, made his Y-shaped incision from the patient's clavicle on both sides to the xyphoid process of the sternum, then down her abdomen to her pubic mound. There was very little blood, and what there was trickled out of the wound onto the table from which it was washed away by a continous stream of water. The table was slightly tilted to facilitate drainage of the water and blood.

The resident peeled back the flaps of skin and muscle tissue from the ribs, and he stepped backward. He glanced at Mae. "First year?"

She shook her head.

"Senior," said Shelly.

The man stepped to the table with the saw, caught hold of a rib. *Rrrrrraa-a-ang*, sang the saw as it cut through the ribs. He pulled the set of ribs loose and laid them on the table beside the body. *Rrrrrraa-aa-aang*, went the saw again.

"Is he a doctor?" asked Bret indicating the Negro.

"Him?" asked the resident. "No. He's just an aide."

He's just an aide. Not a doctor, not a nurse. An aide.

Gwen Hutton turned and bolted out the door of the autopsy room, but the others stood firm.

The last ribs were tough to get out, so the aide jerked and yanked to free the ribs while the body's head beat rhythmically on the table.

People who are so quick to give permission for an autopsy on their family member should see this, Carol was thinking. *Oh God, I hadn't dreamed it was like this. No order, no privacy, no dignity.*

The resident turned and held up a rib for the students to see. "Do you see this black place?"

The students could see nothing but a human rib. A *human* rib.

"Five'll get you ten it's cancer. She had cancer of the pancreas; it has metastasized to the liver, and here it's in the bone."

While he spoke, the other two residents were doing something to the head of the body, and when Carol's eyes went to the body again, the face was folded, the scalp was pulled down over the forehead. *Zzzzzzing*, went a drill on the skull. *Zzzzzzzing*.

No. It wasn't like this. She had always imagined that autopsies were like surgeries. Suddenly she saw that the autopsy room resembled the operating room, the table of instruments, the cabinets, the stainless-steel tables, the tile on the walls, everybody gowned and gloved. It was an operating room scene with all the hope gone out of it.

Rrrrrrring. The aide deftly lifted the top off the body's skull.

A resident was weighing the liver and speaking into a tape recorder attached to the table.

"I'll take all five pounds of the large intestine, please." Shelly laughed nervously as the resident weighed the intestine on a butcher's scale which hung from the low ceiling.

Meanwhile the friendly resident cut the brain loose from the brain stem, lifted it out of the cranial vault, and placed it on another scale.

Carol's limbs had thawed a little now, and when she was sure that the raw, cut-up-chicken smell which permeated the place wasn't going to make her ill, she moved so that she could see into the cranial vault.

With the top of the skull removed, she could see inside; a sleek, whitish pink vault molded and smoothed by a sculptor's hands, fashioned for the seat of the body's mind and perhaps its soul, the brain.

The brain. The brain of a lady, a mother, probably. Somebody's beloved wife. The brain had caused her to love, to sing to her babies, to read recipes. Maybe she had gone to college.

The brain was gray. Just as A&P textbooks described, gray, with convolutions and fissures. They had examined a brain floating in a jar of formaldehyde, but it looked impersonal and unreal. This brain had ceased to function only an hour ago.

Whack! The resident looked at Carol. The brain lay

in halves under his knife. He smiled. "First autopsy?"

She nodded, offended.

"The first is always the worst, honey. Next time, you'll feel more at home in here."

"I would never feel at home in here."

"How would you feel going out with me to dinner sometime?"

"After seeing you work, I'd be afraid to."

The resident threw back his head and laughed, then shrugged and went back to work. *Whack!* She stared as he cut the brain into small slices.

She looked at the body again. Most of the organs had been removed now and the body was a gaping cavity. Incredulously, the legs and feet were intact and there was worn fingernail polish on the body's toenails.

By the time the residents moved to the male body, Carol's thoughts were more organized. She watched with cold, remote curiosity, and noted the arrangement of every organ in the man's body. It was amazing. It was like nothing on earth, the human body constructed for a human life. It *couldn't* be an accidental evolution. It was like seeing the insides of a machine; every organ, every vessel had a purpose—all the systems were created for a purpose, each system was assigned a special function and yet each functioned as part of a whole.

Carol and Mae left together. "I'm going to write about this and send it to the newspaper," Carol threatened. "People are so curious about what their family members die of that they allow this when it isn't necessary."

"But isn't there a purpose for it?" Mae said.

"There's no excuse for the indignity of it. And do people know their loved one lying in the casket is without a brain or any organs?"

"I'll never sleep again," Mae said. "Never."

"I don't know whether to let you in or slam the door in your face."

"What?" Duane asked incredulously as he stood on the porch of her apartment.

"You looked right at me in the corridor at Bennet and didn't speak. Are you ashamed of me or something? Look, I have feelings, buddy, and I don't appreciate your attitude."

"Oh, come on, Carol, I was on rounds. That was Whitehall himself directing rounds. Whitehall, the chief of surgery. Could I break out of our serious little group and say howdy to a pretty student nurse? The others would have ribbed me about that and Whitehall wouldn't have liked it. He's all business."

"You could have winked."

"You had that male student with you and *I* didn't like that."

"Don't change the subject."

"Carol, if you were an ordinary-looking girl, I'd have . . . winked or something. But to draw the attention of the others to you as cute as you are? I'd have had every med student on my back. 'Who's the nurse, Duren? What's her name? You friendly?' " He spread his arms wide. "So I'd be badgered. Why get it going?" He smiled. "Carol, let me in. It's cold out here. I'm sorry if I hurt you."

She hesitated, stood aside; he walked in, she shut the door.

He turned toward her. "I guess I'm a nerd, huh?"

"Yes."

"Carol, I'm only human." He took her by the shoulders. "I was scared. That's the first time I was ever around Whitehall. He was taking us to see one of his surgery patients. He was firing questions at us. I was . . . simply scared."

"You still could have nodded at me or something." She turned away and walked to her couch. Tucking one foot under her, she sat down.

He stood over her. "You had a bad day."

"More or less."

He sat down beside her. "Tell me about it. What now? Another hysterectomy you didn't approve of? See a cryosurgery?"

She sighed and told him about the autopsies. "I'm really disenchanted with medicine, Duane. I don't like some of the things I'm seeing. Nice people aborting viable, normal fetuses for no reason, slaughters they call autopsies, ants in people's wounds. Grouchy doctors I can take, but not nerds like that gynecologist Mae saw do cryosurgery."

Duane was grinning as he listened to her. "Carol, sweetheart, that's life."

"It isn't life; but if it is, I don't want to see any more of it."

He put his arms around her and pulled her against him until her head rested on his shoulder.

"Don't laugh at me. I didn't expect the hospitals to be like the ones on TV, but this is awful," she said.

Duane laughed softly. "My little nurse," he said. "I love you for your femininity. In spite of your curiosity and your drive to learn everything you can, you're about as scientifically minded as a kitten. Without autopsies we wouldn't know much about anatomy. We wouldn't have learned a damned thing about the human body. We never could have done surgery. Nobody would know where to cut to find what."

"Don't laugh at me. I know all that. It was done with such . . . such disregard for their humanity."

"Carol, those residents have probably performed four thousand autopsies. And the aide is there to help with the muscle work."

"They didn't perform, Duane, they just butchered and recorded what they observed."

He laughed again. "Did all the students feel like you?"

"There were some more curious than I. Two put on gloves and handled the organs." Shelly had, and so had a quiet, older student named Betty. "But everybody was offended by the manner in which the autopsies were done."

"Again, you've seen something I haven't. I've seen one surgery. I haven't seen an autopsy. I've dissected a cadaver though, but you . . . My God, it's incredible what you've experienced, Carol, for just a nurse."

"*Just* a nurse."

"Just *my* nurse."

Some of her hurt and anger at him were gone now. Maybe he did have a good reason for ignoring her that morning. She thought she knew him well. His father and mother had been divorced before he'd graduated from high school. His father was an executive, his mother was a real-estate broker married to a banker. Duane was intelligent and lonely and needed a quiet listener who could share his interests and his frustrations. And she had grown to love him in spite of herself.

Duane needed her, needed her as a girl, as a woman. She knew he had fought the need, had reasoned about it, thought it out, and had come up with the conclusion that if they started having sex, he'd get in too deep and his grades would slip. Having sex with her, he'd said once, wouldn't be like doing it with other girls he had known. *So he had known a few.* With her he knew he'd get in over his head, he said. She knew he hoped to finish medical school and wanted to put off any "permanent arrangements" as long as possible. But if they decided on some permanent arrangement—and she would prefer marriage because of her own convictions and because of her parents—she could help them through his residency by working as a nurse. Residents make very little, not enough to live on. With Carol's income—None of these plans had been discussed. They had just been hinted at.

"But you won't give up, will you, Carol?"

She sighed against his chest. "No. I love nursing. I love the hospital atmosphere; and most of all, I love my patients. But I'm like Bret. I'd sure like to change a lot of things. Maybe become a supervisor, a nursing director, go clear to the top and—"

"As a nurse? You think you can change things as a nurse?"

She raised up to look at him. "Why couldn't I?"

"Darling, nurses don't have any leverage in hospital management and politics."

"Are you saying that nurses have no say about policies in an institution where they're employed?"

"God, no, baby. Not over stuff that doctors do, like autopsies and unnecessary abortions and indiscreet gynecologists. Don't go thinking you can. Just because you've gained a little medical knowledge, don't forget you're still just a nurse."

"*Just* a nurse again."

"Just, baby. I've gone through four years of premed, almost four of med school, and I'll go through four or five years as a surgical resident. That's a hell of a lot of education. Why should *I*, for instance, let some nurse have a say in my business affairs?"

She stood up. He pulled her back down to him. "Don't leave till I tell you, Carol. You're getting snooty on me with no cause."

She struggled to get up again, but he held her down. "Let me up, Duane. You've hurt me. I thought you respected my nursing."

"Not to the extent you're talking about."

"Let me up, please. And I think you should leave. I'm upset enough without—"

"No. I feel like taking off your T-shirt." He grabbed her wrists and pressed them against the back of the couch.

"Duane . . . what's wrong with you tonight?"

"Tension. Pressure. Think I came up with the right answers when Whitehall asked them? No. He directed one question to me all morning. One. Did I answer correctly? No, I blew it. I was so rattled I couldn't tell him how the Guillain-Barre syndrome progressed. All I could do was spout what it was and I think I kept telling him it was an acute idiopathic polyneuritis disease. It's sort of rare. I knew the disease, but I went blank. I could have killed myself afterward."

"Oh, Duane, nobody knows everything."

"*I* do. He didn't even bat an eye. Didn't seem to *expect* me to know. That's what bothered me the most. That he didn't expect me to know. I wanted him to *know* that I would know. He keeps an eye on senior med students who have applied for residency at Bennet. Damn it, and I blew it. I knew the syndrome, but I couldn't get it out of my brain. I guess I wasn't expecting a surgeon to ask a question like that. But the patient he had done surgery on whom he wanted us to see was also suffering from Guillain-Barre syndrome."

"Duane, you're hurting my arm."

"You're supposed to be my tranquilizer, Carol. I came over here for some sympathy and you've got your back up because I didn't say howdydo in the hospital corridor."

"I'm supposed to be your tranquilizer? What about me?"

"Your pressure is of your own making. Nursing school can't be that difficult. And tonight, I need help."

She took his hand away from her thigh. "Not that kind."

"Yes, that kind."

"No, Duane."

"Why?"

"You know why. I'll never allow it."

"Frankly, my dear, I'd rather rape you anyway."

"Ha! Fat chance. We've been seeing each other for almost a year now and frankly, my dear, I don't think you can get it up."

His face turned scarlet and he took hold of her T-shirt as she fought him half-laughing, half-crying, still hurt and angry. But he did not laugh. Suddenly he stood up, red-faced. "Damn you, Carol, you can do it every time." He strode for her door just as he'd done a dozen times before . . . maybe two dozen times before.

This was a typical evening. About once a month he got out of control, then took his frustration out by slamming her door. But he always telephoned back later. Carol had an awful fear that he'd leave some night and never call again.

"Carol, sometimes—" He sought for words as he glared at her still sitting on the couch. "Sometimes I think I almost hate you."

"Only when I turn you down, Duane."

"I'll find me a . . . a girl."

"Go ahead. But be sure you don't get involved."

He left and slammed the door as usual.

She rested her head on her knees for a long time; then stood up, went to her door, threw the dead bolt, and hooked the chain lock. Then she took a shower, put on her Snoopy nightshirt, lay down on her bed, and waited for his call. It didn't come. Just as she had feared, it didn't come.

She turned off her bed light and stared up at the ceiling. A little moonlight streamed in through the Venetian blind at the window. She knew she wouldn't sleep, as Mae had said. Maybe none of the students would sleep tonight.

She thought of Bret, of his anger at Duane, and probably at her, too. He was strange. He had comforted her, but had made no comment. Only that he didn't understand, and he had said something about blind ambition. Yet, there had been something nice in his comfort, something undemanding and unselfish that she liked.

Tears slipped from her eyes and down the sides of her face onto her pillow. Her eyelids grew heavy, she drowsed. *Rrrrrang.* She jumped. It was the saw in the autopsy room. She pulled the covers up over her head, tensing, freezing, almost holding her breath.

The body's head beat a steady rhythm on the table as the aide jerked at the ribs to loosen them. Knock knock knock. She broke out in perspiration. *Knock knock knock* . . . She jerked the covers off her head and listened. The knock sounded again at her door. She froze with irrational fear. "Who is it?" she called from her bed.

"Me."

She got up hurriedly and went to her door. "Duane?"

"Let me in, Carol; it's cold out here."

She unlocked the dead bolt on her door, but left the chain lock latched so that she could crack the door open about five inches. "Duane, go home. Please," she quavered unconvincingly.

"No way. Carol, I've made up my mind. I'm going to spend the night with you. Now. Let me in."

"Oh, Duane, please. Let's not fight."

"No fight. Just let me in."

"No-ooooo," she groaned.

He kicked the door open with one blow and stood there as she stared at the broken chain.

And she was glad, *glad* it had broken.

He slammed the door behind him, locked it. She

just stood there as he came to her. Came to her and lifted her up, carried her to her bed. He pulled the nightshirt up over her head and off and stared down at her body as he removed his own clothes, and stood naked at last staring down at her.

She reached her arms up to him and he came into them, came down on her body. "I love you; I love you and I want you," he whispered. "I want—I want—"

Had there ever been a moment when his lips had not been on hers or his body on hers or his hands moving over her flesh burning her like this? Never. And nothing had ever existed for her before, but this.

PART SIX

Chapter Sixteen
Medical-Surgical Nursing II

The Emergency Room

After rotating through the cardiac-care unit and surgical ICU, the emergency-room experience was a flop. Nothing much went on there on Monday, Wednesday, and Friday mornings. At the present stage in Carol's education, she was beginning to wonder in what area she would like to work as a nurse. She thought CCU might be the one.

In the cardiac-care unit nothing much went on, but Carol at least had found out what it was like; the monitoring and caring for cardiac patients were fascinating. The thing that impressed her most about cardiac care was that its patients were so afraid. Most were normally well persons who *suddenly* had been struck down by heart attacks and knew their lives *suddenly* were teetering on the brink of eternity.

Surgical ICU was fascinating too, but there were so many monitoring gadgets and IV medications that she wasn't comfortable there. Still, she had learned more in ICU in the three days she had spent there taking care of patients—a laryngectomy with a tracheostomy, and a gastrectomy who had gone bad—than she had learned in her entire Med-Surg I semester on the regular wards.

Compared to the critical-care units ER was a drag.

Her third week of Med-Surg II was spent there, but not much happened. There was a boy who came into ER with a dog bite. She gave a tetanus injection. There were children in with various stages of flu or sore throats. One of the most interesting things that happened was the admission of a man with a broken leg. She assisted a disinterested resident in applying a cast under the direct supervision of a disinterested ER nurse. But mostly what Carol did in ER was run errands.

"Hey, student?" a resident would say. "Fill out a lab request for a culture and sensitivity."

"Take this lab slip to the lab."

"Call x-ray and tell them we need a portable chest and abdominal stat."

Once she observed a semiemergency procedure; the installation of an IV into the subclavian vein in a G.I. bleeder. It was a minor surgical procedure which required that the resident do a cutdown into the vein in order to insert an IV catheter. The procedure was tricky because it would be easy to puncture the lung with the needle if one wasn't careful.

"Student, take his history, will you?" the resident said as he got ready to do the cutdown. "The admissions clerk is busy and so are the other nurses."

Carol, holding the ER admissions sheet on the clipboard, said, "Your name sir?"

"Appleby! Clarence Potter Appleby and I don't understand why I've got a damned bleeding ulcer!"

"Age?"

"Fifty-six! I'm a calm man, I'm not your usual uptight executive!"

"Who is your doctor, sir?"

"Dr. Molly! But he died last October!"

"I'm sorry. Who—"

"Well, it was about time, he was eighty-three! Shoulda retired years ago!"

"Do you have a new doctor?"

"I went to one last December when I started having headaches! Never had headaches in my life until then!"

"His name?"

"Karnes! Dr. William Karnes! But don't call him! Call somebody else! Karnes is a young upstart! Acted like he was scared to death of me! Get me somebody older! I want a doctor that knows his ass from a hole in the ground!"

"Start this IV on Mrs. Pearson, will you Welles?" the nurse asked. "I've got to get this stab wound to surgery."

"But I've never—"

"Here's the IV, the tubing, the intracath, okay?"

"But I've never—I'm not supposed to—I'll try."

The little elderly patient said sweetly, "My veins roll, deary. You'll have lots of trouble finding my veins. They're plugged up, too, with fatty plaques. Right there is where everybody finds a vein. Oh my. Does the rubber thing have to be so tight? Nobody's ever tied it that tight before. Oh. Oh! *Oh!*"

"I think I'm in! My gosh! I think I'm in the vein!"

"Of course you are, deary. Know why? Because you're a red-headed blonde. Red-headed blondes find a vein every time."

"Your occupation, sir?"

"Ranch hand."

"Have you ever had diabetes, heart trouble, kidney infection, blood disease, venereal infection?"

"Nope."

"Any family history of the above diseases?"

"Nope."

"Do you have a physician, sir?"

"Nope."

"Are you allergic to any medications?"

"Nope."

"Ever been hospitalized before?"

"Nope."

"Religious preference?"

"None."

"Do you have any accident insurance?"

"Nope."

"What seems to be your trouble, sir?"

"Ma'am?"

"Why have you come to the emergency room?"

"It's this here. See that blood all over mah shirt under mah coat?"

"Oh! Oh my God!"

"Purt near shot off mah arm with a cotton-pickin' shotgun. Bleedin' like a stuck hog. Reckon it's broke in a couple of places, too."

Sometime during her three days in ER, Carol heard about Felix.

Felix Seifert was a wino who was attached to Bennet Memorial. Felix had discovered every unlocked door in the entire complex and had made it his habit for years to slip in through an unlocked door, find an empty hospital bed, and spend the entire night

he
corri

"Hey,

her, "You

you?"

Carol nodded h

"You are a natural.

after you graduate," and

corridor.

Remember L&D? How could she ever fo

e-
ndle
herself

(915, $2.95)

...ut Sharon finds the work
...mergency arises and she's the
...e thinks to call an R.N., then

...s One!

Available wherever paperbacks are sold, or order direct from the Publisher. Send cover price plus 50¢ per copy for mailing and handling to Zebra Books, 475 Park Avenue South, New York, N.Y. 10016. DO NOT SEND CASH.

unmolested—and in perfect comfort.

Felix didn't show up in the summer, only in the winter when the nights were cold. Then some nurse would wheel an early admit to a room and there on the immaculate sheets would lie Felix, dressed in a filthy shirt, a tattered suit coat, frayed trousers that didn't match—and if they had you wouldn't have been able to tell it because of the filth—his hat over his bewhiskered face, and his muddy boots resting ludicrously on the clean bedspread.

Everybody had heard about Felix, and had started to lock more doors, but somehow he always managed to find a way in. The new administrator hypothesized that Felix was entering during the day when the doors were unlocked, hiding somewhere, and slipping into a vacant room at night. So personnel started locking more interior doors and carrying more keys. They began locking linen rooms, utility rooms, treatment rooms; but still Felix found a way to slip in and to spend his nights in a warm room.

He was friendly, though. Whenever a nurse would discover him lying on a bed and shriek her outrage, Felix would get up, raise his hat to her, smile and plod out through the nearest exit.

But persistent personnel and nailed-shut windows prevailed at last and Felix spent one winter somewhere out in the cold of the inner city. Then he began showing up in ER with chest pain.

Brookline was a huge community-funded medical complex in the city, where most charity patients were sent, but Bennet's budget allowed ten percent of its average census for charity cases. It would have served Felix just as well to be sent to the community hospital, but since he'd become a fixture at Bennet—almost a tradition, in fact—he was admitted there. No doctor ever saw an arrythmia on Felix's EKG. No nurse ever saw an abnormal beat on the ER monitors. Never was there an elevated cardiac enzyme to prove that he was having angina or a heart attack.

Still, you couldn't turn away a man complaining of severe chest pain without observing him for three days in CCU. Hospital policy. So Felix spent three days in the quiet clean comfort of a CCU bed, attended to by nurses and fed a liquid diet, which he was accustomed to anyway.

Felix showed up in ER with chest pain about once a month.

Carol's last day in ER was so boring that she happened to be watching an LVN student catheterize an obese lady with low back pain, when there was a clamor outside the treatment room. Carol went into the ER corridor and watched the fire department ambulance attendants wheel in a patient. As she stood watching, she witnessed all of the forces of an ER come into play. The floor vibrated with residents running toward the patient as he was being wheeled into treatment room number four, the cardiac room. The patient was being breathed with an ambu bag by one of the attendants. Amid the sounds of clattering equipment and brusque commands, the patient was lifted from the stretcher onto the treatment table. Carol saw two residents strapping the automatic cardiac-massage machine onto the patient, saw another tilting the patient's head back and inserting an endotracheal tube. A crowd filled the room: two residents, four nurses, two ambulance attendants. All

Carol could do was stand in the corridor and try to catch a glimpse of what went on.

After ten minutes, a resident came out and went to the admitting clerk at the front desk. "That was Felix in there," he told her. "Only this time he was D.O.A."

"I'll be durned," the admitting clerk said.

Medical personnel vacated treatment room four and Carol looked inside. Felix lay gray and naked from the waist up. Urine stained the front of his tattered trousers. His shaggy head was gray and lay upon the clean paper of the treatment table. How ironic, Carol thought, that Felix in death now lay in the quiet comfort of the hospital on which he had come to depend in life.

She was immediately reminded of how sentimental she tended to be when one of the residents and a nurse bustled into the treatment room. "Never done an intubation? Now's your chance," the resident said to the nurse. "I never had either, but I did it on Felix. There's a trick to it. You've got to get his head tilted back so you can see the larynx. And be sure you've got a laryngoscope that's got a large blade."

Carol watched as the resident flipped open the metal instrument called a laryngoscope. It was outfitted with a tiny light and looked like a shoehorn with a curved handle.

Felix's teeth clicked against metal as the resident inserted the blade of the instrument into his mouth. He showed the nurse how to insert the endotracheal tube stylet into the tube to make it stiffer, then he inserted the tube through the opening in the laryngoscope.

"How do you know when you're in?" the nurse asked

taking her stethoscope out of her pocket.

"You listen. It's the only way. If I'm in the esophagus I'll pump air into the stomach and you won't hear it in the chest." The resident attached the endotracheal tube to the respirator at the head of the table, then turned on the respirator.

The nurse listened to Felix's chest. "Nope. You're not in."

"The hell I'm not!"

"He's bloating, Dr. Bonham." She stuffed the stethoscope back into her lab-coat pocket. "Here, let me try, will you?"

They practiced on Felix for a few moments and another resident came in and practiced, too. They practiced until Carol was sick of it. Two residents and a nurse, practicing on poor ol' Felix Seifert.

Chapter Seventeen

CPR

The cause, or etiology, of Lanelle Godsby's abdominal obstruction was unknown, just as the etiology of Shelly's obstruction had been unknown — until surgery. According to the ER admit sheet, Lanelle had been admitted to ER on February sixteenth with severe abdominal pain and vomiting. Her vital signs indicated that she was rapidly going into shock. Abdominal x-rays revealed pockets of air and fluid in the small intestine and ascending colon. She was taken to surgery immediately because she was shocky and there was no time for an attempt to decompress the intestines using conservative measures. Her surgeon, Dr. Feliciano, removed a large benign polyp from the transverse portion of the large intestine and had to make a decision as to whether to anastomose the two ends of the colon together again, or to form a colostomy. There was some uncertainty as to whether the compressed nerves and vessels which fed the colon could function again. The surgeon decided to give the colon its chance to rally — Lanelle was fairly young and had once been a professional model. Why ruin the anatomy any more than you have to? he reasoned. He sutured the colon ends back together and now the uncertainty still remained: would the bowel be able to function again? Or had the nerves and blood vessels feeding it been compressed by the polyp so long that they wouldn't be able to heal?

Dr. Feliciano told Lanelle that if she did not pass flatus or gas, or if he was not able to hear bowel sounds in the lower abdomen by the afternoon of February twentieth, he would have to take her back to surgery, do a bowel resection, and give her a colostomy. Lanelle had begged the doctor to remove the nasgastric tube that had been installed in surgery to remove stomach secretions, and the doctor had thought, What the hell? The NG tube was removed. He told the nurse who removed the tube that once he'd had a patient who'd caused peristalsis to start in her bowels because she'd begun to vomit. If that happened with Lanelle, all the better.

Lanelle was a fashion designer for an enormous apparel firm; she was thirty-eight, and unmarried. In report the day Carol was assigned to her care, on the morning of the twentieth, the nurses said that Lanelle was extremely depressed. She had not passed flatus and the nurses were unable to hear bowel sounds on auscultation of the abdomen.

In Jenson, all equipment necessary for taking vital signs was already in the rooms. Jenson was the newest of Bennet's buildings and contained all the latest equipment, plus carpeted suites and a surgical suite located on the fourth floor. Carol did not have to roll a mercury sphygmomanometer into the room or find and carry in the anaroid type with its gauge attached to the cuff. In Jenson, each private room contained its own mercury manometer attached to the wall near the head of the bed.

Carol walked briskly into Lanelle's room.

Lanelle was a gaunt woman with long black hair and she lay with the head of her bed rolled up almost ninety degress. As Carol entered the room, she turned her face toward her and Carol could see the dark crescents under her eyes, the jaundice of her complexion.

"Hi. I'm Carol Welles. I'm going to be your nurse this morning. How are you feeling?"

Lanelle looked at her without speaking for a moment. Carol did not understand the expression on the woman's face as she stared at her. She did not know that Lanelle was seeing a young, lovely face with a flawless complexion except for a sprinkling of freckles across the nose and cheeks. Carol's long, thick reddish blonde hair, gathered into a shiny chignon at the back of her head, was beautiful and her light brown eyes, flecked with green, were lovely. Carol did not know that her fresh, young face reminded Lanelle of the beauty she had been just ten years ago, or that her cheerfulness reminded Lanelle that somebody somewhere was experiencing life — *life*, not sickness, not this feeling of impending doom from which she was suffering.

Lanelle smiled. "Your nametag says S.N. Are you a student?"

"Yes. Senior. This is my last semester."

"Carol. Carol Welles."

"Yes. The first thing I need to do is take your vital signs."

"Carol Welles. I see a countryside of green grass, a rail fence, blue mountains in the distance, yellow wild flowers nodding in the sun."

303

"Ma'am?"

"Your name. It invokes an American countryside. Perhaps back east, say in Virginia."

"Oh." Suddenly Carol felt the fear, the despair that Lanelle must be feeling. "I guess you're afraid, aren't you?"

Lanelle's smile grew. "You get right down to the nitty-gritty fast, don't you? Yes, I was afraid until the moment you walked in that door."

Carol wondered what to say to something like that. "Uh—would you mind opening your mouth so I can take your temp?"

Lanelle let her place the thermometer under her tongue, but continued to watch her, never taking her eyes off her face. Carol quickly became self-conscious. After forty-eight assigned patients, not counting the ones in L&D recovery and ER, Carol had developed a certain expertise around patients, a self-confidence that overcame many nurse-patient obstacles such as personality clashes, stubbornness, fear. But this unabashed and open admiration of her caught her off guard.

She wrote down the vital signs in her little pocket notebook.

The doctors' orders included instructions to the nurses to listen for bowel sounds twice a shift. Carol knew what to listen for, the squeaking and gurgling of the bowel which indicated that peristalsis was present. Peristalsis was the wormlike movement of the intestines which caused digested substances to be moved through the digestive tract to the lower bowel for excretion.

"Let's see what's going on in your abdomen," she

said, taking her pink stethoscope from around her neck. "Have you passed any gas?"

"No. Did you know that when you stood in front of the window your hair was the color of the noonday sun? It was as if it had suddenly caught fire, glowed red a moment, then become gold, almost iridescent. How long is your hair?"

Carol said, "Just past my shoulders. But the rules of our school state that we mustn't have hair below our pinna—uh, below our earlobes, so those of us with long hair have to pin it up when we go to clinical." She had learned to pause in the routine of taking vital signs and giving bedbaths to *listen* to patients. To listen to her patients who lay for hours staring at the same asbestos tile ceiling, patients whose minds filled with questions like an underground cistern with water, who became lonely in their fear of the unknown, who were dependent on the bustling, busy personnel who came to and went from their rooms. One person who would listen sometimes made the difference between hope and despair.

She did not hear bowel sounds in Lanelle's abdomen.

While she was helping Lanelle with her bath, the patient never took her eyes off her face. First, she asked general questions like, "What area of nursing do you think you would like to work in?" And, "Have you been in surgery?" Then she began to ask the personal ones. "Do you live with your parents? Do you have a gentleman friend? Has your medical student asked for any permanent arrangement?"

"I'm sorry the bath is taking so long, but I like to

lotion and talcum as I go along. Sort of in sections. I complete one side of you before I do the other side," Carol said nervously.

"Carol," said Lanelle, her eyes shining with some emotion Carol couldn't identify, "you can bathe and lotion and talcum me all you want."

That's when Carol really became uneasy. It was the only time the patient shut her eyes. She was experiencing a quiet, introspective ecstasy that expressed itself only in the look on her face as Carol patted talcum powder on her arms, chest, and legs. The rest of Lanelle's bath was done in a hurry.

"Carol?"

Carol was leaving the room to record Lanelle's vital signs.

"Yes?"

"You'll come back?"

"Yes."

"Because now I feel that I'm going to be all right. I feel my stomach rolling. I think . . . I think I'm going to be okay."

Carol paused, came back, took her stethoscope from around her neck. Duane had given her the stethoscope. "Why is it pink?" she had asked. "Because I've heard nurses complain that the doctors steal their stethoscopes and I guarantee you, Carol, that no doctor will steal a pink stethoscope." Carol listened to Lanelle's abdomen again. There it was, the squeaking and groaning of peristalsis.

"Lanelle, you're right. I think I hear bowel sounds. But I'll send in a nurse to listen, okay?"

"But you'll be back?"

"Yes."

She did go back, but only very briefly to say good by to her patient after she had watched the CPR on Mr. Proctor; and she spent the rest of her time before postclinical reading his chart.

Now, hurrying to postclinical, she was thinking, I *must* find out why Proctor died. I must find out what events or series of events allowed — or caused — such a death. Who slipped up? Who goofed? As Duane would say, Somebody didn't do his job.

She was late to postclinical, but after she told about observing the CPR on Mr. Proctor, and of what she had read in his chart afterward, Ellen Child understood.

They were sitting in a circle in desk chairs in the small conference room; the clinical group was almost the same as last semester's and included Jo, Mae, Shelly, and Carol. Bret had not chosen Bennet this semester, but had chosen Brookline.

The students' training as nurses was nearly complete. Graduation plans were being made by the class president, Frances Gorham, and her committee. Tension in clinical and lecture was getting unbearable again. Students were haggling over the uniforms they would wear at the graduation ceremony. Picking a uniform style for graduates, one that would please one hundred thirty-three women, was, of course, impossible, but the committee was trying. All their anxieties over grades, passing nursing, the upcoming state board exams, and their term theses, narrowed and came to focus on that graduation uniform. When all one hundred thirty-three female students and the three speechless males got together in the auditorium for lecture, chaos reigned and the faction for high collars engaged in verbal battles with the faction in favor of V-necked collars. Then there was the faction in favor of polyester-knit fabric against the polyester-cotton-blend-woven-fabric crowd. When the entire class of nursing students gathered for lecture in the auditorium these days it was like a national convention for the nomination of the president, with every state supporting its favorite sons.

So, with strife having become a way of life with the students lately, the clinical group burned with envy because Carol had actually observed a CPR, and the dead patient's chart was a natural source from which she could write her term paper. The ingredients were all there. A relatively healthy patient had been admitted to the hospital for a simple surgical procedure. He had died twenty-four hours later. Her project would be to study the chart—which she had already scanned—and come up with a nursing-care study.

But Carol wasn't satisfied with that. No. Mae perked up her ears when Carol said, "Ms. Child, I heard one of the nurses mention that there was going to be an autopsy on Mr. Proctor. May I observe it?"

Child nodded, smiling a little sarcastically. "I was wondering how long it would take you to ask. I'll try to get permission. But this is touchy, you know. If I can get permission from the pathologist in charge of the autopsy, you can go. But I'd prefer that you take two or three of the others with you."

Child did receive permission from the young resident pathologist who was to do the autopsy and Carol selected Mae, Jo, and Shelly; all three were intrigued by the situation and went along eagerly.

Proctor was already on the table and the autopsy incision had been made. The anterior ribs had been removed. The resident pathologist was very young and somewhat unsure, but he did know his business. He was disconcerted by the presence of the students, but attempted to ignore them as he proceeded solemnly. He was the only pathologist there. In the pathology lab the resident who had conducted the CPR on Proctor was seated at the secretary's desk writing. He still looked sleepless, puffy-eyed, morose. The swinging doors were left open between the lab and the autopsy room so that Carol could turn her head easily and observe the resident from the vicinity of the dissecting table.

The first impression the students got was that Proctor's organs were encased in great yellow and white globs of fat. The second impression was that the abdominal cavity was full of fluid. *The ten thousand three hundred and fifty ccs of saline?*

"How do you plan to proceed with this autopsy?" Carol asked the resident as he took up a scalpel in hand. He looked at her soberly. He looked tired or subdued, or both.

"First I will dissect the heart to determine if there was a coronary thrombosis. However, it's hard to determine if a patient has had a coronary if it was sudden. You understand that if a patient has a heart attack and lives a few hours, parts of the cardiac muscle will have necrosed—or died—due to blockage of circulation in the area of the heart which the blocked vessel feeds. In sudden death due to a coronary, there will be no dead tissue. Yes, there will be a clot because when someone dies the blood in his body pools in all the vessels including the heart and the pooling causes the formation of clots. Therefore, the clots found in the vessels of the heart have to be studied. If there are old blood cells or fatty substances in the clot, he probably had a heart attack. If the blood cells appear to be new and there are no fatty substances in the clots . . ." The resident shrugged.

The pathologist proceeded then to cut out the heart. He observed it and intoned into the tape recorder briefly, "Gross examination of cardiac muscle reveals normal tissue without necrosis." He placed the heart into a basin for dissection and further study.

He looked at the students. "Next, I will remove each lung and will later dissect the lungs to determine if there was a pulmonary embolus or blood clot in the vessels of the lungs. Then, I will remove and study the bladder to determine if—er, that is, to study it."

He didn't get a chance. Suddenly a tall distinguished-looking, white-haired man entered the room. It was as if someone had opened a window on a stormy night. He said nothing as he came to stare down at Proctor's body.

The resident pathologist clearly became uneasy.

"Well, Benson?" said the tall man.

"I've just begun to proceed, Dr. Tyree."

Dr. Tyree. Proctor's urologist. The one who had performed the T.U.R. on Proctor.

"You haven't done a test on his bladder?"

"No sir, I—"

"You know, of course, that there's a quick and simple way to determine if there is a, uh, problem in the bladder?"

"Yes, but I—"

Tyree turned abruptly, went to one of the cabinets, and as he did so, Carol watched him. He was solemn, energetic, absolutely self-assured, so self-assured that he did not even question the presence of the students, or acknowledge them in any way. He snapped on a pair of surgical gloves and took a rubber catheter from the cabinet. Then he found a syringe; then a solution in a tube. As he approached the table again he still did not look at the students.

"Benson, you'll note that I'm inserting this urinary catheter into the penis?"

"Yessir."

As Tyree did so, he said, "I'll then inject this purple dye into the catheter. If there's a—er, problem, the dye will show up in the abdominal cavity, correct?"

"Well—possibly—"

"Possibly? Where else would it go?" Tyree injected the dye gently with his right hand; his left hand went inside the patient's abdominal cavity. "Hmmmm," he said. "No dye in the cavity, Benson."

Benson said nothing, but Carol saw the purple stain on the glove in the abdominal cavity. But did he get the stain on it from the test tube of dye *before* he put his hand inside the cavity? Or did he get the stain on it while it was inside the cavity?

What both doctors were avoiding saying was that if Tyree had goofed when he cut out pieces of the prostate and had cut a hole in the bladder by accident, then the hole in the bladder would have allowed the saline irrigation fluid to leak into the abdominal cavity, causing Proctor to go into shock.

While the resident watched, Tyree said, "Let's give it another test to be sure, Benson. We must be sure."

Tyree drew up another syringe of dye and injected it into the catheter with a vigorous push.

Carol saw the resident wince.

"Shit," said Tyree. "I pushed a hole in the bladder!"

Purple dye flooded into the abdominal cavity for all to see.

Tyree looked at Benson. "Well, now we can't be sure there was a problem in the bladder before it tore, can we Benson? I apologize. But you can note in your report that we did the test and there was no evidence of extravasation. Correct?"

Benson stared at the doctor; then looked down at the body on the table.

The resident who had attended CPR on Proctor appeared beside Tyree and stared down at the body. Tyree said, "Coleson, we tested for extravasation of the bladder and the test was negative. I inadvertently tore the bladder with the catheter, but we had already done the test. Your diagnosis on the doctor's progress report is wrong."

Coleson only stared at Tyree; the two men stood staring into each other's faces, eye to eye. Carol heard Tyree say in a low voice, "That erroneous progress report, Coleson—Do it over."

Do it over? Carol thought that once something was charted on a patient's chart, it became a legal document.

Coleson stared at Tyree for a long time and it was Tyree who broke the trance and stalked out of the room and out of the pathology lab.

Coleson looked down at the body. Benson proceeded with the removal of the lungs as if it mattered.

The students watched while Benson removed the

lungs and dropped them into the basin, proceeding as if nothing disturbing had happened; except now he was silent.

Carol was thinking that Proctor's autopsy had been performed as an autospy should be, with order, with a purpose; except for Dr. Tyree's intrusion, it had been done with dignity and precision.

Carol became aware that Shelly had put on gloves. She was picking up the colon from the basin and saying, "Give me a sack, I'm going to take this home and have Basil hook it up to what's left of mine."

While Mae and Jo laughed at Shelly, Carol went slowly to the door of the pathology lab. Would Dr. Coleson do the doctor's progress report over?

He was writing on a blue sheet. The doctor's report was a blue sheet. And there was a folded blue sheet in the breast pocket of his shirt.

The next day after clinical, Carol went to the pathology department where records were kept and asked to see Dr. Benson. He came out of an office and Carol said, "Hi. I'm one of the students who observed the autopsy on Mr. Proctor yesterday. I was just sort of curious what he died of."

The resident almost smiled. "We aren't sure, but the diagnosis is MI."

MI. Heart attack.

Carol didn't believe it. It was absurd. In fact, the conclusion absolved the doctor of any error whatsoever and the burden of guilt for Proctor's death fell *solely* on the nurses. It wasn't fair.

But what a study it would be. What a thesis! Carol had great visions of her thesis being so meticulous, so scientific, so interesting that somebody might even want to publish it as they did masters' and doctors' theses sometimes.

It was Friday and she told Duane the whole story that evening. He seemed eager to take her to dinner, but she told him that she wanted to talk awhile. He listened patiently at first as she began to relate the story of Proctor and the autopsy. Then he began to get restless; his face turned white, then red. Then he went berserk. He jumped up from the couch, stood a moment breathing rapidly, and then said, "Carol, you can't pursue this. You've got to drop it. Now. Immediately!"

She raised her brows. "Why?"

"Because you're nosing into something that's not any of your goddamned business!"

"But Duane, I'm only using it as a study for—"

"And going to that resident pathologist—my God! What if he saw your nametag? What if he connects you with *me*?"

She stared up at him as he turned away, then turned back. "And who the hell are you anyway to be spying on somebody like Tyree?"

Angrily Carol replied. "Look, Duane. I'm not accusing anybody of anything. But I am going to medical records to study Proctor's chart, and I am going to do my thesis on it."

"Thesis!" He spat. "Thesis. As if you were working on a master's degree or something. Why don't you call it a term paper? Every time you call it a thesis I feel like throwing up." They glared at each other for a moment in silence. Then he shouted, his face twisting in a mixture of disgust and anxiety, "Who are you? Nothing but a student nurse. Compared to a man like

Tyree, you're nothing. Nothing! Not if you graduate, pass state boards, become an R.N., go on to become a supervisor, go clear to the top wherever the hell that is. As a nurse compared to Tyree you're a pipsqueak! A nothing! Tyree is chief of urology department. He's been a urologist for sixteen years! He'll be my chief when I rotate through urology. Benson will be chief resident when I rotate through pathology. Goddamn you, Carol—Bennet accepted me. I got the letter today. I was going to take you to dinner and tell you, but you hit me with this before I had a chance. You—"

"Oh, Duane. I'm glad you were accepted, but—"

"But you're doing your best to ruin me. What if somebody finds out I've been fooling around with you? And your snooping around trying to find mistakes—" Duane's hands went to his head. "Oh my God!"

"Duane!" she screamed jumping up from the couch. "I'm not trying to snoop on anybody. I'm not trying to accuse Tyree or anybody else of mistakes—"

"*Doctor* Tyree to you, nurse—"

"I'm only going to do a care study, a clinical study about how Proctor's death could have been prevented."

His eyes were full of tears of rage; his face was purple. "But Tyree saw you—"

"No; he didn't pay any attention—"

"He saw you. Benson saw you. Coleson saw you."

"Duane, nobody will see the term paper but my instructor."

"Can you guarantee that, Carol? Of course you can't. And you'll be snooping in medical records, and Tyree may find out and—"

"I'm not snooping. Stop saying that!" Carol cried. "And I'm not condemning anybody. I'm only . . . only doing a study." She began to cry as Duane stood staring at her; then a look of disgust crept into his face.

"Carol?"

She wiped the tears from her eyes with the palm of her hand, and watched him point a finger at her face. "If you go to medical records—if you write your paper—if you pursue this, I'm walking out that door and I'm never coming back."

"You do that then. Because I'm nothing. I'm nothing as a nurse. You just told me that."

"You're not. You're a piss ant compared to Tyree. In fact you're a piss ant compared to Benson and Coleson."

"Get out!" Carol screamed. "Get out. Now! And don't ever come back."

"You intend to go ahead with the paper?"

"Yes."

Duane's face turned purple again. "You little bitch," he breathed, "I hope to God that someday *you* make a mistake and that somebody finds it out and bleeds you good." With that he jerked open the door and slammed out of it.

She stood for a long, long time in the same spot in her apartment, crying and staring at the door where he had left. She loved him, but he had just made her feel very small—like the piss ant.

Tossing and turning and unable to let her mind dwell on any one thought, she cried all night and could not sleep. Was doing her term paper on that particular subject more important than her relationship with Duane? Nothing was more important to her than Duane. Why then did she want to persist in doing the paper on Proctor's death?

Near morning when the sky was beginning to fade from black to ink blue and then to pale gray, Carol came to a conclusion. There was more at stake than just a term paper. She was soon going to be a nurse and with all her study and what little experience she had gained in clinical, a study of Proctor's nursing care, pathology, medical care, and autopsy would teach her more about caring for a patient and about preventing complications than an entire semester's work.

So, sleepless and barely able to keep the tears from her eyes, she drove to Bennet.

On this Saturday morning, there were only two secretaries in medical records. The room was huge and well-furnished with woodgrain-topped metal desks and chairs done in blue vinyl to match the pale blue carpet. Three walls were lined with shelves where patients' records were stored in sturdy manila folders with colorful plastic edges. The wall of manila folders looked like a colorful, computerized display in blue, green, red, orange, and yellow.

One of the secretaries smiled at her as she approached her desk. Carol showed the secretary her nametag. "I'm Carol Welles, a student nurse, and I'd like to see the records of Rupert Proctor. I'm doing my term paper on his case. My instructor should have called—"

"Sure," the secretary said, "she did call and gave me your name saying you'd be by. Have a seat over there at that table and I'll bring his records."

317

Carol obeyed and the secretary soon brought Proctor's records in a manila folder edged in black. Carol opened her spiral notebook, unclipped the records from the folder, and scanned them. It was all there. Everything except for Coleson's original progress notes on which he had written his diagnosis of extravasation of the bladder and gram negative sepsis shock. That had vanished.

THE ANATOMY OF A PREVENTABLE DEATH

A Care Study Offered in Partial Fulfillment of
the Requirements of the Course
Nursing 432 — Medical-Surgical Nursing II

by

Carol Rachel Welles

University of Texas at Eustice
School of Nursing

March, 1979

Mr. P. was born on October 6, 1923 in Macon, Georgia. His mother was in good health at the time. P. weighed ten pounds at birth. His parents were of upper middle-class culture of Caucasian ancestry. Mr. P. attended grade school in Macon where he proved to be an average student. Mr. P. attended high school in Macon and later moved with his family to Austin, Texas, where he attended the University of Texas. Mr. P. took a job with Texaco Oil and Gas Company and was later transferred to Midland, Texas, where he married Miss Laura Grimes. Mr. P. and his wife had three children, two girls and one boy.

At the age of thirty-five, Mr. P. went into business for himself forming the Proctor and Pedderson Oil Company which prospered and formed branch offices in Houston, Dallas, and Oklahoma City. Mr. P. moved to the suburbs of Eustice into an upper middle-class residential neighborhood in 1962. Mr. P. was a Mason, a member of the Elks Club, was active in the Episcopal Church, and served once as a member on the school board in Eustice. At the time of his demise he was chairman of the board of Petro Chemical Corporation.

Medical History

At the age of sixteen, Mr. P. was diagnosed by his family physician as suffering periodic bouts of asthma for which he received no treatment other than the use of a nebulizer and bronchodilator. In 1968, Mr. P. was diagnosed and treated by Dr. P.L.E., an internist, for gout. In 1978, Mr. P. was diagnosed as suffering from essential hypertension and fluid retention for which he was maintained on Lasix 50 mg p.o. daily.

During February, 1979, Mr. P. experienced painful urination which progressed until urination became nearly impossible. On February 17th, he was seen by Dr. T., who diagnosed benign prostatic hyperplasea and recommended immediate transurethral resection of the prostate.

On February 18th, Mr. P. was admitted to Bennet Memorial where he requested a private suite in the Jenson wing. Routine admission chest x-ray revealed no pathology. Routine admission CBC showed normal values, and routine urinalysis was normal.

Surgery

On February 19th, Mr. P. was given preop medication of Demerol 75 mg and atropine 0.4 mg. At 7:30 A.M., Mr. P. was taken to operating room number six in the surgical suite where he agreed to a spinal anesthetic to be administered by Dr. R., anesthesiologist.

During surgery, Mr. P. remained alert but drowsy.

According to the surgery report there was a slight trabiculation of the bladder necessitating that the fibrous bands extending from the prostate to the bladder be excised; otherwise the transurethral resection went well with no complications. The anesthesiologist's report showed all vital signs and the monitor blip remained stable throughout the surgery.

When the surgery was completed, Dr. T. installed a three-way urinary catheter which hospital personnel at Bennet refer to as a Murphy drip because it resembles a slow-drip abdominal-feeding procedure.

Mr. P. was returned to his room at 11:50 A.M.

Postoperative Period

11:55 A.M. The nurse in charge of the floor reported that the Murphy drip was running at sixty drops per minute and that drainage from the catheter into the catheter bag was clear. V/S. temp ninety-nine, pulse seventy-two, resp. fourteen, BP 130/74.

Throughout the rest of the shift the patient rested quietly.

3:00 P.M. The private-duty nurse reported patient became nauseated and vomited 100 ccs of dark-green fluid. Drainage into catheter bag was bloody. Dr. Tyree was notified and ordered hydrocortisone, one hundred milligrams intramuscularly, and it was given by the private-duty nurse.

4:00 P.M. The private-duty nurse reported Mr. P.'s intake and output. Eight hundred ccs of Ringer's lactate had been given intravenously and six thousand ccs normal saline via the Murphy drip. There were five thousand ccs urine and saline in the catheter bag.

5:00 P.M. The patient complained of abdominal pain. Private duty nurse administered Demerol, seventy-five milligrams intramuscularly.

7:00 P.M. Patient complained of being cold. Hydrocortisone 50 mg was given by private-duty nurse.

8:30 P.M. Mr. P's IV infiltrated and a floor nurse restarted it.

9:30 P.M. Patient became nauseated, but did not vomit.

11:00 P.M. Nurse reported the amount of Murphy drip given since 4:00 P.M. as six thousand ccs. There were two thousand seven hundred and fifty ccs in the catheter bag.

12:00 midnight. Patient complained of nausea, chills, and "sweating." The nurse gave hydrocortisone, fifty milligrams.

12:30 A.M. Nurse noted patient's face was "puffy" and pale. Patient's abdomen was firm but not tense. Patient became restless and could not sleep. Nurse administered Vistaril, fifty milligrams for sleep. Pulse, eighty beats per minute, faint but regular.

3:10 A.M. Six thousand ccs of saline had been given via the Murphy drip and four hundred ccs Ringer's IV. One thousand ccs in catheter bag.

4:10 A.M. Vital signs: pulse eighty, respiration eighteen, blood pressure 170 over 110. Patient became "breathless" when he changed positions.

4:30 A.M. Patient became restless. Nurse uncertain as to whether or not he was cyanotic. She also wondered if he was having a reaction to hydrocortisone.

5:00 A.M. The patient's IV infiltrated. The floor nurse was called in to restart the IV and was unable to restart it. She called the resident on duty in the eastern wing of Jenson.

Vital signs: temperature ninety-seven, pulse one hundred, respiration thirty-two, blood pressure one hundred and thirty over eighty-five.

5:15 A.M. Resident doctor appeared to restart the IV. Immediately placed patient in Trendelenburg position.

5:30 A.M. EKG. Vital signs: pulse unrecordable, blood pressure ninety? respiration thirty-two.

6:00 A.M. Blood pressure zero. Blood sample taken for electrolytes and ABG's.

6:30 A.M. Patient became unconscious. Resident did a bilateral suprapubic tap. Two hundred ccs returned.

6:45 A.M. Blood pressure zero.

7:00 A.M. Resident administered one ampule sodium bicarbonate.

7:15 A.M. Cardiac arrest.

Doctors' Progress Report*

Feb. 19. 11:15 P.M.—Checked pt. on final rounds. Pt. restless, nurse sleeping well. Ordered Vistaril 50 mg for sleep (for patient)

L.T., M.D.

*Quoted verbatim from doctors' progress report

Feb. 20. 5:10 A.M. I was called by the nurse in charge of third floor of Jenson wing to restart an IV.

Upon entering the room I immediately noted the patient's rapid respiration, thirty-six min. Skin pale and cold and clammy. Two plus edema in all four extremities. Face edematous, extreme ascites. Abdomen very tense. Pulse over one hundred beats per min. Determined the pt. to be in shock, placed him in Trendelenburg position. Ordered EKG, ABGs, and lytes stat. Nurse reported zero BP. EKG showed atrial tach with occasional PVCs about four per min. and elevated P wave on Lead II.

6:45 — Restarted IV in L. antecubital space. 'Lytes, ABGs showed potassium deficiency and extreme acidosis. One amp. sodium bicarb given IV.

7:15 — Pt. arrested — ceased to breathe, I was unable to palpate either carotid or femoral pulse.

Precordial thump was unsuccessful. Initiated cardiac massage and mouth-to-mouth resuscitation while nurse called for help. Male nurse took over massage while I administered breaths until crash cart and nurses appeared. Electrodes to cardiac monitor applied. Revealed ventricular fibrillation. O_2 by ambu bag.

Quoted verbatim from doctors' progress report

7:20 — Xylocaine 50 mg given IV.

Placed on respirator via face mask by resp. therapist.

one amp. bicarb given.

7:25 — Suctioned pt. trachea and installed endotracheal tube. Resp. therp. attached endo to respirator.

Nurse reported no BP.

Xylocaine drip instituted — 50 mg in 500 ccs D5W for arryth.

Aramine drip instituted — 100 mg in 500 ccs D5W for BP

7:30 — 400 joule by defibrillator.

Monitor showed ventricular fib.

7:32 — Defib.

7:36 — Defib. Monitor showing progressive digression from course v. fib to fine fib.

7:38 — Intracardiac injection of epinephrine 1:1000.

Monitor pattern showed momentary conversion to course fib and digressed to fine fib.

Continued cardiac massage.

Resp. giving breaths with 20% O_2 15/min.

7:45 — Defib.

Monitor showed fine fib.

8:05 — Asystole.

No BP, pulse, or spontaneous resp.

8:10 — Pronounced pt. dead.

Diagnosis: myocardial infarction due to stress of surgery. Recommend autopsy to rule out pulmonary embolus and other factors.

P.C., M.D.

There was an estimated eight thousand ccs of clear, nonpuralent fluid in the abdominal cavity. Culture taken of fluid, but microscopic exam showed no organisms.

Gross examination of the bladder showed no tears other than that caused by the overinflated catheter bulb when gentian violet was introduced for the second time to determine if extravasation of bladder had occurred. There was no dye in abdominal cavity after first injection of dye.

Gross examination of the kidneys showed they were enlarged and toughened, indicating a certain degree of renal insufficiency.

Dissection of the celiac artery showed excessive plaque formation.

Dissection of the liver showed a degree of congestion. Right-sided failure?

Dissection of the lungs showed very little congestion.

Dissection of the heart showed a possible very recent myocardial infarction. Coronary arteries showed some occlusion with one artery ninety-five percent occluded. No necrosis. Weight: six hundred gm.

Subcutaneous emphysema due to resuscitation attempt.

Diagnosis: MI resulting in cardiogenic shock and death.

B.B., M.D.

**Quoted verbatim from pathology report.*

Hypertension: Etiology of essential hypertension includes family history of high blood pressure, stress, obesity, high dietary intake of saturated fats or sodium, tobacco, aging. Hypertension does not usually produce other pathological effects until vascular changes in heart, brain, or kidney occur. Hypertensive crisis is caused by discontinuation of hypertensive medications, high salt intake, or added stress. Symptoms are headache, drowsiness, vomiting, shortness of breath, heart failure, tachycardia, tachypnea dyspnea, cyanosis, edema.

Obesity can lead to complications such as hypertension, cardiovascular disease, diabetes mellitus, renal disease. Obesity is an additional risk to surgery patients. Gout rarely causes serious complications, but one of the complications is hypertension and chronic renal failure.

Dissection of Medical Management

The patient's Lasix which he had been taking for years for fluid retention and high blood pressure was not continued during hospital admission.

The transurethral-resection type of surgery is considered a less traumatic choice of prostate surgeries for the poor risk patient, but this type of prostate surgery has a higher risk of septic shock than other prostatectomies.

The installation of three-way bladder irrigation ensures continuous bladder irrigation, aids in keeping urethra patent, combats swelling, and discourages growth of pathogens in bladder.

Hydrocortisone 100 mg was ordered. It is a steroid used for its anti-inflammatory effect, to combat gram negative bacteremia. Side effects include insomnia, congestive heart failure, hypertension, edema, hypokalemia, hyperglycemia When administering hydrocortisone IM, monitoring of electrolytes is imperative to detect depletion of potassium.

The doctor did not order electrolyte studies.

Vistaril 50 mg was ordered for sleep. It is usually give for anxiety and nausea.

Resident doctor placed patient in Trendelenburg position — head lower than feet — the usual shock position, when he detected shock.

Resident ordered EKG, electrolytes, and ABGs. He also did a suprapubic tap to determine if there was fluid in the abdominal cavity.

Resident conducted CPR in orderly and correct fashion.

Though Dr. T. had been called at 5:15 concerning his patient, he did not make his appearance until autopsy.

Mr. P.'s surgeon, Dr. T., was allowed to test extravasation of the bladder by injecting a dye into the urethra.

Nursing Assessment and Dissection of Nursing Care

Benign prostatic hyperplasia: Etiology is

unknown but hormonal changes seem to be a factor. Symptoms include difficulty starting micturition, feeling of incomplete voiding. Possible complications include infection, and renal insufficiency.

Transurethral resection: A resectoscope is inserted into the urethra through the penis and under direct vision, the surgeon is able to remove pieces of gland at the bladder orifice with wire loop and electric current.

Doctor T. should not have ordered hydrocortisone on a hypertensive patient because it promotes fluid retention and high blood pressure.

After the initial vital signs when the patient was admitted to his room from surgical recovery, there was no indication in the nurses' notes that vital signs were taken until 4:10 A.M., a fifteen-hour lapse of time.

At 11:00 P.M., if the nurse had reported the six thousand ccs of irrigation instilled, with only two thousand seven hundred and fifty returned, Dr. T. might have suspected extravasation of the bladder and taken measures to prevent complications.

According to the doctors' progress notes, at 11:15 P.M., Dr. T. checked the patient on his final rounds and there is no indication that he noted the intake and output. He did mention that the nurse was dozing.

At 12:00 midnight, when the patient complained of nausea, chills, and sweating, the nurse should have suspected shock, possibly septic in origin. Symptoms of septic shock are chills, fever, tachycardia, hypertension. As septic shock progresses, the BP becomes low.

At change of shift there is no indication that the nurse in charge of the floor checked the patient's vital signs or his intake and output. (At Bennet, charge nurses are responsible for all patients under their care including those for whom private-duty nurses have been hired.)

At 4:00 A.M., the nurse again should have recognized signs of shock and the wide difference between the amount of saline solution instilled and that which returned in the catheter bag. At this point the doctor might have been able to repair the bladder and save the patient. At 4:30, when symptoms of shock persisted and patient became cyanotic, the nurse failed to report symptoms to the doctor. Shock might have been reversed at this point.

At autopsy, the surgeon should not have been allowed to do a procedure on his own surgical patient with questionable cause of death.

Conclusion

Since the pathologist reported no microorganisms were found in the fluid culture taken from the abdominal cavity at autopsy, gram negative sepsis shock due to extravasation of the irrigation fluid into the abdominal cavity was ruled out. However, the abdominal cavity held over eight thousand ccs of fluid at autopsy. Also, edema was present indicating that there was fluid retention and probable hypervolemia due to excess fluid in the circulatory system. Electrolyte studies, ordered by the resident, indicated that the patient was suffering severe potassium depletion possibly caused by the hydrocortisone, vomiting, and lack of potassium intake, IV or ingested. The elevated T-wave on the EKG indicated hypokalemia (low potassium) and its effect on the myocardium; low potassium weakens the cardiac muscle. The congested liver found at autopsy indicates a certain amount of right-sided heart failure.

It is therefore my opinion that Mr. P. digressed into right-sided heart failure due to: weakening of the cardiac muscle, hypertension, and hypervolemia. He then proceeded into cardiogenic shock. When the resident placed him in the Trendelenburg position, the weight of the obese abdomen together with eight thousand ccs of abdominal fluid, compressed the diaphragm into the already weakened heart, compromising it further and leading to cardiac arrest.

> *Grade 80*
> *Good, Carol. This paper was well-researched. Good luck in your future professional endeavors.*
> *Ellen Child, R.N., M.S.*

Carol had waited until she had reached the elevators before she looked at the grade on her term paper. Then she exploded. "Eighty! That's a C!" she cried as she stood holding the paper in her hand.

"Well, I got a ninety-eight," Jo said tonelessly, "and that brings my D up to a C. Mae got a ninety-three. That brought her D up to a C, she says. I think this term paper passed Mae and me both."

"I'm glad . . . but my paper an eighty? Jo, it was better than that!"

"My gosh, what d'ya want, Carol? You already have your A. One eighty isn't going to hurt you."

"This . . . this paper was my nursing career. This paper represents what I've learned as a future nurse. This paper cost me Duane. And I'll be damned if I'll let some half-assed instructor give me a C on it!"

"Holy smoke!" Jo exclaimed as Carol strode away from her and down the corridor. "Some people are never satisfied!"

In a blind fury Carol hurried back toward Child's office. She had tutored Jo and Mae through Med-Surg I and II. Before every exam she had met them in the university library where she had gone over medical terminology, and explained disease processes and diagnostic procedures, over and over. Sometimes even meeting them before preclinical and after postclinical.

She hadn't worried too much about Jo. For some unknown reason Jo had been making A's on her nursing-care plans lately, and *higher* A's than Carol's. Carol suspected Jo of copying old care plans of Shelly's.

But Mae? Mae hadn't been making it. Unless she made a good A on her term paper and a passing grade on her final, she wouldn't make it. D was not a passing grade in nursing school.

Yet *they* made A's on their term papers while *she*, their tutor, made a C. It was not only absurd that her paper had been given a C, but it was humiliating as well.

Carol rapped too hard on Ellen Child's door.

"Come in."

Carol went in. She knew that her face was red and that her eyes were filled with tears.

"Sit down, Carol. You look very disturbed," said Child. When Carol was seated beside her desk, she asked, "Now, what is it?"

"This paper. Why did I get an eighty on it?"

"Because I felt the paper deserved an eighty."

"Ms. Child, I am the only student who went to medical records to do research for her paper."

"I know. I gave you ten points for that."

Carol's face flushed. "There's nothing wrong with its presentation."

"Well . . . I gave you nine points there. You were very scanty with your nurses' assessment and too heavy on the medical assessment."

"I don't understand."

"Carol, don't you feel you're overreacting to this grade?"

"No."

"You are. It's probably the stress of graduation. Two of my students have been diagnosed with ulcers."

She didn't want to hear that garbage. "What's wrong with my paper?"

"Nothing. Except your approach. We instructors asked for a nursing-care study. From you I got very little nursing-care study and more of a report. If I'd asked for an investigative report, to submit to the *Informer* scandal magazine, I'd have given you a ninety-five and if you'd used names in your report instead of initials, I'd have given you a hundred. But Med-Surg II was not a course in investigative reporting and I asked for a nursing-care study. Jo gave me a nursing-care study because she's an experienced nurse and knows what I wanted. She also knew what I wanted on her nursing-care plans. Mae gave me a nursing-care study because she's a natural as a nurse; she's caring, possesses integrity, and intuitively knows how to manage patients and she is eager to learn. She will barely pass nursing school, but she'll make the best nurse of any of you. I gave you an eighty instead of a *lower* grade because a nurse sometimes needs an analytical mind, a determination to see things done properly. You'll probably make a good nursing supervisor someday, but you're going to have to practice at thinking like a nurse first." Ellen Child leaned back in her chair and draped her fashion model's body in an unfashionable slump. "But perhaps I'm old-fashioned. When I was in nurses' training ten years ago, we were taught never to question a doctor. We were taught never to put soiled linen on the floor while we made a patient's bed, just as you were taught. However, our reason for not putting soiled linen on the floor was so that if the doctor walked in, he wouldn't see a messy room, poor man. We learned to turn the pillowcase opening away from the door so that the *doctor* wouldn't see the unneat pillow inside. Things like that. Now nurses question. Nurses don't give a damn about whether a doctor sees a sheet on the floor or not."

Carol smiled in spite of her persistent anger.

"Tell me, Carol, what do you think happened with Mr. Proctor?"

Carol looked down at her hands; then up at her instructor. "I think Dr. Tyree accidentally cut a hole in Proctor's bladder during the T.U.R. procedure. I think that the irrigation fluid leaked slowly from the bladder into the abdominal cavity. I think maybe when the excised prostate bled, which isn't unusual, that Dr. Tyree ordered hydrocortisone to combat inflammation and gram negative sepsis shock, trying to cover all the bases he could. Why he neglected to order electrolyte studies with the hydrocortisone I don't know. Also, of all the things he could have ordered, why did he order a medication that could compromise Mr. Proctor's preexisting complications? Had he forgotten Proctor's high blood pressure, his tendency to retain fluid? I think the private-duty nurse was negligent in not reporting the ten thousand three hundred and fifty ccs discrepancy between the fluid that went into the bladder and that which came out. In fact, that was stupid. The floor nurse was negligent because she didn't check on the patient. Mr. Proctor had asked for a suite on a general surgical floor in Jenson instead of in Baskin on the regular urological ward where nurses are especially experienced in checking urological patients. I think the resident goofed in placing Proctor in Trendelenburg position. I think Dr. Tyree suspected extravasation of the bladder and destroyed the evidence at autopsy. I believe he located a hole in the bladder during the first dye test and destroyed the evidence by pushing the catheter through the hole and claiming he accidentally tore it. I believe he was afraid of a lawsuit. Proctor was wealthy. I think Dr. Tyree threatened Coleson with just a glare when he told him to redo the doctors' progress report. I think—".

"Okay. If you were a nurse, say on the seven-to-three shift, and knew what you know about this case, what would you do?"

Carol looked at her instructor. "I . . . I . . ."

"Go on."

"I . . ." She shrugged. "What *could* I do?"

"Yes."

"I could do nothing."

Child nodded. "Exactly. The negligent private-duty nurse was not on your shift. If she had been, you could only kick yourself for not checking the patient, but the damage would have been done. So you'd remember to mark her off the list of recommended private-duty nurses at the nurses' station. So! From your nursing-care study you've learned what you *can't* do. What did you learn that you *can* do as an R.N. in charge?"

"I can watch every patient closely," Carol said passionately, "no matter who's taking care of him—another floor nurse or a private-duty nurse—and no matter how serious the illness is or how uncomplicated the surgery."

"Is that possible?"

"I don't know. I could only try."

Child smiled. "Now you've given me the only

337

nursing-care plan I really wanted from your report, Carol." Child sighed. "However, I can't help but feel that your natural curiosity and your persistence in searching for the facts behind every doubt will benefit patients someday in a way that the traditional nursing role doesn't." She smiled then. "And don't worry about the eighty ruining your four point zero average. It hasn't. And Mae has made her C and Jo has made hers and they'll both make good nurses. Good grades don't make a good nurse anyway. Dedication does." Child handed Carol back her paper. "Now, my advice to you it to take your term paper with its eighty, Carol and . . . *burn it.*"

Carol left Child's office subdued. And while she was on the floor with the administrative offices, she decided to stop at Lena Black's office.

The nursing-school director looked up from her cluttered desk when the receptionist let Carol into her office. "Yes?"

"I'm Carol Welles, a senior. I would like to find out my grade status."

Black had the figures in front of her already. "Welles, Welles, Welles," she said moving her finger up the long computer printout sheet. "Carol Welles. You're number four in your graduating class."

Number four. Her spirits soared, and they soared all the way to her apartment. She tossed her books onto her couch and took the term paper from her notebook.

Good grades don't make a good nurse anyway. Dedication does . . . Now, my advice to you is to take your term paper with its eighty, Carol, and . . . burn it.

Well, she couldn't burn it; she'd have to tear it up instead. She took hold of its pages in order to rip them in two, stood a moment, then turned and went to her closet where she kept her file cabinet — and carefully filed the term paper under G, for General Nursing.

PART SEVEN

Chapter Eighteen

Graduation And Other Final Things

"You've got a mole here on the perineum, Mrs. Bingham. I do not like that mole," Dr. Simon said taking the scissors off the instrument table beside him. "So I am going to take that mole off."

While he snipped the mole off Perry Bingham's anesthetized perineum, Carol suctioned baby girl Bingham's mouth with the bulb syringe. Once the cord had been cut, the doctors would hand the infant to the nurse, and if the mother was awake, the nurse would show the infant briefly to the mother. Then she would place it under a warming light in a crib with a tilted mattress. The tilted mattress facilitated drainage of amniotic fluid and secretions from trachea, mouth, and nose. Drops of an antibiotic ophthalmic solution were placed in the infant's eyes.

Although the obstetricians would be intent on suturing a patient's episiotomy or delivering the placenta, they were aware of the baby's well-being, although once delivered, the baby was actually under the care of a pediatrician even before he left the delivery room.

"Carol, make the kid cry," Dr. Simon said.

Smiling, Carol thumped the bottom of baby girl Bingham's foot. The infant responded by screwing up her face, mewling, and then howling her rage at being so abused; and while she howled, her lungs were filling with oxygen insuring the continuous "pinking up" of her extremities.

"Joy, have you got a test tube for this mole?" asked Dr. Simon. "I want pathology to take a look at it."

The other nurse in the delivery room held the test tube so that the doctor could drop the excised mole into it.

Two of the three-to-eleven nurses entered the delivery room, gowned and masked. "It's going to be a long, hot fall, mark my words," one of them said. "It's got to be ninety degrees out there."

"Boy, am I glad to see you," Joy said. "Carol and I have had a hell of a day and Mac is beside herself. C'mon, Carol let's go home."

It hadn't been a hell of a day at all, just busy. There was a difference.

"Go on, I need to finish suctioning this kid," Carol told her, and by the time she left the delivery room, Joy had already vanished.

Mac was striding back from delivering a patient to L&D recovery; so Carol concluded that all of the three-to-eleven shift had arrived and had taken over for her and the rest of the seven-to-three shift. That's the way it was. Changes of shift in L&D happened right in the delivery rooms if nobody was in labor to report on. Oncoming shifts came in gowned and masked; off-going shifts saluted and left. It was less confusing that way.

Carol walked out of the delivery area pulling off her mask, which she tossed expertly into a trash can as she passed by; then off came the cap when she was near the nurses' station. She was already untying her gown just as the telephone rang at the desk.

Mac answered it. "Carol?" she said and held the receiver up in her hand.

This may be it. This may be Mom, Carol thought. She took the receiver, put it to her ear. "Carol speaking."

It was her mother. That was it then; Mom telling her that she had passed the state board exams. "With flying colors, Carol!"

"Thanks, Mom," she said and put the receiver into its cradle. Because she knew she would be moving to a larger apartment, Carol had given the state board examiners her parents' address, for she had had a horrible fear that the state board results would get lost in the mails.

Mac had already left now. There was no one at the nurses' station, no one in labor. No one to shout her good news to.

In the lounge behind the L&D nurses' station she changed from the scrub dress into her uniform. She couldn't resist removing the nametag: CAROL WELLES, G.N. and replacing it with the one she had kept in her uniform pocket for three months, which read; CAROL WELLES, R.N.

She smiled slowly as she studied herself in the mirror over the wash basin. The letters on the name-tag were backward, of course, but it didn't matter. She was Carol Welles, R.N.

She took the sweater from her locker and folded it over her arm, lifted her handbag from the locker hook, and slid the shoulder strap over her shoulder as she left the lounge.

You are a natural. Remember, L&D after you graduate, Dr. Cooper at St. John's had said.

Carol smiled as she remembered applying for her first job after graduation.

"You can name your hours, the area in which you want to work, and everything. They'll take you any way that they can get you, there's such a demand for nurses," the graduate nurses had said to each other. That was only partially true.

Carol had picked Bennet and CCU and the day shift in which to work.

The personnel director accepted her at Bennet, but not for CCU. Second choice was L&D, second choice was three-to-eleven, and that's what she got.

But that had been two months ago. She was still working in L&D, but a position had been vacated on day shift and Carol had taken it. She loved L&D; Bennet's large labor and delivery area was in the second newest wing of the hospital. Bennet was large enough to be rapidly acquiring all the newest equipment, a sonogram, a uterine-contraction-and-fetal-heart-tone monitor, and other things which would insure a patient a safe delivery.

Charlotte was in L&D, too, at St. John's. Mae was in ICU at a suburban hospital, and Jo was in surgery at another suburban hospital. Bret was employed at Veterans. Shelly—

346

Carol shook her head sadly thinking of Shelly as she paced down the long corridor with its polished tile floors and newly painted green walls. The thought of Shelly reminded her again of graduation night.

The nursing-care plans had become a thing of the past in May. They had grown like carcinomas from their original five to ten pages, to twenty and thirty. If the students had been allowed to keep them, and had put them together, they each could have published several thick volumes of some of the most dull nursing books in history, provided they could have ferreted out a publisher for them. But instructors knew—probably from personal experience—that students tended to help each other out by passing on their old care plans to lower classmen, and so after the students were allowed to see their grades and where they'd messed up, the care plans were handed back to the instructors. No one knew what happened to them after that.

Finals had been given the second week in May. The weather was very warm; nevertheless, Jo and Mae had sought Carol's warm side continually, especially right before each exam. Carol had been tutoring Jo and Mae for three semesters, and right before finals, the tutoring, like labor pains, had increased in frequency and intensity.

Meantime, the high-collar and the polyester-knit factions had won and the students had each been fitted at Best Uniform Shop in a uniform a size too small. Student caps had been tucked away in cedar chests and real nurses' caps with wings and black stripes had been ordered. The nursing pins had come in and each student had crowded Lena Black's office to see them.

Students had had their pictures made cheaply by passport photographers and had embarrassedly submitted them along with their applications to take the state board exams.

Only one hundred and thirty-six students were to graduate out of the original two hundred and seventy-two who started. The attrition rate of the med-vets was nearly one hundred percent. Two were all that was left of the original nineteen. And there was Bret. Rio, the LVN who didn't like to wash his hands, had failed Pedi. Jason, who dissected the mouse at Carol, Mae, and Charlottes' table in A&P, had dropped out in Psych. Nobody knew why.

Should old suspicions be forgot and never brought to mind? Or should old suspicions be forgot along with champagne, punch, and wine? It had been decided during lecture period in the auditorium of the university that the graduation party would be held after commencement, and that punch and champagne would be served with cake.

Faculty and students had decided that the ceremony would include their filing into the auditorium carrying votive candles as the school band played "Largo," speeches by the salutatorian, and valedictorian, Lena Black, and Dr. Winters, the president of UTE. Then the students would file by Lena Black to receive their nurses' pins.

Shelly had made valedictorian, Charlotte

salutatorian—and the graduation party had turned out to be a disaster.

Shelly's entire being had come to focus on graduation, on whether or not Basil Novak would be there to hear her speech. If Basil loved her and intended to keep his promise to marry her after he established private practice, Shelly was convinced that he would attend her graduation. Graduation was the supreme test of his love. It was a conclusion Shelly had come to on her own because she claimed that Basil had once promised that he would attend.

Carol was almost as tense as Shelly, wondering if Duane might possibly slip in to see her graduate. If he did, then he loved her. If not, it was all over. They had not seen each other since he had left her after their argument over her term paper. Neither had he called her. Until graduation night, there had still been hope. Yet, she wasn't sure she would take him back even if he begged to be taken back.

Shelly's speech was bright and witty. Charlotte's was short, and she was perspiring so much that Carol could see the drops of perspiration on her forehead even from the back row of the graduates' section. But surely after these commencement exercises were over, everybody would be okay again, Carol reasoned.

The large carpeted foyer of the university's administration building was the site of the commencement party. After the ceremony, one hundred thirty-six graduates uniformed in white poured through the auditorium doors into the foyer of the building, while the school band played a march from Aïda. The faculty, pouring punch and cutting the cakes, was already behind the long tables covered in white cloths. Family and friends congratulated the identically uniformed graduates and joined in the fun of the party. The students had decorated the foyer with streamers of white and blue—the school colors. Carol was disappointed that her parents did not join the party because they refused to participate in any activity where alcohol was served. Jo had no family either, so she and Carol stood together drinking their champagne and eating their cake.

"You seen Shelly?" Jo asked suddenly.

"No."

"I'm worried, Carol. She's capable of . . . no tellin' what."

Carol wasn't thinking about Shelly; her eyes were searching the crowd for Duane. The cake sat in her stomach like a ball of lead and the champagne was beginning to boil up in her throat. Suddenly she was aware that she was very weary.

"Let's ask around if anybody's seen her," Jo said. "If Novak didn't show up—"

Carol was too wrapped up in her own misery to care much, but she followed Jo around as she weaved her way through the crowd, first to Bret.

"You seen Shelly?" Jo asked.

Bret was standing with one of the other male graduates drinking punch. "No." He looked at Carol.

"Well, I'm afraid for her, Bret. You know how she was looking for that doctor to be at the commencement," Jo said.

"I know. I'll keep a lookout for her. In fact, why don't I see if I can find her car in the parking lot?" Bret said.

"Perfect," said Jo.

Carol followed her through the crowd of hilarious, loud, excited people wondering what was so hilarious about somebody graduating, wondering why all these people were so happy when she—

Jo found Ellen Child in the crowd. "Have you seen Shelly?"

Child said, "No. I haven't." Child knew Shelly's obsession with Novak's appearance at graduation and a look of concern came over her face. "I'll watch for her," she said.

Jo threaded her way through the crowd; Carol followed, mute and sick. She wanted only to go home now.

"You seen Shelly?" Jo was asking Mae.

Mae was laughing, surrounded by family and friends. Her two girls, aged ten and twelve, freckled and red-headed, were eating cake and drinking punch beside her. Mae's face grew solemn, "No, I haven't. Not since we filed out of the auditorium. Oh. You don't think . . ."

Jo and Mae looked at each other silently. "Look," Mae said. "I'll help you look for her. Let me ask some of the instructors."

Jo turned to Carol. "Shelly doesn't have any family. Nobody I can call. Got a quarter, Carol? I think I'll call her apartment."

Carol took her purse of small change from her pocket and gave Jo a quarter. Jo said, "There's Charlotte. Why don't you go ask her if she's seen Shelly while I try to telephone her apartment."

Carol threaded her way through the crowd to Charlotte. When she came close, she was suddenly astonished by the look on Charlotte's face. Her eyes were glazed, her complexion jaundiced.

"Charlotte?" Carol said taking hold of her arm.

Charlotte looked at her, bewildered. "Ca—Car—"

"Charlotte, are you all right?"

Charlotte's husband, Ted, came smiling to them, a glass of punch in each of his hands. "Hi, Carol."

"Ted . . . look at Charlotte."

Charlotte dropped with a thump on the floor.

Carol was aware of confusion around her, of people exclaiming, bumping into each other as she knelt beside Charlotte.

Of course, it was a diabetic crisis. But which one? Was she going into diabetic ketoacidosis, or hypoglycemia? Was it diabetic coma, or insulin shock?

Graduate nurses were anxious to demonstrate their expertise. Carol heard them calling for water. Somebody said Charlotte was diabetic, better call an ambulance.

"Put her head lower than her feet."

"Her pulse is rapid. Is she diabetic?"

The two kinds of diabetic crisis were similar, but there was one main difference. In diabetic coma the skin was hot and flushed. Charlotte's was pale and cool, and she was perspiring, so it must be low blood sugar, insulin shock.

"Give her the punch, Ted," Carol commanded. "There's sugar in it."

Ted was on his knees with a glass of punch in both hands. "But how do we know?"

"We know," said Bret as he knelt beside Charlotte. "Better give the punch." Bret lifted Charlotte's head up off the floor. Another graduate placed a damp cloth on her forehead. Bret took the punch from Ted and told Charlotte, "Hey, drink this, Charlotte. Drink it!"

Charlotte was barely able to respond, but she swallowed the punch slowly.

Carol, bathing Charlotte's face with a washcloth, was aware of the wail of an ambulance approaching, approaching slowly. She was also aware of Bret's tenderness with Charlotte, of his ability to take control, to command obedience from a patient while being gentle at the same time.

Ambulance attendants waded through the crowd. Somebody mentioned diabetic coma. Charlotte was lifted onto the stretcher.

"Please go with her, will you, Carol?" Ted asked. "I'll bring the car."

Bret's hand fell briefly on her shoulder, and Carol felt herself moving forward through the crowd behind the stretcher carrying Charlotte.

We know, Bret had said. Yes, after two years of prenursing courses and two years of intensive nurses' training, *we know.*

"Help me?"

The ambulance jerked forward in the night, lights flashed outside. The inside of the ambulance was dimly lit, and the ambulance attendant was hanging an IV over Charlotte's head. "Will you help me?" he asked again. "Tie the tourniquet while I attach this needle."

"Sure," Carol said and suddenly, she was no longer Carol feeling sorry for herself. She was no longer just a frightened friend of Charlotte's. She was Carol Welles, G.N., Graduate Nurse, and Charlotte was her first patient.

"Can you start the IV? I can, but I've just learned and I'm not too good at it," the young, red-bearded attendant said.

Well, Carol had only started one—in ER on little old Mrs. Pearson. "All right." She took the needle which the attendant had attached to the IV tubing. "Charlotte, a little stick," she said.

We'll go inside that vein right there. Okay? the anesthesiologist, Dr. Pashi, had told her in the operating room just before Reba Flowers' surgery. *Then when we've gone through the skin, we'll angle over and go into the vein. You'll feel it pop when we go in.*

She felt the vein pop, blood backed up into the tubing, Carol released the tourniquet, and threaded the catheter through the needle. "Tape?"

The attendant handed her some tape and she

354

began to tape the hub of the IV intracath to Charlotte's arm.

"Boy, we're lucky tonight. To have a nurse along," the attendant said.

I started the IV. I am a nurse. Just a nurse? Just my nurse . . .

The ambulance siren wailed, the vehicle swayed from side to side, automobile lights flashed in the night.

Charlotte's eyes were open, her pulse was about one hundred and ten beats per minute. Charlotte would not die; she was only on the verge of coma. Charlotte would live because medical people knew what to do.

The ambulance pulled up in front of the huge sliding doors of ER, Bennet's ER, where Carol had spent a boring three days in training. Carol jumped out of the back of the ambulance and Charlotte's stretcher was brought out and wheeled through the doors.

"You a nurse?" asked a resident doctor at the ER entrance.

"We are both graduate nurses," Carol replied. "She's in insulin shock. She's diabetic."

"Too much stress from graduation tonight, huh?" said the resident. Carol was surprised at his acceptance of her diagnosis. But after all, she should know, shouldn't she?

Later, she and Ted sat in the ER waiting room waiting for Charlotte's own doctor to telephone the resident in

charge of ER and to give him orders for Charlotte.
The resident had told them that he had done blood
and urine tests and that Charlotte was indeed in
insulin shock. He had given her an injection of glucose.

Carol was leafing through a *Times* magazine when
they first heard the wail of another ambulance
outside the door of ER. She raised her head,
listening, as the wail died abruptly on a low pitch.
Carol stood up and went to the door of the waiting
room from which she could see the ER entrance; the
hair on the back of her neck prickled.

The same attendants who had brought Charlotte
to ER now wheeled in a stretcher hurriedly. ER personnel converged on the stretcher as it was rolled
into treatment room one, the trauma room. Carol
thought of Felix Seifert as she left the waiting room
and went to the door of the treatment room. Two
residents, two nurses, and the two ambulance
attendants were working over the trauma patient.
Somebody hung an IV. The cardiac monitor
suddenly showed a blip on its oscilloscope over the
head of the treatment table. The blip did not bob.
Asystole. Straight line. Just as it had done when they
had brought in Felix Seifert.

Carol watched as the residents who were bending
over the patient raised their heads to look at each
other. Somebody flipped off the monitor.

The two attendants started for the door of the
room. The one with the red beard jerked his thumb

toward the patient on the stretcher. "Another one of you?" he asked Carol.

The residents and nurses paused and watched as Carol entered the room; she knew, already knew who lay on the stretcher with its blood-soaked sheets. The face was covered with blood; the short, black hair was matted. It was Shelly.

After Carol had left Charlotte in her hospital room and Ted had driven her back to her car on the university parking lot, she drove home in the dark, still night. She thought once, Maybe *I* should consider driving off a highway bridge on the interstate as Shelly did. But then she told herself, Hang on. This loneliness and depression is just a letdown after graduation.

She pulled into the parking lot of her apartment complex, came to a stop in the parking lot outside her apartment door. Before she got out of the car, she saw a movement in the shadows of her porch, but it did not occur to her to be frightened; for she was thinking of Duane. *Oh dear Lord, let it be Duane.*

But it was Bret who stepped out of the shadows as she stood beside her car. Carol shut her eyes a moment, opened them, said, "Bret, you startled me," aware of the slowing of her heart now.

"Sorry. I heard about Shelly."

"I was in ER when they brought her in. She was

D.O.A., Bret." Carol stepped upon her porch beside him. "Maybe I shouldn't have called Jo at the party, but she was so worried. It was awful, Bret. I'll have nightmares for weeks." Carol shuddered. "Did Jo tell everybody?"

"She did. It threw cold water on everybody's fun, but Charlotte had already done that anyway. How is she?"

"She'll be okay. It was insulin shock brought on by exhaustion, as we all know. Would you like to come in?"

"Yes. That's why I'm here."

Carol unlocked her door and the two of them went in as she flipped on the light of her apartment. Bret, hands in his pockets looked around. "Nice," he said.

"Now that I have a job, I'll move to a larger apartment," she said dropping onto the couch. "Sit down, Bret. In a minute when I've gotten my nerves together, I'll fix us something to eat and drink. Sandwiches and champagne. I was planning to celebrate by myself, if necessary." She laughed mirthlessly.

"A sandwich and champagne sounds great," he said and dropped into a nearby chair. "And I hope celebrating by yourself won't be necessary."

Bret gazed around him. She watched his handsome profile as he studied her meager furnishings without seeing them; then he smiled at her slowly. "So you have a job."

358

"Yes. Jeez, I didn't realize that I haven't had a chance to talk to you in several weeks. I took a position. Guess where?"

Bret grinned. "Bennet."

"That's right. Guess what department?"

"Mmmmm . . . CCU."

"No. At Bennet you're required to work on the floor a year after graduation before you can rotate to any of the critical-care areas."

"Okay. I guess OB."

"Right."

"Labor and delivery?"

"Yes. I start Monday. How about you?"

"I'm in charge of fourth floor south at Veterans. Where else?"

They were silent for a while.

"Lousy graduation night isn't it?" he said.

"Yes. It *was* lousy. Why did you come here tonight, Bret?"

"Figured you needed somebody to talk to after Charlotte's collapse and Shelly's death, and . . ."

"And?"

"He didn't show up, did he?"

She leaned her head back on the couch. "No."

"He's never called since you had the fight over your term paper, has he?"

She jerked her head up to look at him. "How did you know about that?"

"Charlotte told me."

"So you came here to comfort me tonight?"

His eyes shone, looking at her, directly at her. "If I can."

They looked at each other silently for a long time, two people alone on the night of their graduation, alone but now *not* alone.

Finally she said softly, "I think you probably can."

Now, approaching the exit of Bennet's Markson wing, dressed in her uniform, she was Carol Welles, R.N. By now *he* would be Duane Duren, M.D., or Dr. Duane Duren. Bennet had accepted him into its residency program and he would be taking his residency in the hospital day and night. She could not help but wonder as she went out through the door how long it would be before they met in the corridor somewhere, or in an elevator, or in the cafeteria.

My little nurse. I love you for your femininity. . . . Darling, nurses don't have leverage in hospital management and politics. . . . Carol, sometimes—sometimes I think I almost hate you. . . . I love you, I love you and I want you. I want—I want—Compared to a man like Tyree you're nothing. Nothing! Not if you graduate, pass state boards, become an R.N., go on to become a supervisor, go clear to the top wherever the hell that is. As a nurse, compared to Tyree you're a pipsqueak! . . . I love you and I want—

When they did finally come face to face with each other someday, when it had become apparent to him

360

that her paper had not exposed anyone's mistakes and that no one had linked her to him, and that his residency at Bennet was secure—what then?

Bret met her just outside the door. She paused, stood smiling, waiting for him to see the nametag pinned to her uniform which read, CAROL WELLES, R.N. He grinned, gave her nametag a thump with his finger. "Me, too," he said.

Then he took her hand and walked with her to the parking lot reserved for Bennet Memorial's nursing staff.

ROMANCE AT ITS BEST!

TIDES OF ECSTASY   (1079, $3.50)
by Luanne Walden
Meghan's dream of marrying Lord Thomas Beauchamp was coming true—until the handsome but heartless Derek entered her life and forcibly changed her plans . . .

DESTINY'S PASSION   (1061, $3.50)
by Lucy Cores
When the beautiful Clare is swept off her feet by Russia's handsomest prince, memories of her love for a Lord are rekindled. But no matter who her heart truly lies with, Clare is forever bound to DESTINY'S PASSION.

ECSTASY'S TREASURE   (1053, $3.50)
by Jean Haught
As determined as she was beautiful, Paige vowed never to be owned by any man—no matter what! But when she met Kyle Brenner, she found in a stranger the one man who could make her a prisoner of love . . .

PASSION'S TEMPEST   (1067, $3.50)
by Nicole Duval
Chantal has the face of an angel and the body of a seductress. And when fate brings her into the arms of a rugged pirate captain, she's overcome in a struggle—and overwrought with passion!

SAVAGE EMBRACE   (1069, $3.50)
by Alexis Boyard
Primitive passion consumed Sylviane when she saw the powerful Indian warrior. It didn't matter that he was uncivilized and she was of noble birth. He was the man of her dreams—and she swore to make him her own!

Available wherever paperbacks are sold, or order direct from the Publisher. Send cover price plus 50¢ per copy for mailing and handling to Zebra Books, 475 Park Avenue South, New York, N.Y. 10016. DO NOT SEND CASH.

FASCINATING, PAGE-TURNING BLOCKBUSTERS!

YOU WILL ALSO WANT TO READ . . .